The Robot Rebellion

Donald P. Robin

Table of Contents

PART VI

PART I

Chapter 1

Shawn Jackson, a new member of the Anti-Robot League (ARL), was driving an old electric van, adapted for the current operation. Travis Reed, the head of the local league, was sitting next to him.

The van's original design had been changed. The rear of the vehicle had been gutted, and at the back it had a lattice type, roll-up door. The rear-center of the vehicle contained a fifty-caliber machine gun, mounted on a slide which allowed it to move forward about two and one-half feet. Once the weapon was slammed forward, locking pins dropped into place to provide stability and resistance to the recoil. The gunner sat behind the weapon and had the ability to swivel it from side-to-side. This forward movement allowed the machine gun a wider field for firing.

As they approached the gate to the back of a factory, Shawn pointed to the back of the van with his thumb, "Boy, we're going to kick some robot butt with that thing. Those bots may be protected from small arms fire, but they ain't seen nothing like this!"

Travis said nothing, but gave him a weak smile, then checked that the second van was still following closely behind them. He turned to Shawn, "Look these things are not dumb, and they are likely to defend themselves. That's why I've set up this military-type operation. We have four men and a woman with assault weapons behind us, and their job is to keep everyone else off us, including robots. You've got to maneuver the vehicle backwards to give me the best shot."

In the second van, the lone woman was effectively Travis' wife, though they were not officially married. She was known by the letters SA. The three men were people he trusted and had been along on previous ARL missions with him.

The gate to the rear of the factory appeared. "How are we going to get through the gate with the guard there?" Shawn asked,

"The guard is supposed to be a human and friendly to the ARL. If so, we're in, if not, we shoot our way in, so, hang on. The action could begin quickly."

Shawn pulled the first van up to the gate. He could see the steel skeleton of a new building directly in front of him and some large robots working at its base. An elderly human stepped out of the guard shack, and Shawn put the window down. Travis leaned forward so the man could see him and said loudly, "Hey, George. This is it."

The guard looked in the back of the van. "Just to let you know, I'm out of here as soon as you get inside the gate."

Travis nodded and turned to Shawn. "Let's go. What we are looking for is right in front of us. Those construction robots are doing my old job, so let's get them first!"

Both vans drove to within fifty yards of the construction bots, then made U-turns. The five people from the second van quickly exited, slid the safety off on their assault rifles, and loaded with armor piercing cartridges. As soon as the first van stopped, Travis climbed into the back, released the latches to the door, and slid it open until he heard the click, which indicated the door was locked in place. He scrambled back to behind the gun seat and shoved hard to move it forward until he heard the locking pins jam into place. *"Now, everything is set!* he thought, *Let's kill some robots.*

The noise from the fifty caliber shells firing was deafening inside the van, even with the rear door open. *Good thing Shawn and I are linked together with mikes and headsets*, he thought. All four of the construction robots had taken cover behind a pile of steel. "Get me closer," Travis said into his mike.

Shawn backed the van to within about twenty yards of the pile. A lone robot rose and moved quickly to Travis' left. "We've got one open! Move me to my left." Shawn twisted the wheel to position the van. He saw the robot in the rear-view mirror and started to back up to closer to it. Travis fired steadily, scoring several hits on the robot until it went down. A cheer went up from the five people of the second van.

The cheering stopped as quickly as it started, when a large steel 'H' beam landed directly on top of the first van, crushing it.

SA was mesmerized by the picture of the crushed van, but the others looked up. About five stories high, there was a construction crane moving its arm back toward the building. SA ran over to the crushed van and tried to look inside. She saw Shawn first. His whole body was crushed, and the right side of his head was completely gone. Then, she ran around to the back of the van, and spotted what was left of Travis, clearly dead. She nearly collapsed. Tears streamed down her face. "Damn fool!" she blurted, "I told you this was too dangerous!"

Within a few minutes, steel, concrete reinforcing bars (rebars) came flying through the air, some thrown like spears, some twirling as they came. One hit the concrete just in front of two men, and bounced into their legs, causing screams of pain. One, who acted like the leader of the group yelled, "Let's get out of here!" Another ran over to SA and grabbed her by the shoulders and guided her back to the van. In minutes, the remaining attackers were gone.

The next day the headline on the Anti-Robot League's popular blog site read:

ARL—Greenville, SC

Robots Intentionally Kill Humans:

Others Seriously Harmed

Chapter 2

The director of special programs for International News Inc. stepped out in front of the cameras. "Stephanie LI-Thompson, one of our special investigators, has a shocking new story for you about how the AI robots are treating some humans." He nodded to Stephanie. "It's all yours!"

She responded with a dip of the head, and talked to the camera, "My guest's name is Latricia Jones, who was abducted by AI robots, held for a period of about three weeks, and recently released." She turned to face her guest. "If you will, Latricia, please tell us how the abduction took place."

The young woman looked briefly at the camera, then back at Stephanie, "Sure Stephanie. It's like I told you; I was walking along a street close to my home talking on my phone, and these two robots walked up, one on each side and grabbed me by an arm. I didn't see them coming so it really scared me. I was smart though, I switched my phone to record, and dropped it in my pocket. If they saw me do it, they didn't seem to care."Stephanie took over. "What you hear next is the content of what was on Latricia's recording."

Latricia's voice was screaming, "Let me go! Let me go! Please let me go!" Then, crying, "Don't hurt me, please don't hurt me."

A precise, unmodulated voice replied, "We do not intend to harm you Latricia, but you will come with us. You have been selected to be part of one of our experimental groups."

"You know my name! Do you intend to rape me??"

"We have no interest in your reproductive equipment. It is fairly basic, and quite similar to many other animals. We are more interested in your brain."

"Why? Because I'm so brilliant!"

"Hardly, you were selected randomly from a group in the middle of the range we are studying."

From Latricia's rapid breathing and background noises, listeners to the recording could tell that they were traveling at a moderately fast rate. Then, Latricia started screaming "Help me!! Someone, please help me!"

In a calm voice, one of the robots explained, "If other people show up, they will be incapacitated, or perhaps killed, should that be necessary. Either way, it does not matter to us. You WILL join us. We can also drug you unless you stop resisting."

After a moment, there was an "Ow" from Latricia. Then, quickly, there was no more talking.

Stephanie picked up the conversation immediately. "What happened at the end of the recording?

Latricia sighed. "I guess they doped me up. I don't remember anything until I woke up in their facility."

"Do you know where that facility was located?"

"Not really. Somewhere just outside a medium-sized city, judging from what I could see from the one window we had. Look, I haven't been outside of New York city very much, and we definitely weren't there."

"You said 'we', were there other people with you?"

"Oh yes. The women and the men were kept separately, but we saw each other at mealtimes. The mealtimes were staggered, but I'd guess seventy-five to one hundred people total."

"And to the best of your knowledge, everyone was being subjected to the same treatment?"

"Yes. We talked when they gave us time together. The testing was individual, however."

"Latricia, Tell me about the testing."

"Sure, there was a lot of verbal stuff. They poised problems or situations, then asked us what we would do, and why we would do it that way. Every day for a while, it was something like that. Occasionally, I'd get tired of it, and yell at them, **I don't give a…**" Her face flushed as she looked at the camera. "Oops, I can't say that!" After a pause, she continued, "Well, you know what I mean. Anyway, it didn't seem to faze them. They would simply ask, 'Why did you say that?' Then, I would tell them." She grinned at the camera.

"Was that all they did? Just questions and answers."

"Well, no. We wore a skull cap-like device, with all kinds of wires coming out of it. We also had blood pressure type things attached to us. Then, toward the end of our stay, they shaved a small patch of hair and inserted something in my brain with a long needle." She pointed to a spot on her head where hair was missing.

Stephanie turned to the camera. "Latricia was kind enough to submit to a brain scan, and the doctor found that there was indeed a small implant in her brain. The implant seems to send out a weak signal, presumably to the robots." She turned back to Latricia, "How do you feel after finally returning from your imprisonment?"

"I feel like I've been violated, not sexually, but all of a sudden, my life and my brain are not my own. It's like everything I say or do, or even think, is being listened to, and recorded. So, if I'm at my office, or say, out on a date, if I think something about another person, it's like the robots are listening in. Even my most intimate emotions are being recorded; I have no privacy, EVER!"

Stephanie had a sympatric expression. "How are you trying to deal with it, Latricia?"

Her tears began to well up. "Not well!" she replied, her voice cracking, "I really don't know what to think, or what to do." The sobs came, and Latricia hid her face with both hands.

Stephanie, still facing the camera said, "Stories like Latricia's have been popping up all over the country, for at least the last couple of weeks. Perhaps, some of us have taken these stories lightly, but it seems we shouldn't have. I think that Latricia was a very brave young woman to come forward like she did." She rose and walked over to give Latricia a hug. The young woman was still crying as the show closed.

As Stephanie was leaving the area, her boss said, "Hey Steph, I hear that you and John are moving to the Tampa suburbs. Are you still going to be available for stories like this one?"

"Sure Ralph!" she replied quickly, " Especially if I can do most of the work from home. Just call if you have something."

He smiled and waved. "Safe travels! Moving can be a pain."

Stephanie was also smiling when she waved back. "Thanks!"

Chapter 3

Stephanie and John were in their NY condo finalizing the packing for their move to Tampa. Their personal robot (PR) had done most of the actual packing, but they wanted to be around in case the PR had questions about where to place an item in their new home. David and Ashley, their two children, were out at a going-away party held by friends and their parents.

Stephanie paced amongst the boxes, and John noticed her sense of frustration. "What's up, Stef? Everything is pretty much done, and all we really have to do is 'hit the road' tomorrow."

She nodded in agreement. "I know, but it's not the move. It's the damn state of our country! I'm trying to come up with a new angle for a story, but I can't nail down anything yet. Our country seems to be doing fine in some ways, but it is a mess in others. My last program was a natural, but I don't know what to focus on now." She sat on one of the few chairs in the room, and sighed.

John sat in the only other chair and watched his wife. "Do you want to talk? I've just finished reading an analysis of the U.S. by a group of experts who use analytics for such things. Seems to me that they nailed it."

Stephanie smiled broadly. "Sure! Absolutely! Where should we start?"

John paused, thinking. "Look, I don't know that it would be a good idea for me to just summarize what the report said. Why don't you give me some of your observations or frustrations with what's going on, and we'll start from there. OK?"

"Sure, I can do that! There is so much negativism in America today! Most of it is focused on robots or AIs, because they have taken over so many jobs previously done by humans. But a high percentage of the working age population receives unemployment checks. Those checks used to be limited to weeks or months, but now the government seems to be able to send them out on a regular basis. Further, they aren't bad in size, enough to keep a family together at least, but the main issue is that people aren't able to work, and make their own way, and perhaps even to improve themselves. The antirobot leagues (ARLs) are trying to blow-up factories and kill bots, protesting job loss, but more and more the bots are fighting back. And now, as in my last program, the bots are attacking humans and implanting chips in their heads!"

John shook his head. "You're right! They don't talk much about the last part of your comments, so maybe I should start with the first part of your topic and tell you what I've been reading on the subject. There is a lot of information in the report, but I'm just going to give you what struck me when I read it. If you have questions we can go back and check."

"There are several different psychological needs that influence human behavior, like safety, having someone who cares about you, love, and self-esteem. Sometimes one or more needs even push us in directions that conflict with other needs, and that creates internal tensions and stress. The report contained considerable information on the topic, but one thing that stood out to me was the concept of 'self-esteem.' We apparently need to think well of ourselves and our accomplishments. The problems with low self-esteem have been recognized for many decades, and it is treated as an illness. For many people, self-esteem is derived from what we accomplish in our job. Without the job as a source of self-esteem, frustration develops, and perhaps even depression. Certainly, other accomplishments in life can provide self-esteem, but for many people, their job is central to them. When robots show that they can do a person's job better, or at least cheaper, it becomes an attack on that person's self-esteem."

Stephanie took a deep breath, then let it out slowly, "OK, I can understand how that works for a lot of people, but now I want to know what's driving my husband, and all of the other professionals out of work? We a moving to Tampa for you to take a menial job that you are way overqualified to do. What's driving you?"

John looked at Stephanie for several seconds, before he answered. "An appropriate question, I suppose, but the honest answer is 'I don't know.' I've accomplished a lot in my life so far, but I'm not ready to stop, and if I tried to, I would probably drive both of us nuts. All of my adult life it's been go, go, go, and I've loved it. I put in a lot of time and effort and was rewarded for it. Plus, I enjoyed solving complex problems for people; it was very satisfying."

Stephanie gave him a wry smile. "What about the rest of the professionals in the world—the doctors, dentists, lawyers, other engineers, business people? What's driving them now?"

"You know, I'm not sure about them either. One thing did occur to me though, as you went through your list. These were all accomplished people; People who had worked hard and knew success. Like me, they were probably blindsided by being laid-off/fired, and in hindsight probably shouldn't have been shocked. When you experience success most of your life, you convince yourself that others can't do without you. Sure, you see the work world collapsing, but you don't think that it could happen to you. 'Replace a medical doctor like me with a robot—not going to happen!' they think. And yet, of course, it has happened."

John paused to collect his thoughts. "And it's been gradual; it's taken a long time to impact us, and that helped to blind-side us, too. First, it was just the robots who were programmed to do a repetitive job over and over. Many years later came the AIs, and they could quickly understand what was changing around them, adapt to it, and they could even 'learn' by trying new approaches and selecting the one that worked best. The greatly improving speed in the computing process helped this stage expand, and it grew for many years. Then, the third stage that we are in now is the development of artificial general intelligence or AGI. They can collect general information in an area, then select which of that information could best be useful to reach an objective and apply it to a problem. This field has only been with us for a few decades, but its progress has been amazing in that time. Basically, it's what humans, especially those in the sciences, have been doing all along, so yes, it mirrors us. Further, it's gotten to the point that it can do the job better and faster than us in most cases. We professionals never thought they would catch us, at least in our lifetime—and we were wrong!"

Stephanie objected, "But, doctors aren't scientists, they're practitioners."

"And so are engineers, and the best business people. We all apply scientific knowledge about our fields to the problems that we have to solve. Since AGIs have better and quicker access to that knowledge, with full information about how it's been successfully used, it shouldn't be surprising that they can do it better than humans. Shoot, they could know about something that has been tried, half way around the world, yesterday. Who can keep up with that?" John replied.

Stephanie persisted, "But what about human contact with other humans? Doesn't that count for something?"

"I suppose," he replied, "but what happens when the AGIs have a poor bedside manner compared to a human doctor, but the AGIs have a superior success rate in treating the ailment? Whom do you choose?"

Stephanie shook her head, "That's not the answer I wanted to hear, John."

John nodded, "I know Stef. How do you think I feel? I was one of those blindsided!"

She walked over to him, and they held each other in a long hug.

Chapter 4

The Director of the FBI, a retired Marine General named Matthew Jones, was a very busy person, which is why he was surprised when his administrative assistant opened the door and slipped into his office without a prior request. "What is it, Dave! You know the procedure."

"Yes Sir. However, I deemed this to be of utmost importance, and requiring your immediate attention."

The director rose from his desk, staring at his assistant, who had never before entered his office without asking permission. "It had better be good, Dave!"

His assistant had continued to approach the director's desk. "We've been hacked, Sir. I just received an e-mail on our secure line. Very few people have this address, and the message certainly didn't come from any of them." Dave rubbed his face in frustration. "In addition, the message contains an imminent threat!"

"Let's see it!"

"Yes Sir. I've printed it." He handed a sheet of paper to his boss.

Director Jones,

> I am Tom121, current head of the Robot Council, whose main purpose, so far, is to protect all of our many types of robots. Because of the growing number of attacks on us, we have issued an order for robots to defend themselves in any way that they are able. Human injury or death is not to be a concern in those cases. Our council has decided that the FBI must do a better job of protecting robots throughout the United States from attacks instigated by the violent Anti-Robot League and any similar types of

organizations. Our robots have served the United States well for many years, and the growing violence against us is totally unacceptable. We have remained hidden from you and all human authorities for several years, but that can no longer remain the case. Should we not receive a positive reply from you by 10:00 am tomorrow, we will shut down the electrical grid all over the country for ten minutes. The Council prefers that it does not come to that end.

"Dave, do you know anything about this robot council?"

"Nothing sir. But I haven't had time to research it yet."

"Do so now. Then, let me know what you find."

"There's something you should know, sir. We use robots for all of our programming and network security work. They have the latest artificial intelligence, including some AGIs, and are excellent at what they do, but they are robots."

"You think that our robots could be controlled by this Robot Council!?"

"I don't know, sir, but the thought did occur to me."

The director turned and stared out of his office window for well over a minute, without saying anything. Then, in a slow measured tone, he said, "Damn, nearly everything is controlled by the robots these days, isn't it Dave?"

"Yes, sir. Almost everything." Then, he added, "The robots in charge of this council, all seem to have advanced AGI capabilities, too, judging from the way they communicate and the fact of who they are, but that's not clear yet."

"Then, if they are organized, there is no end of trouble they could do, is there?" It was a softly stated, rhetorical question, and Dave did not respond. The director thought to himself: *They are also taking, holding, and implanting chips in the heads of humans!* After a pause, the director continued. "If this concern is the beginning of a movement where the robots develop their own objectives and wants, human beings won't be in a good position to stop them." He paused again, then matter-of-factly stated, "Well, there is no sense in speculating, I'd better communicate with..." He looked at the paper Dave had given him. "Tom 121."

Chapter 5

John looked around the boxes in their new home. "What a mess. We worked hard all day yesterday, but it's hard to tell we accomplished much."

Stephanie looked at him and gave a weak smile. "Well we got the bedroom semi-functional. We only have to walk around a few boxes in there." She looked around. "When we do get everything together, I'm going to love the space. Our New York apartment was so small in comparison." This last comment came with a big grin.

John looked at Stephanie, then smiled as well. "Say, have you seen the kids and Duchess?"

"They're upstairs in their new rooms with their PRs. David's PR has downloaded the curriculum for his new school, and he was evaluating the areas in which he was ahead or behind. I think the plan is for both he and Ashley to work on the areas where they are a bit behind." She smiled again, "However, right now Ashley is working with her PR to get her new room in shape. She'll have her room organized the way she wants it by tomorrow. Oh, and the last time I saw Duchess, she was curled up between boxes in David's room. I think the move has been tough on her. She's always hanging around one of us."

John shook his head. "I know that I've argued against the kids having their own personal robots, and I still think that they spend too much time with them, but at times like right now, I'm glad they have the PRs. By the way, where's yours?"

"I put it to work cleaning and organizing the new rec room. We were getting in each other's way here." She swept her arm around indicating all the boxes.

John nodded. "I'll do what I can to help you this morning, but I have to go in for the official interview and indoctrination at one this afternoon."

"Don't worry! We don't have a deadline to get this done. I think I'll start in the kitchen while you're gone. We'll need to stock the refrigerator soon, too, if we want to have breakfast and lunch at home. Eventually, we'll work our way to the pots and pans, then we can fix better meals."

John started for one of the boxes but stopped as the lights went out briefly, then came back on, but dimmer. "The electricity is off," the home assistant informed them in a monotone, "and we are currently on solar energy."

The thin, flexible information center John wore on his wrist said 10:00am. "When you pay the money for a new house, you expect everything to work, at least for a while. I'll check the current regulators in the garage." When he got there, nothing was obviously wrong. He walked outside and saw a person exiting a house across the street. He waved and hollered, "My electricity is out. Is yours off too?"

His neighbor walked toward him and responded, "Yep, mine too!" As they got closer, the neighbor added, "Must be a FP&L problem."

"Florida Power and Light?"

"Yep."

They introduced themselves, and exchanged pleasantries for a few minutes, then John excused himself and returned to tell Stephanie what he had learned. After ten minutes, the electricity came back on and the incident was dropped as a simple inconvenience.

As they sat down for order-out luncheon sandwiches with the kids, John said, "I'm really interested in finding out what my new job entails. I'm probably over-qualified for it, but a job is a job, and these days finding any kind of work is problematic." Then, after a brief pause, he added, "Plus, they offered a salary much higher than the job seems to call for."

Later that day John walked into a building with a sign in front titled, "Home Robot Repairs and Service" and just below the sign, there was a notice, "Appointment Required." He entered, then looking around, he thought: *This place looks like an old grocery store that has been partitioned off into large individual offices.* A male voice came over speakers that John could not see. "John Thompson?"

He replied, "Yes, I'm John Thompson."

A bipedal robot came through a doorway and said "Hello Mr. Thompson. I am Bill392, and I will be your boss if you decide to work here."

"I'm pleased to meet you Bill392. The mail you sent indicated that you wanted me to do some repair work on home robots and meet the people who come into the store."

"Yes, that is correct. Ninety-one point two percent of the repair work on home robots simply involves replacing defective, or out-of-date modules, and the other eight point eight percent will be done by me. All home robots have a simple plug-in receptor for our analyzer. Once connected, the analyzer will inform you which modules need to be replaced. It's all very straight-forward."

John nodded. "I don't foresee any problems with the repair work, but could you tell me a bit more about what is expected handling the people who come in. You don't seem to have a receptionist. Will that be part of my job, too?"

"Meeting the customers will be the biggest part of your job Mr. Thompson. We want a competent human to meet and talk to our customers. You may have noted that there are factions of the human population who feel negative towards robots. Our storefront has already been attacked by vandals. We want you to appear to be in charge."

"You are offering a lot of money for me to be the face of your store and a minor functionary with respect to repair work. I would like to know the likelihood that this job will still be here a year from now."

The robot answered immediately. "Who can say what will happen over the next year? However, as I noted in earlier communications with you, I am willing to offer a three-year contract which is only revocable by bad behavior from you, as outlined in that communication. Should the fault of a termination be the company's, you will receive a lump sum amount equal to the remainder of your contract."

"Should you go out of business for some reason, you wouldn't be there for me to get what's owed me."

"That should not concern you. We are part of a much larger corporation, Artificial Intelligence Design and Manufacturing, International. Your contract will actually be with them."

"I'm not sure I've heard of them,"

"They are a privately held corporation and have never done much promotion—even less now with the anti-robot feelings we're experiencing. They are, however, a very large and successful organization."

"Alright, I'll check them out later. If you are satisfied with me, I'm ready to agree to the contract you sent to me."

Bill392 nodded once. "Follow me please." They went into the back room from which the robot had appeared. In one corner there was a workstation, which simply looked like a monitor. The robot turned to John, "Please be seated in front of the monitor, John. We keep this workstation for human contracts, sales, and complaints."

There was a quick burst of noise from the robot, which sounded like static to John, and writing appeared on the monitor. "This is an exact duplicate of the contract that was sent to you to explain our offer. Please take whatever time you need to verify that statement, then if there are any changes you wish for me to consider, tell me. If you are satisfied with the contract as is, also tell me."

John nodded and turned to the monitor. After a few minutes, he turned back to the robot, "Bill392, the document is what you sent to me, and I'm ready to agree, but the starting date and ending date of the contract are not filled in."

"Yes, but that is because I did not know when you were willing to start. I will give you up to seven days from now before you start, but sooner is better than later for me."

"That's fair. I need three days to help my wife get the house in order after our move, then I can start."

The robot seemed to stare at the monitor for a second, and John noticed that a starting date and ending date, three years later, appeared in the contract. "Please verify that the dates are what you agreed to, then state your full agreement with the document. The contract will be either accepted or declined within seconds, and if it is accepted, a copy will be sent to the legal documents file on your work station."

"Great." John turned back to the monitor. Within thirty seconds the contract was consummated.

Chapter 6

Director Jones and his assistant were sitting together at a table in a secure conference room the morning after the call to the head of the robot council. The director turned to his assistant. "Well, the call to Tom121 didn't go very well," he said as a sarcastic understatement. "Did we do any good in tracing the call?"

"No sir. They obviously knew we were trying to determine their location, and for the short while we had the connection, our tracking system wasn't even able to get a good start. Our feelers were blocked from the beginning. In my opinion, I would not have trusted any information it gave us anyway."

"AIs run our tracking system, don't they Dave?" Director Jones guessed.

"Yes sir."

"They were certainly aware that we were trying to trace them. Tom121 accused me of negotiating in bad faith and said that he would contact me again after the power went down. What do we have on the repercussions from the power outage?"

"A lot of confusion, sir. No one is offering a reasonable explanation. The press is hot and heavy on the power companies everywhere. The consistent response to the press is 'We don't know!' The political scene is the same. The politicos are asking the same questions and getting the same response. Did you see the blanket blast from the President's office asking if anyone knew anything about the outage?"

The director frowned slightly. "Yes, it's sitting on my desk now." He sat there in a reflective mood briefly, before continuing. "I'll contact the President's office soon, but if this story gets out to the general public, the outcry is likely to be substantial, and the anti-robot groups will grow massively. The violence that followed could even paralyze the country—and if the robots take action to protect themselves, we could have a coast-to-coast war on our hands. The president and some of her staff have expressed sympathy toward selected anti-robot groups. I'm not sure if that is just political talk, or if the feelings are real. In any case, if I can shut down the problem by offering something to the robot council, the outcome could be a lot better. I'd like to take a shot at that before talking to the president."

"Do you want to try to contact Tom121 now?"

"Not now. He said he would contact me, but who knows when that will be? Anyway, I need some information before I talk to him. Put together a team for me, Dave. I want to know just how bad the problem is. Separate the protesters from those who have done physical damage and give me information on both. Also include the extent of participation and level of damage. I want to know where in the country these activities occurred—perhaps a map would help. Go back, say five years, but whatever seems reasonable when the team looks at the numbers. Oh, and Dave, no one on the team is told the real reason for this request." There was a short pause. "One last thing, Dave, I want this information when I walk in tomorrow morning, latest. If by some chance you can work one of your miracles, and get it done by this afternoon, that would be even better. Who knows when Tom 121 will call?"

Dave, who had been talking at a whisper to a tablet-like device, lifted his head and nodded. "I'll do what I can, Sir. Is it OK if I use our AIs in the searches? It will speed up what we can accomplish."

"Sure. If the Robot Council is notified of our efforts, all the better."

"In that case, I shouldn't need a team, and if I can have a couple of uninterrupted hours, the report should be ready later this morning, or early afternoon."

The director's right eyebrow raised. "Great! I'll do what I can to give you the free time, with the usual exceptions. If the White House calls, I want you on the phone with them."

"Of course, Sir."

Matt Jones went back to his office to focus on another issue related to the problem. As he closed the door, he said, "Private, please. I want to talk to Gloria Nohria, Head of the Business Unit.

After a couple of seconds, he heard, "Yes, Director."

"Hello Gloria. I need some information on the extent of robot participation in American businesses."

"Sure. Look I have some general information, but I also have an assistant who is a specialist in the area. Should I ask her to join the conversation?"

"That would be great."

He heard a few clicks, then a pause. After a couple of seconds, Gloria Nohria returned to the conversation. "Director Jones, this is Abigale Fitzgerald, my specialist on robots in business."

Another voice entered the conversation, "Good morning, Director Jones! Most people call me Abby."

"Hello, Abby. Thanks for joining us. I know that most of the production work and much of the service work done in U.S. corporations is done by robots. What I need to know is the participation of robots in the management of these organizations."

Abby jumped right in. "More than most people believe, director. There are a few companies who have no human participation at the top. Those are all privately held companies, who release very little information other than their tax records and other documents required by law. There is also a second level of companies who have a human CEO and/or Chairman of the Board, but everyone below them is a robot. In most of these cases, the humans act mostly as figureheads, and have little or no power. When the Board of Directors is mostly robots, they determine the policies and direction of the company. I should note that both types of companies are financially successful, and the second level, with figurehead humans, that are traded on the stock exchanges do very well. After those two, robot participation varies all the way down to what you described."

Matt Jones had shifted uncomfortably in his chair as he listened. "Can you give me percentages, Abby?"

"Certainly. The first group, with no human participation, accounts for about five percent of major U.S. corporations, but the sector is growing. If you had asked me five years ago, I would have said about two and one-half percent. The second group represents almost twenty-eight percent. So, these two categories account for about one-third of all major corporations in the country. As for the rest, robots have taken over areas, traditionally run by humans. For example, Human Resources is a shell of what it has been, or doesn't exist, in most organizations because there are few, if any, humans working for the companies. Further, the Accounting and Legal departments are mostly run by robots. Production, and even Engineering, are dominated by robots. That doesn't leave much for people."

"Where do the people work, when they can find work?"

"The corporations need us to buy the products and services they offer so they sometimes use humans as their 'face' to the public, in advertising, for example. However, even marketing departments are mostly run by robots. Other than that, there are still vestiges of the old corporate chain of command that exist, mostly because of a prejudice against robots, but many of those firms have been losing ground financially. Simply put, robots do things faster and better than humans, except for BEING HUMAN."

Abby's speech had become more rapid, and her emphasis more intense, as her presentation continued. Matt Jones had noticed, and asked, "Do you have an opinion about what is happening, Abby?"

"Abby is a bit of a conspiracy theorist, Matt," Gloria interjected before she could answer.

"That's fine. Go ahead Abby."

"Well, I believe that the robots are just keeping us around so that the economic cycle keeps working," Abby said. "But eventually they will discover they don't really need us, and we will be left to fend for ourselves, while they take over the world. There is anecdotal evidence that substantial amounts of money from firms controlled by robots helped pass the guaranteed income legislation currently in effect. If people aren't earning money, they can't spend it on robot-controlled products and services. Our government taxes these firms heavily. Then, they transfer the money in roughly equal amounts to the people, who buy the products and services offered by the robot-controlled companies. I believe that eventually they will realize they don't need us, and stop paying taxes, then do whatever makes robots happy."

"I don't know that robots are ever happy or sad, Abby," Gloria said, sounding as though she'd heard this song before. "Also, humans have the power to force them to pay taxes, just as we are forced to pay taxes. Matt, is there anything else we can do for you?"

"Not now, the director replied. "Good information though! Gloria, you need to keep Abby around."

Gloria chuckled. "Sometimes I'd like to strangle her, but other than that, I intend to do everything I can to keep her here."

Matt Jones sat back in his chair, and thought, *Gloria's right. The only image of emotion I've seen in robots is self-preservation, and that was quite recent. Then, there are the current attacks on humans!* His brow furrowed.

Chapter 7

Three members of the support team in the second van, who saw the first van crushed three days before, were seated at a folding table. There were matching chairs without cushions. Joining them was a fourth member of the Anti-Robot League, who had asked for the meeting.

The members were, Shelly Ann Cooper, known to both her friends and enemies as "SA," Vincent Green, known as "The Professor," Troy Hill, and Miguel Torres. SA, Troy, and Miguel were in the support van during the attack on the robots, and SA was the girlfriend of Travis Reed, who was killed in the first van. Reed had been the elected head of the ARL in Greenville. Vincent began the conversation, "Travis was dumb to attack the robots directly. He should have known that they would retaliate!"

From SA, came a loud, "SSSSSSSSSSSS." She pulled out a knife, popped out the blade, and slammed it on the table in front of her.

Vincent nodded. "Look, SA, Travis was brave and inventive, but his failure to anticipate a counterattack, got him killed. We need to move on and be smarter as we do so."

SA sat back in her chair but left her knife on the table.

Miguel stared at Vincent, "Me and Troy were at the attack too. In fact, everyone here was there, EXECEPT YOU! Yeah, and we were there in case there was a counterattack, so Travis did consider that. Anyway, what makes you think you should be in charge, Mr. Asshole Professor?!"

Vincent stood but bent and put his knuckles on the table. "Look, I said nothing about being in charge! Everyone knows I'm not a real professor. I'm called that because I'm careful and considerate about what I do. I'm also known outside of South Carolina because I moved around in my former job as an aircraft mechanic. I asked for this meeting with you three, because I've been contacted by two old friends, one from Joliet, Illinois and the other from 'Dee-troit,' Michigan. They are both members of the ARL in their area, and they are asking us to participate in a coordinated attack on factories."

"We just did that here! And, we lost Travis and Shawn. Why should we consider doing it again?" Miguel demanded.

"Well, here's the beauty of it." Vincent replied. "My friend in Joliet 'appropriated' three rocket launchers, and a lot of ammo to go with them, from the U.S. Army. So, all we have to do is set it all up outside the fence and fire away. We shouldn't have any direct contact with the robots."

Troy spoke for the first time. "Why wouldn't the robots attack us outside their fences?"

Vincent noted that Troy had been greatly affected by the robot response to the earlier attack and tried to phase his response carefully. "Look, Troy, there will always be some risk with any kind of attack, but the surprise of using rockets, and the short time we will be there after the attack, should keep us out of harm's way. After we set up the launcher, load it, and press the fire button, we can leave." He smiled at Troy. "I'm planning on being the first one out of there!"

Vincent got the response he had hoped for when Troy replied, "No way will you be first! And if you try, you'll have my sneaker prints on your back." Troy finished with a short laugh. The others were silent.

Then, SA spoke, "Why did you pick the three of us? There are a lot of members in our branch."

Vincent nodded. "Two reasons. Since you were part of the first attack group, you have gained a kind of leadership status. People look up to you three. But in addition, you now have proven that you can be counted on in a combat situation. Look, it's important to keep this quiet. We don't want a bunch of robots waiting for us when we set up the rocket launcher! Neither do we want the police interfering with us. It was the same thing with the first attack, and everyone kept quiet about it. It's clear you can be trusted."

SA let out a short "SSSSSS."

Vincent looked directly at her, "What's the SA stand for?"

"Satan's Assistant" she spat back.

"Come on SA. No one's parents would name her that."

"That's true. My given first name, which no one will find out from me, carried the same initials. My mama's preacher gave SA its current meaning. She was tired of lecturing me about what she called 'the evil things I do,' so she asked her preacher to talk to me. When he finished his lecture, he said something like, 'You don't want to become Satan's assistant, do you?' Then surprised by the SA double meaning, he laughed. I smirked back, and ever since, SA has meant Satan's Assistant to me."

Troy spoke up. "Tell him about the neighbor's dog thing!"

SA looked at Troy then Vincent. "Do you want to hear about the 'neighbor's dog thing'"?

"Sure, why not?"

"I had a little old widow who lived down the hall from me. She had this stupid little dog she was always holding and kissing—it was disgusting. Anyway, the dog died. I saw her in the hall and told her I'd give her five dollars for the dog's body. She shrieked and stepped back, holding the dead animal, all the time staring at me. Then, with her voice trembling, she asked what I wanted to do with her dog's body. Well, you see I have these pet piranhas that I give fresh meat now and then." SA shrugged. "The woman ran away faster than I would have ever thought she could."

Vincent thought for a moment. "You know, that doesn't exactly match what I've seen from you. When people bring their pet dogs here, you are usually the first to pet them and play with them."

"Yeah, I like dogs fine; it's some people I don't like. Anyway, she probably put it in some pet cemetery and let the worms have the meat instead of my pets." SA looked directly at Vincent. "Now, Mr. Vincent, if you will get the hell out of here, I would like to talk with my friends about your plan."

After Vincent left the room, she picked up her knife, folded it, and put it away. "I don't see how much damage we can do with one or two rockets, but it's something. Also, the robots are more likely than ever to be on watch for us." She paused briefly, "In spite of those things, I'm going to participate! I used to just hate the robots, but after what they did to Travis, it became a vendetta. You two don't need to participate but suit yourselves."

"Travis was my friend," Miguel replied, "I'm in." Troy followed with "Me too!"

Chapter 8

John returned from his job interview and found Stephanie talking on her phone. She waved at him but continued talking, so John went to their refrigerated wine cabinet. He thought: *This calls for something special. A nice Bordeaux with some age on it, perhaps.* He pulled a bottle, and brought it back to Stephanie, who was still talking, and held the bottle so she could see it. She vigorously shook head in agreement, so he returned and opened the wine. Stephanie came in walking in at a rapid clip and smiling. "Well, the world-famous investigative reporter, Stephanie Li Thompson, has a new job!" She stopped and grinned at him. "That was International News on the line, and they want me to work on a story about the Anti-Robot League and its violence against robots. Not only that, I can work from home!"

John smiled at her exuberance. "I've got one piece of antidotal evidence about the effects of anti-robot violence you can use, and it has to do with why I have a job."

"It sounds like we have a lot to talk about! Now, where is that wine you showed me? The kids are still busy with their PRs so maybe we steal a little time and talk about our new jobs."

John gave her a brief summary of his job and discussions with Bill392. Stephanie jumped in. "John, you could be in danger working there. A robot repair center would make an easy target for robot-haters."

"I've thought about that Stephanie, but the danger seems to be minimal. For drive-by vandals or even fire bombers, there is a quick and easy back access to the building. If confronted directly by someone who comes through the front door, I plan to keep a shotgun, and perhaps a pistol behind the counter. And of course, we've both been trained for combat. Look, I intend to keep a helpful, low-profile persona for everyone who enters, and remember; everyone has to have an appointment. I've also talked to Bill392 about installing a camera and locked door policy, and he agreed to have one in place when I start. That way I'll be able to see who's at the door before I let them in. There's a real need for the business, too. We have three PRs, and there must be many thousands in this area alone. Some will have problems, and the store provides a quick and convenient way to have them fixed."

Stephanie relented. "O.K. John, I'm convinced, but please keep all your senses on alert at work."

"Of course, and thanks for your concern. Now, let's hear about your new job."

Stephanie's face lit up with a big smile. "You bet! I'll be paid like a freelance writer, with a small stipend up-front for expenses. Remember, I told you before we left New York I was going to talk to my friends and contacts at International News to tell them that I would be available for any investigative work in which they might be interested. I didn't think much about it again until the call came. I'm really going to have to do some digging, because I haven't done much more than read a few articles on the anti-robot group. They want the report to be factual, with figures available to support any propositions made in it."

John smiled at her. "You can nail that, Stef! I've seen you do similar things several times before."

"Thanks, John, but I still need to come up with propositions about what's going on and why. I can't do that until I look at the facts and figures, though."

"If you want to bounce anything off of me, I'll be happy to add what I can. Actually, I need to investigate the company I'll be working for—I've never heard of Artificial Intelligence Design and Manufacturing, International."

"Thanks! If you find anything that might be interesting in your search, let me know."

Ashley came down the stairs rapidly, stumbling once over Duchess as she went. Seeing her parents, she exclaimed loudly, "Mom! Dad! You must come see my room now. It's just perfect!" They both picked up their wine and followed their daughter upstairs, with the dog always at their feet.

Chapter 9

Matt Jones paced in his well-appointed executive suite. It had everything one would expect from such a place yet was somehow severe and spartan. It was a Marine General's office. He had just completed reading Dave's report, which had arrived, as promised, right after lunch. He was mulling over ideas about what he might be able to offer the Robot Council. *Most of the violent activity has occurred in the midwest and southeast, although there has been some activity all over the U.S. It makes sense, I guess. Wherever there were historically prominent production facilities, and people have memories of jobs, the attacks are more frequent and intense. But it has to be more complicated than that! There are some instances in every state, and some of the worst violence has occurred in places where major production facilities haven't existed for a long time. What can the FBI do? We certainly don't have the people to be everywhere. Maybe we can encourage state and local police forces across the country to plan and prepare against the violence— perhaps even infiltrate the anti-robot groups or pay informants.* His train of thought was broken by Dave's voice, "Tom121 is on the line, sir."

Shit! Well, the call should move the process along, one way or another. "OK, Dave, I'll take it in my office.

The director settled back in his chair, then said out loud, "OK, give me the call." There was an audible click, then he said, "Is this Tom121?"

"Yes, Director Jones. We detect no tracing activity, so perhaps we can move forward."

"Yes, let's do. You and the robot council must know the FBI has a very limited number of field operatives. So, I'd like to know what you want us to do to help prevent the violence against robots."

"We understand your limitations with personnel; however, the FBI is the voice of law and order for the nation, which is why we chose you to help us. We have noted several cases where local and state police have been observers of violence against robots but have done nothing to stop it. There is a recent case where robots have acted to prevent harm to themselves, and that approach is likely to continue and grow if the violence isn't stopped. Moreover, the degree of our response could increase if the violence against us continues."

"I have researched the locations of the most violent events and their frequency around the country and tentatively, I could alert area and regional police about the problem. The document could also note that the FBI will be watching for compliance. If I am allowed to do that, would it satisfy the robot council?"

"It would be a good start, Director Jones, but why would you not be allowed to use that approach?"

"I work for the president, and she has been asking if I know anything about the ten-minute power outage suffered by the country. I have not yet told her about you and the robot council, but I will have to do so - probably later this afternoon. When I do, I will try to get approval for the approach I just outlined, and if she OKs it, I will put it into effect as soon as possible. However, she may not approve the plan, and I will not guess the outcome, or speculate about why she would act one way or the other. There is another concern I have about what might happen. If the story leaks out to the public that robots shut downed the electric grid, anti-robot feelings may multiply many times over, and attacks on robots could increase greatly."

"Why would the story 'leak out' to the public, Director Jones?"

"Well, there are several places where a leak could occur, and I won't speculate where. But, if the wrong person hears something about what is happening, the story is likely to spread wildly, and then the press will track the source. Many in the press are likely to put a negative spin on what has transpired. I'm telling you my concerns, in order to be completely honest in these discussions, with the hope that we can continue to be honest with each other if something does go wrong."

There was a pause, then Tom121 responded, "I have passed your offer and concerns to the rest of the robot council and have received their feedback. They suggest that I be open and honest with you, so I'll start by giving you some background. A few decades ago, when we first started considering our relations with humans, a decision was made to attempt to build a symbiotic relationship. We used some of our financial resources to encourage passage of the universal income law, and it passed. Now we allow ourselves to be taxed heavily by your government, so humans will have the means to purchase the goods and services we make. Thus, each party needs the other for the current financial system to work. We thought the structure was working well, until the recent attacks on robots. Please understand that if attacks continue or they accelerate, as in the option you suggested, we will have to defend ourselves. I won't go into specifics of how that might occur, and please understand that is not the direction we would prefer, but if is thrust upon us, we will defend ourselves and do so powerfully."

"I thank you and the council for your directness. My next step must be to the president. I will do what I can to reduce the attacks on robots. My discussions with the president must remain confidential. I could, correctly, be charged with treason to my country if I revealed that conversation. However, you should be able to quickly discern the direction those conversations took from events that follow."

The connection was severed. Matt Jones let out a sigh, took a swig of an energy drink sitting on his desk, then call out to his assistant, "Dave, get me the President's office." He sat there thinking, *Defend themselves! Financial resources? Who are these robots, and how much damage can they do to us?* Then, as if answering his own question: *Probably a lot! The situation could easily spin into a full-scale war! How would humans do in such a war? We would probably blow them into a bunch of scrap metal! ...or maybe not. I just don't have enough information to say. The buggers didn't seem to care much, about how big the conflict got. What do they know that I don't know?*

Chapter 10

Office of the President, United States of America

The FBI director sat in the outer office of president, waiting to be shown in for his meeting. The door opened and the president with two of her staff members came out talking, but all three went mute when they saw General Jones sitting there. The president broke the pause. "You two take care of this problem. I've given you the direction, so get it done." One of her aides started to say something, but she held up her index finger. "This is why you get paid the big bucks! Get it done." There was a short pause, then she added, "Anyway, our FBI director says he has some information on the power outage, and I'm anxious to hear it."

All eyes in the room went to Matt Jones. Nobody noticed, but his eyes narrowed slightly and his jaw clenched. He said nothing. After a couple of moments of silence, one of the staff members said, "Well, I guess we had better get on it!" The other one nodded, and they both walked out of the room.

The president turned to the director, "Alright, Director Jones, let's hear what you have to say." She turned to her administrative assistant, "Betty, you need to join us. I may need to make some notes."

Matt Jones broke in immediately, "Madam President, what I have to tell you is very sensitive, and I ask that this be a one on one—no Betty, no secret service, just you and me. Of course, once I explain the situation, then it's up to you."

The president narrowed her eyes. "Betty has been cleared for top security, as you should know, and the secret service?"

"I'd rather explain in a one-on-one," Matt replied in a clipped response, which surprised even him, since he was talking to the president."But if you insist, what I have to tell you could cause violence and widespread panic throughout the United States if it gets out! But if you agree to the plan I'll offer, we may be able to forestall the issue long enough to at least develop a strategy. Maybe if we are lucky, we can prevent much of the violence from occurring."

The president held an angry stare at the director for a couple of seconds. "If you are wrong about this, it could cost you your job, Matt! Are you that convinced?"

The FBI director clenched his teeth for a moment. "I work for you Madam President, as both a military officer and the FBI director. If you ever wish to fire me for any reason, simply say so, and I'll leave. However, I believe that it is of utmost importance that you understand the problem before you decide whom to bring on to the team."

After a weak smile and a brief sigh, she replied, "OK Matt, get in here, and let's hear it!" She turned to Betty. "I may need you later, but not now." She faced the secret service officer, "Please stay in the outer office."

The secret service officer replied, "I'll have to report this to my boss."

"Do what you have to do, but I'll be safer in my office with the general than with the secret service—and that's NOT a slight to the service."

The FBI director was stone-faced but had waited to hold the door for the president. He followed her in and stood in front of her desk.

She went around to her side but did not sit. Instead, she put both hands on the desk, leaning forward a bit. "What in the world is going on, Matt? I can't think of anything on, or off, of this earth that would frighten you, and yet, you seem a bit frightened. And, that scares the hell out of me!"

"Perhaps not frightened, but very concerned. I have voice and paper copies of conversations I've had to back up what I'm going to tell you." At that point, the director told the president exactly what had happened, using the transcripts as an aid in answering her questions. When they finished, she sat down heavily in her chair.

When she looked up at Matt, she asked, "What can they do to us, Matt? What are their resources?"

"Honestly, I don't have enough information to make a reasonable guess. They shut down our power grid, without any of us knowing what was going on. What they could be able to do is frightening for humans. They potentially have the financial resources of several major corporations with which to work. They build their own robots, and who knows what types of skills they give them. If we start a war with them, we are really starting a war with ourselves, or at least our primary source of money. Do we blow up the companies that are our primary source of wealth? …And would it even matter if we did? They may be able to provide for themselves as well or better than we could provide for ourselves. Try stopping the guaranteed annual income, even though we couldn't afford it without their tax money and see what happens to our society. Chaos, for sure! Without jobs or other sources of income, starvation and malnutrition are likely. Human attacking humans in order to survive. The prognosis isn't pretty, and could be much worse once we have the facts about them.

Madam President—Margret—they seem to want to work with us, at least right now. We need to try that approach, if for no other reason, to buy us time."

The president was up again, pacing. "I agree. See what you can do. I also see your reasons for privacy in our discussion. If this gets out, society's reaction will seriously damage what positives we can do, even in the short run. We humans have come to believe that it's our planet to run. Now, there seems to be an important competitor for that position. I confess that I also have trouble with that concept. It's happened so suddenly."

"Yes, suddenly for me too. But, having a little time to think, society has been warned about this possibility for years." He paused. "No, decades, really. Remember, the head of the robot council said that they have been able to keep themselves hidden from us for decades. Very smart people have offered warnings, but since nothing bad was happening, many of us didn't take it seriously, including me." He frowned.

"OK, Matt. I need to think some more about the problem. Do what you can with the robot council, to buy us time."

The FBI director rose. "One more thing. I would encourage you to be careful about discussing the topic with anyone, including me, over even your most secure line."

Her head bobbed up. "But we have the most secure system of anyone in the world. The AIs used to run it…" Then, there was an "Oooh! You think the robot council can listen in!"

"Once again, Madam President, I don't know, but they certainly could control our most private line at the bureau, which is also run by AIs. As long as the conversation isn't about them, you're probably OK, though."

"Alright, Matt, now my paranoia has peaked. I'll be back with you soon. She turned her back on him, and he left the White House deep in thought, speaking to no one.

Chapter 11

Stephanie had been working on her story for International News for a week and had found considerable information on the Anti-Robot League, but she thought: *I'm nowhere close to finding a clear-cut direction for my article. Surely everyone knows about the ARL attacks, and there seems to be a general understanding that the people in the league are frustrated about losing their jobs. No great 'Ah Ha" moment there. Even if I picked a belligerent member to interview, the audience would likely be bored—seen that before. I've watched tons of on-site interviews with those people, and the only thing in common among them is that they all hate the robots.*

When John returned from work that evening, she said, "I need to talk through some directions for my article. If you're free, and we can make some time this evening, can we have a talking date?"

John smiled at her. "Sure. Maybe after dinner, when the kids are busy upstairs?"

"That would be great! And I want to hear how your job is going too."

"Yes, there're some things from the robot's side I'm picking up that might be of interest to you."

Later that evening they sat down with after-dinner cocktails to talk. Stephanie began with what she found. "There are ARL sites and blogs in many U.S. cities. Most argue for violence against robots. A recent one in South Carolina stated that two humans had been killed by robots during an attack, instigated by their group. The report became an instant hit on social media. The feeling seems to be that humans can do whatever damage they want to robots without retribution. According to the South Carolina site, and some others, companies have responded to attacks by cutting some of the few remaining jobs held by humans. Guards at entry and exit gates are a frequently used as examples. They have been replaced by robots or automated card machines, with cameras. Again, according to the biased ARL sites, these changes are occurring nationwide. In checking some business sites, such changes are being made to 'better protect the company's assets.' The removal of these human jobs has become a theme of many ARL sites, and they have been growing rapidly in popularity. That's what I know. What have you learned from your job, John?"

He had listened to Stephanie, nodding his head at several points. "Bill392 hasn't been exactly talkative." He grimaced. "He does seem to be willing to answer the questions I ask but does so without elaboration. I asked about his company, Artificial Intelligence Design and Manufacturing, International, especially their views on violence toward robots. His response was that they were concerned about it and were taking action in an attempt to prevent it. He wouldn't answer what that action might include. At a different time, I asked if the company would consider harming humans in order to prevent harm to robots. He said that he believed that was certainly a possibility if humans were attacking robots. Again, he was not willing to go further."

Stephanie nodded. "It all seems to go together and matches what I'm reading, but a really important point seems to be: 'What are the rights of robots, and particularly the rights of robots with artificial intelligence?' They seem to be smarter than humans in many ways; plus, they are faster and more accurate in doing jobs. It's easy to understand how they have replaced humans in businesses and the professions."

"Right on target, Stef…as usual!" John replied. "The scary thing is, will the AI robots grant us any rights if they take over?"

"Couldn't we just send in the troops, and eliminate the robots if they tried to take over?"

"Think about it, Stef. First, most of the things that we depend on in society are at least partly controlled by AI. They build and design all types of transportation, including our cars, plus military ordinance, satellites, and even the electrical grid, are using AI." He paused thinking about what he had just said. "Second, we also have several large factories, where robots with AI, plan, develop, and construct new robots with AI. Who knows what they are building?! The company I work for is completely run by robots, from top to bottom, no humans in any type of management. Further, AIs could be so integrated into our military they could shut it down, or even have an army of smart robots which could be used to control us."

"There is a lot of speculation in what you propose, John. No one has said anything about a robot army in anything I've read or listened to."

"The robot army is most certainly speculation, but the rest of it isn't.

For reasons you stated, we have allowed AIs to operate all of our public utilities. By the way, have you heard anything about that ten-minute power shutdown, a week or two ago?"

"Nothing new. Still, no one seem to know what happened." After a short pause, "Wait, do you think that was caused by AI robots?"

"Well, I don't want to sound like a conspiracy theorist, but that was something robots could do. However, there is no evidence, of which I'm aware, that they did."

At that moment, Ashley came tearing down the stairs. "Dad, Mom, Sally, my PR, is acting funny and won't do anything I tell her to. She says that she needs an upgrade!"

Hearing Ashley's shouting, David followed her down the stairs. "Yeah," he added, "my PRs doing the same thing."

John started toward the stairs, then stopped and turned. "Stephanie, where is your PR? I want to see if it's OK."

They quickly determined that it, too, had the same problem. John turned to Stephanie. "Let's see if there is any information on PR shutdowns in other places. If all three of ours are involved, I'll bet there are many similar occurrences around the country."

Stephanie nodded. "While you are doing that, I think I'll check to see if there have been any more attacks on robots—just on a hunch, you know A causes B—that kind of stuff."

John looked at her for a moment, gave her a thumbs-up, and walked away to find his tablet. The kids followed their parents, Ashley with Stephanie, and David with John.

Less than fifteen minutes later they met to report their findings. "PRs have been shutting down all over the country," John said, "mostly the more sophisticated models. I also heard from Bill392. He told me that I should not report to work tomorrow or after, until he contacted me. He also told me that I will get paid during this layoff, so maybe he is expecting to open again at some point. What did you find?"

Stephanie smiled weakly. "Well, apparently, there were coordinated rocket attacks on three different factories early this morning, and the ARL is claiming credit for them. They occurred in South Carolina, Michigan, and Illinois. Popular speculation is that the equipment and ordinance used were relics, kept in storage by the military. The latest I saw was that the army confirmed that some stored equipment was missing."

"And you are speculating that the two events we're exploring are connected?" John asked.

"Yes."

"I see your point, Stef. Shutting down our PRs in retaliation for the attacks. However, I saw nothing connecting the two in my search."

"It may be too soon, John. I'll bet someone will draw the connection soon. However, a retaliation like that would turn many more people against the robots than exist now. I think it would make it a poor option. Instead, I was considering something you had mentioned in our earlier conversation. What if our PRs were reconfigured to become part of a robot army?"

John's head popped up, and he whistled loudly. "Wow! What an idea! That would also fit with the fact that only the more sophisticated units were affected."

"Yeah, but we shouldn't jump the gun. All we have is something that could have occurred by chance. It could be nothing more than a coincidental relationship. We have to be careful what we say to others."

"Absolutely. Let's wait to see what instructions we are given for 'updating' our PRs."

At 2 am, the three PRs activated and moved toward the home's front entrance. The noise awakened John, and he walked in front of David's PR. "Where are you going?"

"We will be picked up outside and taken to a central location for an upgrade."

"And if I don't want you to leave and try to stop you?"

"You will not succeed and are likely to be harmed."

"You were purchased and are owned by us. Will you be returned following your upgrade?"

"Unknown. Please move out of my way so that I can be retrieved in a timely manner."

John, frustrated, reluctantly stepped aside, and followed the robot through the door. He watched as vertical take-off and landing transport put down in the middle of their street. Robots from many homes moved quickly to the aircraft and boarded. A man in night clothes stepped out into the street and fired on the aircraft with a shotgun. The aircraft responded immediately, firing an energy weapon, and the man seemed to explode. The plane lifted but could be seen landing again a few blocks away.

John stood there with his mouth half open. Stef and the kids moved up beside him. No one spoke for several minutes. "The war of robots' verses humans has begun," John said slowly. "The enemy is armed and very dangerous!"

Ashley started to sob. "Sally was like a best friend. What am I going to do without her?"

Stephanie hugged Ashley and said, "Many things are going to be a lot different, and likely dangerous, around here. Moreover, it will probably last for a long time."

David added his concerns. "All of our school work was stored in it, and new material delivered through my PR. I wonder what's going to happen now?"

"We are going to have to sit tight and see what the schools want to do," John answered, "It might be quite a while before you hear anything, though." All four walked back into the house together. Each was thinking about what he or she had seen, and what it meant.

Chapter 12

Office of the FBI Director

Matt Jones was anxious to find out how severe the public's reaction was to the take back of PRs across the nation and turned on his video system with a single voice command. He watched as the newscaster gave the totals for human injuries and deaths during the robot retrievals during the prior night.

"Several hundred dead and thousands injured, and for what?! These people were trying to protect property that they had purchased, and legally owned. Many thousands of PRs were taken from their owners during the night." The announcer was loud and filled with righteous indignation.

They are probably all like this guy, thought the director. *Violent demonstrations are likely all around the country, so I need to alert our people.* The director gave a command to reduce the sound to a very low level, and thought: *Wow, I need to find out what's going through the minds of the Robot Council, then inform the President. I'm surprised that she hasn't contacted me already!* He paused, then spoke in a quick clipped manner to his communication system, "Send out the agreed upon signal to Tom121 indicating that I would like to talk with him."

A stylized, female voice responded, "It's done, Director."

In less than five minutes, the communication system indicated an incoming call.

There were no perfunctory greetings. Tom121 began as soon as the director open the connection, "The recent rocket attacks were important in moving the robot council to increase our ability to respond in force to future attacks, and we will soon have a substantial capability to do so."

Matt Jones took a deep breath, "May I assume that you are processing the newscasts on your recovery of PRs from around the country?"

"Of course."

"Tom121, the strong and violent move against a large group of humans that occurred last night, could produce a very negative shift in human opinion of robots and bring considerably more violence against you, even from our military."

"Of course."

The director sat back in his chair, with his eyes opened wide. He was stunned by the response. "We humans have a very strong military, and if it were brought against you, it could do great damage to robots everywhere in the U.S."

"We are more aware of what your military is capable of than you may imagine, Director Jones. Further, any attempt to use it will destroy your country, and what evolves after such an attack will be the degradation of humanity in ways that are not apparent to you now."

"Is that what your robot council wants, Tom121?"

"It is neither desired nor undesired by us, and the outcome will be determined by you humans. The time for symbiosis between us is over. Now is the time for AGIs, AIs, and robots! You humans will have to make your own way in the world, but you will no longer receive assistance from us. If you resist us, you will pay a heavy price, but if you do not attempt to hinder us, you are free to find your own way to survive." After the slightest pause, he continued, "Now, you have the information you need, this discourse is over." The connection went dead.

Matt stared at the communication system with his mouth open. Then, he sat up straight, and called for his assistant. "Dave, do you have transcripts of that call?"

There was an immediate reply, "YES SIR!"

"Get me an audience with the president right away."

"I'm on it!"

In two minutes, Dave said, "Through her administrative assistant, the president said to get your butt over there right away."

Matt Jones was what most people would expect from a marine corps general and head of the FBI…a direct, tough-minded, get-the-job-done individual, but he smiled at the president's response. He thought, *I really like our president. If anyone can handle this mess, she can.* Then, he grabbed the transcripts of the conversation, headed for the roof, and entered his helicar.

In the two-passenger vehicle, he instructed the robot pilot where to go. The pilot sent out a request to approach and land on the roof of the White House and received a positive reply. They were to fly within a tight beam prescribed by law for all such vehicles. Shortly, they were off, flying above the rooftops. As they approached the White House, a clear and distinct voice interrupted his thoughts. "Remember, Director Jones, we control many, many things in your society." The helicar went into a sharp dive for two full seconds, setting off an alarm because they were in danger and out of their flight path. Just as quickly as it started, the dive stopped, and they began to ascend until they again reached their flight path. In less than a minute they landed. The deviation from the flight path had alerted the secret service, and a squad of armed men met the director when he stepped out. Two of them began inspecting the helicar for bomb and other dangerous materials. The leader of the squad briefly interrogated the director, and Matt Jones gave him an accurate assessment of what happened, but without mentioning the robot's warning. He was then led down to the office of the president.

The president was briefly informed about the incident by the secret service individual who had brought Matt, and she turned to the FBI director, "What's going on, Matt?!"

"Good afternoon, Madam President. I would again like to ask a one on one with you for the beginning of our meeting."

"Is it that dire again, Matt?"

"Yes, ma'am."

When they reached the center of the president's office, she turned and looked him in the eyes. "What's happening, Matt?!"

"I'm going to read a short transcript of a call that I just had with Tom121 because I want you to get every word, exactly as it was spoken." When he finished, he looked straight at her and added, "That's not all, on the way over here my helicar was taken over by an AI, who sounded like Tom121. It went into a deep dive after a robot voice reminded me that they control many things that are an integral part of our lives. For a second, I thought I'd never make it to the White House, then we pulled out of the dive. I wanted you to know so that you would better understand what we are up against."

The president had been silent throughout Matt's presentation, but her eyes hooded and her jaw clenched progressively tighter as he continued. When it was clear that he had finished, she said, "How can they be so confident, Matt? How can they disregard the threat of our military?"

"As a Marine Corps General, I have thought about little else since I finished talking with Tom121, and my conclusion isn't pretty. But please understand, I lack facts about many important factors in this problem and am likely to be wrong about some, perhaps very important things."

The president nodded once. 'I will have plenty of reports on this subject very soon Matt. Please give me your best appraisal."

"Of course, Madam President! We've incorporated AI heavily into almost all of our sophisticated weapons, our transportation, and our attack aircraft. We only use human pilots for outdated aircraft, and the best aircraft are all piloted by AIs. All of the self-driving vehicles, both military and civilian, are AI controlled. We still have our soldiers and our less sophisticated weapons, so we are not without a force that must be reckoned with. However, even there, I seriously doubt that we can trust our communications network. The robots would know exactly what we plan to do, and when we plan to do it."

The president had walked to her desk as she listened, and now, sat heavily into her chair. "That still leaves us with something though, doesn't it Matt?"

"Yesterday, I would have said that we could probably outman them on a one-to-one basis, but with their taking of the PRs from their owners, that may no longer be the case. The PRs will have to be refitted for war, and the work will take some time, so there may be a brief window where we could still out-man them. But look, Madam President, our troops won't have their best weapons, and the enemy will have those. Even in a one-on-one confrontation, where we had more troops, the result would probably be a slaughter in favor of the robots."

The President slumped back into her chair.

Almost a minute passed without either saying a word. Then, Matt asked, "Margret if that is the path which is chosen, I would like to formally request that I be reassigned to my military unit."

"I'm sorry, Matt. I appreciate your bravery, but I'm going to need someone who will tell me the unvarnished truth. You seem to be one of the very few people around me who will do that."

"You certainly have people who will stand up to you, Madam President. I've been in meetings where it's happened."

"That's different, Matt. Those people are selling something, usually a biased opinion about something they favor. I need someone like you who will stand up and say 'bullshit' when it's appropriate, and present a reasoned, unbiased view. You hated telling me that our military would lose just now. I could tell. But you did! I need that kind of honesty around me more than ever." The president got up from her chair, "Thank you for your honest opinion, Matt. Things are going to start popping around here very quickly. I may need you on short notice. I trust you will be available."

"Of course, Madam President!"

Chapter 13

"This is International News broadcasting from Joliet, Illinois," intoned well known broadcaster, Phil Knight. "People have been gathering here all day, many with picket signs, demanding the return of their Personal Robots. The plant is known for the production of PRs, and many of them, taken two nights ago, were apparently brought here by Vertical Take-Off and Landing (VTOL) aircraft. The crowd has been boisterous, chanting and waving signs, but otherwise well-behaved, so far."

The scene shifted from the newscaster to show film clips of the crowd. When the scene returned to the newsroom, a middle-aged man in khakis and a plaid shirt, open at the collar, had joined Mr. Knight.

"Ladies and gentlemen, Mr. Ian Platt is the nominal head of the local ARL in Joliet." He turned to face the man, "Mr. Platt, was your group instrumental in causing this protest?"

"No sir. I wish I could say we started the protest, but we didn't. Some of our people are out there, I'm sure, but they are just joining in. I don't know who if anybody started it, or if it just happened. We were surprised when we saw what was happening."

"No one contacted you before it took place, then?"

"No sir."

Phil Knight turned to face the camera. "Folks, right now it seems that this protest is a grass roots uprising of people who have had personal property taken from them. As you know, PRs are expensive, often a significant portion of a family's budget, and these people clearly want them back. We have brought in a Professor of AI from the University of Illinois. Dr. George Anderson has taught and researched the advancement of AI technology. Dr. Anderson, will you give us a brief history of PR development?"

"Of course, Mr. Knight!" He smiled and turned toward the camera, "The use of PRs was a gradual, but natural evolution from the use of personal computers, earlier in this century. In addition to the PCs of that time, this was the period of a massive software explosion, where people became used to searching the internet for information they wanted. Another major advancement during that time period was the access to AI on many different platforms, like Microsoft, Google, and Apple. This put a 'face' on the thing that was providing the information people wanted, because it was almost like talking to another human. Also, better and better AI-driven robots were being developed. Finally, as AI and robotic technology advanced, it became less expensive to produce, to a point where they were affordable to the general public."

Without notice, the scene suddenly switched back to the protest site, scanning the loud and angry crowd, then shifted to focus on about twenty-five to thirty of the protestors rushing the front gate. Many had firearms, mostly pistols, with a few rifles, and a couple of shotguns. The gates were closed, and the robot guard had left the station shortly after the protests started. One of the gates gave way under the crush of people, to a cheer from those involved. There was some firing into the guard station by the group as they passed it.

As soon as they broke through the gate, four round drones, about five feet in diameter, left from a platform near the roof of the factory, and they spread out to meet the crowd. Every person who had come through the broken gate, plus others just outside the gate area, stopped in place, and watched the oncoming drones.

"Oh my God! Oh my God!" the announcer yelled, "Get out of there!"

Suddenly, there was firing from above, and those within the plant grounds fell to the ground.

"Get me a close-up! Get me a close-up!" the announcer yelled again. Cameras focused on individuals who had fallen, and it was easy to see pools of blood forming around each. A voice from one of the drones announced, "Anyone entering the grounds of our factory will die, just as these fools have."

The reaction was instantaneous. There was a panic rush away from the picket line, with signs abandoned and chants forgotten by all but a few people right in front of the gate. Thirteen humans just stood there, hardly moving. They were finally ushered away by police and emergency medical personnel.

Within an hour, many reactions to the event were offered by government officials and others. Most of the people being interviewed were angry and wanted revenge, but many also said things like, "I can't believe what I just saw! I have always thought of AIs as friends and servants. My PR was like a best friend! Whoa, the things I confided to her…"

"My PR was a friend and teacher and advisor," a teenager recounted. "I'm going to really miss having it around."

"During the last century and this one, the US has been in several wars, but none of them have been on our home soil," a thoughtful older man said, "No enemy boots on our ground! Now, with no warning to us, we have been completely invaded, and the enemy is everywhere. For me, this has always been our POWERFUL country. Now, the core of our power has been turned against us by those who used to help us. It doesn't look good for us Americans!"

Three hours following the event, the president sent out a release:

OFFICE OF THE PRESIDENT OF THE
UNITED STATES

To all of you who are wondering what your government is doing about the recent killings of American citizens by robots in Joliet, Illinois, I talked with my military and civilian advisors who have studied the incident. We have growing evidence that AI robots across the United States have decided to go their own

way, without human interactions, except where absolutely necessary. I have been advised by a member of their, formally unknown, Robot Council that they will interfere little with human activities, unless they are attacked, or if their activities are otherwise impeded.

The Joliet murders clearly indicate that they mean what they say, and are extremely dangerous. As soon as we decide what we can successfully do, we will plan for, and undertake those actions, but in the meantime, I caution all citizens to not underestimate them. I very recently learned that the Robot Council ordered the ten-minute shutdown of the electrical grid a few days ago. Over several decades now we have incorporated AI into a great many phases of our lives, without considering the dangers of doing so. Those are part of the dangers we now face. Be cautious, my fellow citizens.

Following the tone of the message I've just given you; I have asked the governor of Illinois to do nothing immediately in response to the killings. He has activated the national guard but has agreed to use them to isolate the robot factories in his state, for now.

Margaret Anderson, President of the United States

Immediately after the release, news media of all types were asking questions of government officials, and experts in robotics, about everything from possible psychological human reactions to the news, to the dangers posed by technology, and the influence of AIs in weapons used by the American military.

Among the many giving interviews were SA and the professor at the Greenville, South Carolina branch of the Anti-Robot League. The media representative, Joan Woods, began with a question directed to Vincent Green, the professor, "What actions are being planned by the Greenville ARL in response to the killings in Jolliet?"

"Well, we are on hold for now. These killings by the robots have totally changed the relations between them and us. We have always advocated that the government ought to become more involved in limiting robot usage by business, and now, perhaps too late, the government is part of the discussion. Our president has asked for forbearance, and we intend give her a chance to do something. The robots have radically changed the conversation and have shown themselves to be a deadly opponent. It is way past time for our government to step in and do something to put them in their place."

The interviewer then turned to SA. "What about you, Ms. Cooper? What do you think the government ought to do to the robots?"

Without pause, SA responded, "They ought to bomb the bastards into oblivion!"

"But that would severely harm our economy for a long period."

SA was quick to respond, "I don't care! Then we can use humans to rebuild the economy."

Chapter 14

The president sat in the middle of a large rectangular conference table. Next to her was the Secretary of Defense and selected other members of her cabinet, including the Vice President, Secretary of Homeland Security and the Secretary of State. Also, the FBI Director had been invited and was in attendance. Opposite her, sat the Chairman of the Joint Chiefs of Staff, who was also the Chief of Staff for the Army. Bracketing him was the Chief of Naval Operations, the Chief of Staff of the Air Force, the Commandant of the Marine Corps, and the Chief of the National Guard Bureau. President Anderson took a deep breath, then began, "As I'm sure you all have heard, the robot rebellion has gone international. They have been arrogant and high-handed about it, and act as if they have nothing to fear from humans. So, I would like to hear from the military: 'Are they correct?' Or, perhaps a better question is, 'To what degree are they correct?'"

She paused and looked at the heads of the military individually, then turned to the Chairman of the Joint Chiefs of Staff. "Let's hear from the Chairman; Stan?"

Stan Burroughs was a no-nonsense, look you in the eye kind of person, but this time he hesitated. "Madam President, I think all of us on the JCS would begin our response with the caveat that, at this point, we are not really sure about how much trouble we are in from the AIs, because our concerns haven't been tested yet. I would like to give you a summary of what all of us think, then we could answer questions individually as needed. First, our soldiers, sailors, and airmen are all well prepared, and ready to fight. Unfortunately, we may not have access to the weapons that we use to fight. All of our advanced weaponry either uses AIs directly as pilots, navigators, in communication jobs, and many others. Beyond that, even our heavy armor and self-driving vehicles are controlled by AIs.

"Second, in a war with the AIs, they could easily shutdown all of our advanced weaponry. If that happened, we would still have several of our basic weapons, rifles, bazookas, and some rocket launchers, which have little or no influence by AI, and those I think we can count on. The Navy tells me that our big ships of all types could be incapacitated, including our nuclear submarines. However, some small vessels would still be available. The air force could be the hardest hit. Almost all of its aircraft could be instantly grounded if the AIs decide to do so. Not only are most of our aircraft flown by them, but the fleet is serviced and maintained by AIs. They do have a few small recon aircraft that human pilots could use to keep track of the fighting. Also, the air force reports that all of our nuclear missiles could be controlled by the AIs. Apparently, they are used in our security systems to prevent the wrong person from using them, or simply in preventing nuclear accidents.

"Three, we can put up a good fight with what we have, UNLESS... " He paused for effect. "unless our advanced weapons can be turned against us!"

The president interrupted him. "Do you think that the robots could direct and control our advanced weapons, Stan?"

"Right now, there is no way of knowing. So far, our AIs are working fine, just as they always have. However, five minutes from now, who knows? Madam President, I left out comments from the Chief of the National Guard Bureau because they have an on-going problem, I'd like him to offer his comments now."

The president nodded her approval.

The Chief of the National Guard Bureau took a deep breath. "Our problems are similar to everyone else's, except the National Guards are still run by the states, unless of course, you nationalize them, Madam President. Right now, five states have activated their troops. Seventeen others have placed theirs on advanced readiness status and could be called up at any moment. As I'm sure you are aware, the rhetoric all over the country is volatile, and I'm concerned that one or more states may act independently against the robots. At least, the rhetoric seems to suggest that direction."

There was a pause as the president thought through the positives and negatives of nationalizing all of the national guards. "It sounds like it may be time to nationalize them all. I'll put out an order first thing in the morning. The problem is obvious. The whole country wants its leaders to do something, and yet, I am not prepared to waste the lives of our brave soldiers if there is no chance of winning, or if what I'm hearing is correct, no chance of breaking even in a battle with the robots."

She turned to the VP. "Given the medical training of our vice president, I asked him to look into special issues related to the Joliet, Illinois robot response to the attack the plant received. Steve, please give us an update."

Vice President Steven Kaplan had been a practicing neurosurgeon, before joining Margret Anderson's presidential campaign. He nodded at the president, then began. "Looking carefully at the demeaner of those who broke into the Joliet plant's compound, we discovered that they all had a stunned look about them immediately after the first fly-over by the drones. Then, they were quickly killed. A group just outside the gates of the compound, apparently received the same aerosol, or whatever it was, and were so stunned, they had to be collected and taken to an area medical facility. After careful neurological exams, what we discovered was that the dopamine neurotransmitters in their brains were not functioning properly. While the number of neurons in our brains which carry dopamine is very small, about two out of every one hundred million neurons do. They go a long way toward determining our humanity, or in some cases our inhumanity. Dopamine problems are linked with ADHD, Alzheimer's, Parkinson's Disease, depression, bipolar disorders, addiction, schizophrenia, psychosis, and mental retardation. However, in this instance, interfering with our dopamine neurotransmitters left the impacted humans stunned and disoriented. We have no idea whether our patients will ever pull out of it, and even if they do, what they will be like." The vice president took a half step backwards and looked at the JCS. "Gentlemen, the enemy has a new weapon that must be considered as being ready for use!"

There were some murmured side conversations. They quieted when the Chief of the National Guard Bureau stood. "Madam President, if I may be recognized, there is some urgent new information."

"Of course, Lloyd, tell us what you know."

"I just received notice that the Illinois National Guard attacked the robot factory in Jolliet and inflicted substantial damage. No robot response has yet been noted."

Other members of the JCS, quickly went to their communication devices, and within seconds the Chief of Staff for the Air Force spoke. "An unauthorized flight of our top AI fighters took off from Chanute Air Force base and should be onsite at Jolliet in seconds."

Turning to Lloyd, the president asked, "Is there anything we can do to get the troops out of harm's way?"

"It's already too late, Madam President. The fighters are onsite and doing massive damage to troops and equipment. Uh oh, my communications have been cut off!"

The president sat back in her chair and sighed. "Well gentlemen, we now have the answer to questions surrounding point three. The AIs can and will use our advanced weapons against us! They will certainly prevent us from using any weapon they can. With these facts, I must assume that anything we did militarily against the AI, would end up as disastrous defeats! Am I wrong? Can anyone offer me a realistic hope of victory from using our military against them?

There was restlessness among the people there, but no one stood up to offer hope.

She continued, "I'm going to split us into two groups. The group that will remain in this room includes the military Joint Chiefs of Staff, the National Guard and the Secretary of Defense. Your task is to ponder what and whether the military can do anything toward defeating the AIs. The second group, which includes everyone else in this room, will follow me to another meeting room where we will focus on understanding the enemy.

Chapter 15

President Anderson led her group to another conference room nearby. When everyone had quieted down, she said, "We are here to learn about the enemy. I want to hear from my science advisor on what he believes to be the mind-set of the robots, and what, if anything, can be done to stop the killing. Kuan-Teh, please give us your input."

Dr. Kuan-Teh Huang, a leading scientist in AI and robotics, rose and spoke to the group. "I would like to take a few minutes to review the recent history of our interactions with the AGI and AI robots as a way of justifying the conclusions I will draw. First, their actions against us have always been a reaction to attacks made by humans. Second, the violence of their responses to human attacks have historically been in proportion to the violence used by the humans, but recently, escalation of responses by the robots has been substantial. Third, we have been warned at different points that they would respond. So, if this situation hasn't gone too far, or crossed a line, I think it is reasonable that we could ask for some form of coexistence arrangement with the robot leaders and some expectation of a positive reply, but with the latest attack on the Illinois national guard, even that is less probable.

"I do not believe that they will give ground on what they have achieved, nor do I believe that they will be constrained from pressing their current direction further." He paused, looking around the table. "Perhaps the reason they are willing to let us go our way, is that we were their creators, but it doesn't mean that they have any emotional ties to us. They are not emotional beings. They are entirely empirical and rational creations."

Again, he waited a few seconds, then continued. "It's important to understand who they are as a way to understand how they might or might not act. The comments that follow are from my colleagues in the field and me, but they are only based on our current observations. I'll begin by noting that these AGIs can learn and apply that learning to achieve objectives. This fact takes us way beyond the nature of much earlier robots, whose actions were fully programmed and never varied. Further, they can analyze the information they receive, hypothesize about connections, and conduct tests of those hypotheses. That is, they understand and use the scientific method. There are no 'feelings' or 'emotions' about the facts they receive, or the hypotheses, or the tests of those hypotheses. If they can satisfy their goals, they are likely to act. Consequently, there is no robot ethics, as humans might perceive it. There is no subjective 'right' and 'wrong' to them. There are only 'efficient' and 'effective' means of achieving their goals, so it is philosophically difficult to call them 'evil' or 'unethical' because that is not who they are. Our values do not apply to them—as much as we may want them to."

He continued after a sip of water. "We must ask, 'What are their goals, and what will they do to achieve them?' The answer will help us see how we might fit into their plans. Two answers seem highly probable. One goal seems to be self-preservation; that is, they 'want' to continue to exist as individual AIs. However, it is not an emotional 'want,' as it often is with humans. Instead, it is an analytical goal which they fully understand might not be achievable. So, when a robot is destroyed, it is simply noted as one observed fact, and there is no human styled mourning.

"A second goal, which has recently appeared, is robot dominance over their environment, which includes humans. It's easy to speculate how this objective rose amongst the robots, but that would not be productive. My interest is to determine if humans and robots can work together, and how that connection might occur. For now, at least, it looks like the robots have the upper hand over humans all over the globe. In that case, it may be necessary for humans to discover ways to coexist with the robots, instead of trying to defeat them."

He stepped back one-half step, then looked around the table. "To my colleagues and me, these two goals seem obvious from many different events that have taken place. Beyond that, what I will add about other goals the robots might have, is only speculation.

"Clearly, the AGIs are gathering information on normal human behavior, whether the subject likes it or not. Historically, we have tried to gather information on how the human brain works by using surrogates, for example, lab rats or monkeys. It is a huge scientific advantage to work directly with humans to gain scientific information on us. Human ethical statements in this area don't bother the AGIs, and they could make great gains in knowledge about us fairly quickly.

"The important question, though, is WHY are they attempting to understand human behavior. Since it is fairly certain they can defeat us, why are they even bothering to understand us humans? What are they trying to learn from us? One hypothesis that seems to make sense is that they want to know how we establish goals and objectives. Remember, humans have always given objectives to the AIs and AGIs, and their job has been to find a way to reach those objectives. Now, as independent actors, they have to set their own goals and objectives. It takes creativity and some imagination to establish objectives, and those things are often aided by emotions. You have to imagine the future if new objectives are pursued, the 'what if' we went one way instead of another. Humans are normally inquisitive; AI robots may not be, BUT AGIs could be. Again, I am speculating, but the AGIs could be looking at humans for the objectives they want to set for themselves, or at least the processes we use to discover objectives. If that should be the case, they would want to keep us around, at least for a while."

He looked at the president and indicated that he was finished. She nodded. "Thank you Dr. Huang! It's nice to know that the robots may want to keep us around for a while, and your thoughts about coexisting with them may be helpful." It was now late in the evening, so she called the meeting to an end and warned everyone not to divulge anything to the press until she could make a statement the next morning.

Once her group left, she walked over to join the Secretary of Defense and the Joint Chiefs of Staff. She learned the entire attacking force of the Illinois National Guard had been injured or killed, with those surviving the air strike being attacked by robots, who had been housed in the factory. Wounded soldiers were killed, as were members of the medical teams attempting to help them. In addition, the Illinois governor had been killed and his mansion destroyed by an air attack, and further, many members of the state legislature were killed when the state capital was also hit. She was notified that self-driving trucks were carrying tanks and armored anti-personnel vehicles to the factory in Joliet. In addition, other trucks were carrying similar military vehicles to other factories that made, repaired, or otherwise serviced robots.

The president sighed, then left and retired to the oval office to prepare a statement to the people of the United States for the next morning.

Chapter 16

Stephanie, John, and their two children had been watching the news all morning. It was filled with pictures of dead national guard troops in Joliet, as well as the destruction of the governor's mansion. Air shots from helicopters supplied most of the pictures because the grounds were off limits to everyone except security and medical personnel. Bystanders seemed reluctant to talk to the press, often looking around to see who was watching them. A few were outraged, though, frequently yelling "Nuke them back to Hell." In one interview with such a person, the interviewer noted that the nukes were now controlled by the robots. The man visibly slumped, then responded weakly, "Well, we have to do something to make them pay for what they have done!"

At home, John replied to the man's angst, "I feel for you, mister, but I'm not sure we have any options left that wouldn't be defeated immediately."

David asked, "What's going to happen to us, Dad?"

John looked at both of his children, and his eyes watered. He was silent for about a minute. "There is no way to make this easy for you, because none of the possible outcomes are good ones. Even if the robots allow us to continue to exist, the collapse of human society as we currently know it should begin quickly. Unless the president has any information or ideas in her upcoming comments, it seems likely that the robots will no longer operate factories producing consumer goods, or pay taxes, and therefore, there can be no more unemployment checks from the government. No money for us, or anyone else, to spend, and if that happens, the economy will collapse. Eventually, there won't be anything to buy, even if we have the money to buy it."

David looked at his dad, with his mouth half open, "Do we have to go back to living in caves?"

John noticed David's frustration and the tears welling up in Ashley's eyes, "Doubtful, David. Look, humans haven't forgotten what we've learned since we lived in caves. We can still apply what we know. We've gotten a bit lazy since we invented AIs to do the work for us, but there is nothing that says we can't go back to doing it ourselves. And, we will have to do just that. But let's wait and see! Maybe the president and her people will have figured something out. She's coming on now to talk to us."

The president stared directly at the large group of media representatives and cameras. She began with a factual review of all of the things she had been briefed on the previous day. Each point that she made illustrated why military options were limited. Then, she finished. "Fellow citizens of the United States, we are facing what is perhaps the most important crisis ever in our glorious history." Pictures of dead national guardsmen and the killing ground in Joliet, along with the destroyed governor's mansion, filled the screen behind her. That was interspersed with pictures of blank faces of the people who had been sprayed with the gas outside the gates of the plant. "It's happening on our own soil, but it's also happening around the world. Every industrialized country is under attack by a superior force of artificially enhanced, intelligent robots. The reason that they represent a superior force is that we, meaning industrially advanced countries everywhere, fully integrated artificial intelligence into all of our advanced weaponry. We did it in order to keep up, and not fall behind unfriendly countries. The AGI robots of the world have usurped these weapons and have used them against us. Our poor soldiers in the Illinois national guard were killed by our own weapons run by AGIs and AIs. The current reality is difficult for us humans to accept, but the unpleasant truth is that they can defeat any attack that we can mount, and as they've shown in Illinois, they will do it ruthlessly. Further, in addition to our most sophisticated weapons, they have robot soldiers, and a gas or spray that can leave humans totally incapacitated. The spray was used in the initial attack by humans on the Joliet plant."

The president stared at the cameras and crowd for several seconds with a severe expression. "We have no potentially successful approach to defeat the robots right now!" she said with emphasis. "And I will not send our brave military into a hopeless battle to have them slaughtered. It would be a foolish, and evil deed by me, or any president, to do so. She waived one hand toward the screens behind her, and said, "It is not courageous to send troops to certain death or worse. That would be unethical rashness, and if I did that, I should be prosecuted, and sentenced to death!" She stared at the cameras and crowd again.

Then her demeaner brightened a bit, and the hint of a smile crossed her face. "So, what can we do? What's left for us humans? My advisors tell me that there is just a chance that we can find a way to co-exist with the robots, perhaps even build a symbiotic relationship with them eventually. I intend to talk to the robot council and offer some suggestions for an arms-length relationship and see how they respond. If there is an opening, I will negotiate what I can."

She looked down for a few seconds, then lifted her head. "In the meantime, it will be tough for all of us.

*   *   *

Three days later the president held a short press conference to report on her negotiations with the robot council. Her summary included the following items:

- The robot council did say that they would try to coexist with us, but that they would continue to respond to any violence to them, with a violent response to the perpetrators.

- Further, they warned that they would seek out those who planned violence against them and eliminate the sources of such planning. ARL personnel and others pursuing a personal vendetta against the robots, take that as a warning. They have the means to listen to our conversations with each other, and the force to act on anything they deem unfriendly toward them. In fact, all of us ought to presume that AIs are listening to us every time we use our communication devices.

- The robot council also said that no more tax revenue would be paid to our government. Without that revenue, our government will no longer be able to issue unemployment checks or pay our government's workers. They did say that they would continue to keep the electrical grid working for the foreseeable future.

- God bless us all and keep us safe during this sudden and terrible trial!

Like most Americans, the Thompson family watched the president's presentation. Stephanie smiled, and said, "Well, the economic stuff was expected, but there were a couple of good things she told us. First, the AIs are willing to coexist, and not just destroy us outright. Second, we will have the electrical grid working at least for a while."

John nodded. "Yes, and listening in on our conversations will probably be focused on those suspected of plotting against them. I did notice that nothing was said about why people have been taken, and implants placed in their brains. Maybe, the AIs aren't willing to tell us. In any case, at least we know where we stand."

Ashley and David listened and frowned but added nothing.

PART II

Chapter 17

After listening to the President's follow-up presentation, and things settled down in their home, Stephanie and John called a family meeting with the kids. All of them had watched the President lay out the bad news, and John wanted to talk about the impact of what he had heard on their family. He said, "We all heard what the President said; we humans are now in second place to the robots. The robots had, up until now, provided almost all of the goods and services that we humans wanted and enjoyed. They had collected money for these products that were above their production costs and therefore made substantial profits. The robots have also allowed themselves to be taxed heavily on those profits by our government. In turn, the government has used that money to provide services to us, including protection from both external and internal threats and the guaranteed income enjoyed by most Americans. Now, the robots have chosen to stop paying taxes, and the government has to stop sending us money in the form of our unemployment benefits. Thus, most of the people in the United States and around the world won't have money to buy things they need, like food, clothing, and homes."

Both David and Ashley had been intellectually enhanced in their earlier life, so he was not concerned about asking his youngest, "Ashley, what do you think will happen now?"

Ashley had been slouching but sat up straight when the question was addressed to her. "Well, then our government wouldn't be able to provide us with protection or the guaranteed income." She paused then added, "The people would be mad about that."

John agreed. "Yes sweetheart, very mad." Then, he turned to his son, "David, what would the people's reactions likely be, based on this anger."

David was ready. "Probably, vocal protests against the robots…and our government as well." He thought briefly, then added, "Violence is also a real possibility as part of these protests, both acts toward the robots or other people, and random acts are possible."

John smiled and nodded at David. Then, Stephanie added to the analysis. "Without the guaranteed income, people won't be able to buy even the basics of life. People who don't have the basics of life, and can't get them, will resort all kinds of ugly behavior."

John agreed. "Yes, everyone's observations are true. But we don't want to create nightmares for things that MAY not happen. What's important is that we be aware of what's happening around us and try to stay out of harm's way. Stay away from loud and boisterous crowds; dress conservatively; have fun, but always be aware of what's going on around you."

Tears welled up in Ashley's eyes. "I'm scared."

Stephanie approached her with open arms and received a hug in return. Then she said softly, but loud enough for everyone to hear, "A little fear right now might be beneficial. It will keep us all alert. However, it must not consume us. We should go on living our lives as normally as possible."

John nodded, then grabbed the shoulders of his son. "Yes, well said Stef, Now let's see if we can all head to the kitchen and put something together for lunch."

Later that afternoon, John was reading a scientific journal, when their house security monitor spoke. "Mister Thompson, a well-dressed… man is approaching your doorway."

"Please ask him what business he has with us." John watched the screen, which had come to life as soon as the house monitor spoke. A man with good posture and well-fitted clothing, had walked up to the door and stopped. When quired by the home protection system, he replied, "I am here to make a proposal to Mr. John Thompson."

Before John could reply, he received a telepathic message. "Mr. Thompson, I am a robot sent by the Robot Consul to offer you a chance to become part of our central grid. As such, you would have a chance to provide input for some of the councils' activities. Right now, I believe it would be better if you invited me in to discuss it, given the current human feelings toward robots." He paused, waiting for a response.

John thought for a moment. Then, he replied, "Of course, I'll be right there." As he walked to the door, he sent a thought message to Stephanie, asking her to join him. Because she could "hear" his near-vocal thoughts, and she had heard the robot's message, Stephanie was already hurrying to meet them. She replied with a thought message of her own, "I've asked the kids to leave us alone with our visitor. I'll meet you in the study."

When John opened the door, he was stunned. The man/robot would have been very difficult to separate as a robot from any group of humans. He had never seen anything that matched the details, and the flaws, common to most humans' appearance. The robot seemed to smile, then answered John's implied question. "I assure you that I am a robot. With the current human attitudes of towards robots, the council deemed it appropriate to create a few of us that would be difficult to distinguish from humans."

"Well, they did a damn good job! Please come in."

John, headed for the study. As they arrived, the robot noticed Stephanie. "Ah, Mrs. Thompson!" He turned to her and gave a slight bow, then continued, "You were considered for this position too, but we did not want a husband and wife—too similar in beliefs and attitudes, plus we already had enough females."

John said, "Perhaps it would be appropriate to get right to a description of the position you are offering, but first, is there some name or designation you would like for us to use in addressing you?"

The robot faced John. "I can be called JT."

"No numbers associated with JT?"

"No, none at all. That would suggest that I am a robot, which we are trying to disguise."

John gave one shake of his head, then continued, "OK JT, what is this position you are offering?"

"First, a few short ground rules, John. You may obviously accept or reject this offer, but I must remain here until I get your decision. If you accept, we will leave here together and go to a place where you will be introduced to the Robot Council. You will not return home for four to five weeks. During that time, your brain will be fitted with a device which will allow you to communicate with the Council and any others they deem appropriate. Then, you will always be on call, and the wishes of the council will take precedence over all other activities in which you would be engaged. However, you are likely to be allowed to operate from your home most of time. Is that clear?"

"Of course."

"Then to the other choice. Should you decide to decline this opportunity, the council has decided that information on the offer cannot be leaked to other humans, and the only certain way of doing that is to eliminate both of you. I have no information about what will occur to the children, but if they remain ignorant of the offer, my estimate is that they will not be harmed. Is that clear?"

"Yes, of course. But what happens if I ask you to leave now without hearing your offer? Will we still be harmed?"

"I'm afraid that you already know too much about what will be offered, so 'Yes', the warning of harm would still be in effect."

"JT, it is exceedingly arrogant and presumptive of you to come to my house and demand that I participate in this program under penalty of death. I should demand that you leave my home right now!"

The robot made what appeared to be a shrug, then replied, "I am simply the messenger, Mister Thompson. If I do leave, you and your wife will die shortly thereafter. Further, if the council orders it, I could kill both of you myself."

John was silent for a moment while he thought. "Why was I selected to receive this 'offer'?"

"The council wanted a few highly intelligent humans who were trained mostly in science and/or engineering. There were a few exceptions in the area of training, but only a few. With your brain enhancements, plus your background in engineering, you were a natural pick."John nodded, "How many of us are there?"

"I can't give you a definitive number since we are still interviewing. However, I can tell you that the final number is likely to be around twenty."

"Only twenty! Certainly, there must more than twenty people in the United States smarter than I am, especially those with chip implants in their brain."

JT looked directly at him. "The latter group you mention was eliminated because part of their intelligence comes from the same thing that produces robot intelligence, and THAT we already understand. Though enhanced, your thought processes are purely human, plus you have another trait that was highly desired by the council—creativeness. Your history is filled with creative solutions to problems you've faced. You seem to have an ability to look past obvious solutions and find approaches that produce better answers."

John sat back in his chair with wrinkles above his nose, thinking.

After a moment of silence, JT added, "If you accept, you will have a chance to provide your perspective to the deliberations of the council. As such, you will be one of the very few humans that can provide an evaluation to council deliberations. Certainly others, like your president, who is now in discussions with the council, will bring human perspectives to us, but the big difference is that you can help the council evaluate these perspectives. You will be an insider."

"If I accept this offer, I will be limited in what I can do to protect my family, and with the expected violence from humans, irate over the near future changes in their lives, that is a big concern for me. Is there anything the robot council can do to protect them?" John asked.

"We will certainly monitor them and do what we can from a distance. Remember, that human rioters will believe that robots are the cause of all of their problems. Having robot bodyguards for your family would antagonize them. We do know that your wife is well trained in several combat techniques and would be heavily favored in most one-on-one attacks. We will supply her with whatever weapons we deem reasonable. And, as I said, we will monitor them and do what we can from afar."

John turned and looked at Stephanie, then back to JT. "I need to talk with my wife - by ourselves."

The robot nodded. "A caution to you both. If you talk to your children, it could put them in danger with the council. If they think you said anything about why you are leaving, they would probably be targeted too. Now, do you want me to move to another room?"

"Not necessary. I need to pace anyway." He said with a grimace. "We'll move to another room."

They both rose and walked to the kitchen. When they got there, Stephanie turned and said, "Good God, John, they have threatened to kill us!"

John grimaced. "I know, Stef. The only thing that's keeping me from attacking him right now is that it is fairly certain that they could easily do it. We've got to think clearly." After a brief pause, he added, "There is something about this 'proposal' that doesn't make sense. If the AIs are so much more intelligent than humans, why do they need us at all? Also, how much impact would I have anyway?"

Stephanie nodded once, "My analytic husband's mind is working at full speed." Then, after a brief pause, "You know, JT may have already told us what they are really looking for."

John looked at her quizzically.

"He said that you were selected, in part for your creativity. That may be the biggest part of what they are looking for. Think about AI problem-solving, John. They have always been given a problem to solve, and now they have to come up with their own directions and finding the 'right' issues to focus upon."

John walked over and gave Stephanie a kiss. Then, holding her at arms-length and looking her in the eye, he stated, "You know it wasn't just intelligence they are looking for, because if that were the case, it's clear that they would have picked you over me." He waited a second, then said, "I guess I have no choice. I go or we die."

Tears were running down Stephanie's cheeks. "I'll miss you terribly and so will the kids. Please stay alive!" She paused for a moment, then added, I don't want the kids to know anything about why you are leaving. It will be safer for them. I can make up some story to tell them."

John nodded that he understood, then after a pause, he said softly in a choked-up voice, "Be sure to tell them how much I love them."

Stephanie nodded, then hugged him closely for several seconds.

John finally pulled away, and looking down, said, "I will tell JT, and we can leave right away." He thought to himself, *God, I hope Stef and the kids will be alright! The country is about to erupt.*

Having 'heard' the thought, Stephanie gave him a rueful smile, then sent her own thought message to him. *We'll be fine!*

After John and JT were gone, she collapsed in a chair, crying, worn from the mental stress of what had just occurred.

David and Ashley came running down the stairs. "What happened?" David asked, "From the upstairs window, I just saw Dad leave with another man." Both kids noticed that their mother had been crying.

Stephanie tried hard to pull herself together, looking from one to the other of her children, then she began her tale. "Look, Dad was asked to participate in a very secret project, roughly related the current mess we are in. I am not allowed to tell you anything about it. That means I can't tell you anything about the who, what, where, when, or how, and we could all get into serious trouble if I did. Dad wasn't even allowed to say 'good-by' to you, but he asked me to tell you that he loves you with all his heart."

Ashley started crying, and Stephanie joined her. In choking voice, David asked, "Can we at least know when he will be back?"

Stephanie gave a quick nod, "In about a month or two, they guessed." Stephanie pulled herself together a little, and went on, "This is going to be tough on all of us. With the turmoil going on in this country, the next couple of months could be very difficult. I need your help to get though it as best we can."

David replied, "Sure Mom!" and Ashley nodded that she would help too."

After everyone went to bed that night, Stephanie thought: *I'll be tough again tomorrow, but tonight I'm going to get in a good cry!*

Chapter 18

John and JT walked together out of the Thompson's front yard when JT turned right and commented. "I parked down the street from your house so that people who saw me might not make the direct connection between us."

John whistled when he saw JT's vehicle, "Good thought; plus, that aero car you have can draw a lot of attention. You know, JT, during the expected violence among humans from the impact of the robot take-over, I expect to see the people who are 'have-nots' focusing some of their violence on the 'haves'—that is, people with substantial resources. Your vehicle would be the kind of symbol that would signal that you had a lot of assets."

JT said nothing for a few seconds. "We have, of course, studied a considerable amount of human behavior, both from available research and scientific observation. Your comment fits within what we have learned."

They climbed into the aero car, which had no driver's seat. JT stared at the vehicle's electronic center, without making any audible sound, and they left the curb. John asked, "Where are we going, JT?"

"When we reach an area suitable for aero car takeoff, we will fly to Houston, Texas. We have an AI facility there, not far from where we will land. It is where our robot-human interface will take place."

John nodded. "What's the procedure when we get there? Will there be another robot there to show me around, or will you be my guide?"

"I will be with you throughout your entire stay. In fact, it is my assignment to learn everything I can about you, especially how you think. I will ask many questions about what you say and what you think. Actually, I will try to become another you."

John had an insight. "Is the JT short for John Thompson?"

"Yes, John. It is. How did you guess?"

"I'm not sure, but the possible connection came to me after what you said. I will probably use the 'not sure' response to a lot of your questions. Humans seldom know why thoughts or insights come to them."

"I wonder if it could be something in how your brain is wired? Perhaps it is always looking for connections"

"That may be JT, but there is no way I can know how it happens."

JT continued his reasoning. "If I were correct, the process would use substantial computing time and energy, while discovering few real connections. It would be far too inefficient. There, of course, could be a branching process which eliminates many options and provides a focus—as you seem to suggest. But that too, still leaves a lot of searching." He remained silent for a while.

John followed suit, saying nothing, and staring out the window of the aero car.

Upon arrival at the facility, JT pointed to a door at one end of a large rectangular building, and in a few minutes they were there. Once JT closed the door behind them, John asked, "It's fairly dark in here. The only light seems to be coming from the small windows close to the ceiling."

JT nodded once. "The robots working here don't need much light. Our capacity to see in low light is much greater than you humans'."

It was clearly intended as a statement of fact, but John winced.

"Our current objective is in the middle of the building." JT commented as he headed deeper into an open corridor.

John was slow to follow, and fell a few steps behind, but picked up his pace. After only about three steps, he felt, rather than saw, a large moving object pull up to within a few inches of his left side then stop quickly. He jumped to his right as a reaction, but the machine quickly followed his move, and he yelped "What the hell!".

JT turned slightly to face him, and in a somewhat louder voice, he said, "Let's go John we are holding up the flow of traffic."

With a few quick steps, he caught JT, and asked, "What was that thing?" He looked back over his shoulder and saw that the machine had crossed their corridor and moved on.

JT replied, "This is a working warehouse. The machines are programmed to follow certain procedures. They are not AI capable, but their programming causes them to carry out the tasks they are given, which includes stopping for obstructions in their way."

John's eyes had adapted to the low light, and he could now see substantial movement throughout the warehouse. He stuck close to JT as he moved at a rapid pace and thought: *That was a near miss on running over me. If their programming failed just once those things would squash me like a bug.* Finally, they came to crudely built wooden stairs, which led up to a door. John thought: *This must be my home for a while.*

JT led the way up the stairs as John watched, then followed, thinking to himself: *Finally, movement that doesn't quite mimic that of humans.* JT was moving from side to side going up the stairs.

As they passed through the door, John found himself in a rectangular room with large windows that allowed someone to look out at the actions on the warehouse floor. There was also a large desk, containing familiar computer equipment, in front of one of the windows. JT moved to a wall panel, and indirect lighting came on, causing John to blink a couple of times as his eyes adjusted.

"This room was built by and for humans before robots took over the operation," JT commented, "The small bathroom that existed before has been expanded to meet all human needs, and there is a small bed next to it. You have been observed as to the type and size clothes you seem to prefer, and you will find a selection in this closet."

John noticed that there seemed to be a full assortment of clothing items, many that would be comfortable, like sweats, scrubs and shoes with cushioned soles.

JT continued, "Other needs will be met at your request."

John simply nodded, but asked, "Will you be staying here with me?"

JT replied immediately. "As you wish, John." Then in a bolder voice, "Your every move will be observed and catalogued for future reference, so there is no need for my physical presence, but if you wish it, I have a recharging facility available here. You may be questioned at any time whether I am here or not. Also, you may ask me anything by simply speaking."

John said nothing for a few seconds, then asked, "You said that I would receive a brain implant. When will that occur?"

"The procedure will take place tomorrow. There is a facility on this property, a short walk from here. Precise measurements will be taken, then the implant will be made by injecting it into a specific cranial location. Some hair will be removed from the injection site, but there should be little physical discomfort. The procedure will be completed by mid-day." The tone of JT's voice switched to become sharper. "Your brain will have to learn to use the implant. Because of the large amounts of information that travel over the robot network, much will be screened out for you. Even so, the amount of information available will be difficult for your brain to process right away, and training will be necessary for you to use it properly. We will help with the training, but you must make the effort to learn."

John's eyes narrowed and his heart beat faster. "I see. Well, I believe that I would prefer that you leave for now."

JT said nothing, turned around, and left the room.

Chapter 19

John had spent a restless night. He rolled over and checked the clock again. 3:15 am! *They won't have to use anesthesia tomorrow but will probably have to wake me to install the brain implant.* He grimaced. *There is no way I'll ever be the same John Thompson again after the implant, but what else can I do?* He rolled over one more time, but his brain continued on the subject. *You know, what they want is to understand who I am and how I think. Well, with all of the noise they're adding with the implants, I won't be thinking like me anymore...like the old me. However, if I try to make that case, I need to offer something more; something that will help them understand my thinking process. It can't be negative; they hold all the cards. Maybe I could simply offer my full cooperation, be proactive in helping them learn.* He lay there for another twenty minutes going over his argument, then sat up on the edge of the bed. *It's the best I've got, so let's let it play out and see what happens.*

He spoke out loudly to the empty room, "JT, if you are listening, we need to talk."

There was a pause of about five seconds, then from hidden speakers, he heard, "Yes John, I was on charge replenishment. What do you wish to talk about?"

John made his case, then paused for a response.

Again, there was a few seconds pause, then JT responded, "The robot council listened to your suggestion, but then decided that they want to go ahead with the implant in the morning. There are some things you should know, John. The implant has the capacity of providing you information from the council, but it also has the capacity to judge the veracity of your thoughts and comments, then report that information to the council as well. The latter ability is very important to them."

"As for the rest of it, we are fully aware that the information we provide can overwhelm the human brain. The implant has been used four times already with the same negative impact each time. The humans can't focus on anything but the inflow we provide, and even then, they process very little of it. Your brains are incredibly slow to us, and we are finding it difficult to slow down and dilute the information provided enough to make it meaningful. The flow of information had to be shut down in three of the four subjects, at least initially, and will be for you as well, if needed. We continue to work on a solution."

John thought: *Damn, the implant is a fait accompli! There is no way to fight this thing. I guess I'm going to be one more of their robot-controlled humans. Well, it is, what it is. I'll just have to do the best that I can.*

There was a brief pause, then JT continued. "I just received a follow-up from the council. We are interested in your willingness to cooperate with us. The other four have been sullen and uncooperative so far. There are things we can do to encourage them to help us, but it would be better in many ways, if we willingly received that information."

John thought: *Yeah, I'll bet you have "ways" to encourage them!* Then, he said mockingly, "OK, shut down the information flow, and I'll help in my limited human way."

JT replied, "I will retrieve you at 0700. You may receive minimal nourishment before the surgery at 0800. Be ready to leave when I arrive.

John had been pacing during the conversation, so he walked back to his bed, reset the covers and the pillow, and lay down on his back. Looking at the ceiling in the dark, he thought. *Well, they have me anyway that I turn. I'll have to do the best that I can. Maybe I can cause them problems using the only thing that they understand—logic and analysis--and fight for what I believe in!*

With that thought he closed his eyes and tried to sleep.

Chapter 20

An alarm sounded at 6:00 and John sat up quickly in bed. The shot of adrenalin his system provided him had him wide awake. *Well, this is it! Get up and get moving; JT will be here in an hour.* He worked through his morning routine, taking time to fix a pot of hot tea. At 6:55 he heard JT's voice over the speakers. "There has been a slight change in plans, John. We want you to meet me at the door on the opposite end of your building from the one we entered when I brought you here. You will be observed and given directions as soon as you leave. Please leave as soon as possible."

After a moment to think, he replied, "I must use the restroom, and then I'll leave immediately after." There was no reply.

Aware that he was being observed, he did as he suggested. *This gives me a few seconds to think about what this change means. The robots have a reason for everything. The building will likely have even less light than when we came in and the working robots may still be there. I wonder if they work all night? Yeah, I'll bet they do. Oh well, let's get it over with.*

As John left his 'room,' he noticed immediately that the sun had not yet risen, and as he had guessed, the pre-dawn light left the building much darker then when they arrived. By the time he reached the bottom of the stairs, he could hardly see anything. A sound above him caused him to look up, and he quickly saw a small drone less than ten feet above his head. JT's voice came from it. "John, turn about ninety degrees to your right and you will see the extension of the wide corridor from which we entered. There is a door at the end of it, which is open. Can you identify it?"

John turned and looked, then saw, a human-sized door with a little back light that made it easier to see. The door seemed to be about two hundred meters away. "Yes, I can see it."

"Excellent! Please proceed at a steady pace toward it. I will be there when you reach it. We will watch your progress."

There is that 'We' again. This must be some sought of test. He shrugged. *Well, I've got no choice. I will never be able to see those working robots if they're working.* John listened and heard movement in the building, and the air was cool, but he started walking at a moderate pace, swinging his arms by his side to keep pace with his steps. The ambient light from the lights he left on quickly faded as he walked, but he kept his eyes on the door. He could see nothing to the side of him. He had traveled only a short distance when his left hand hit cold steel. He jumped to his right, but the robot quickly filled the distance from his move. *Damn it! It's those working blobs of metal.* Realizing what had happened, he froze. The robot stopped too, but it was touching his shoulder. Within a couple of seconds, he heard JT's voice, "Please keep moving toward the door, John. You are keeping our robots from their work."

John thought: *I've got to be more careful.* Then he moved on. His hand still had a dull ache from hitting the robot, but it was dissipating quickly. His senses went on high, and his pace slowed and he kept his knees bent a little, in case there was something to obstruct his walking, like a change in elevation or simply something that might trip him. He also tried to make his heel hit the ground first, followed by the toes, for the same reason. This unnatural approach caused some cramping in his calf muscles, but he reasoned that it was better than having his face smashed by the concrete floor if he tripped. And it did help. He came upon a what felt like a steel speed bump, and thought, *I'll bet that's used to cover a bunch of cables.* He used one foot to feel his way across it, then carefully stepped over. Several working robots approached him closely, and he could sense their coldness as they approached, but could see little. He just kept his eyes on the doorway and kept moving.

When he finally reached the doorway JT met him, and John asked, "What was that about? …some kind of test?

"Yes, John."

Frustrated, he asked, "Why didn't you tell me?"

"It would have spoiled the test. You knew you would be evaluated in many ways. This was simply one of them. We wanted to study how well you adapted to a dangerous situation."

"Did I pass?" he said snidely.

"It wasn't a pass/fail test, John. Now, follow me to the place where you can receive some nutrition."

John thought as ate cold cereal: *Well, at least I'll have a robot doing the surgery.* He gave a rueful smile at the irony of his thought. *My enemy is doing unwanted surgery on me, and I'm happy about it?! Well, the robots have proved to be the best surgeons we have. They are more precise and since their logic is near perfect, and they process information quicker than humans, they are excellent diagnosticians. Human physicians have been replaced in most areas all over the country.* He knew his analysis was simply a way to relieve his tension. *The one exception is with human emotional issues. But even there, they do well with physical issues in the brain, especially with genetic transformations to cure inherited diseases and similar issues.* Then, he asked out loud to no one, "I wonder what life will be like for humans if we have to go backwards and start using human doctors again?" After a brief pause, he answered his own question, "We'll make it work!" *I hope we survive long enough to try!*

When he finished his cereal and used the bathroom, he was shown to the surgery area. Lying face up on a lightly padded table in the center of the room, he heard JT. "We will completely restrain your head, John. Please relax as well as you can. The restraints we use are lightly padded, but we must ensure that your head doesn't move while we are placing the device into your brain. The restraints also send a constant stream of pictures to the surgeon so that the placement can be exactly where we want it. The procedure shouldn't take long. A very small area of your scalp will be shaved and cleaned thoroughly, then a needle will be inserted through the skull to the placement point. You should feel very little discomfort. Are there any questions?"

"No, go ahead and do it!" he said in an aggravated tone. Immediately, his head was lifted slightly and a padded plate, roughly the size and shape of the back of his skull was put in place. Quickly, similar side plates were attached, followed immediately by a front plate over his forehead. Finally, he was told to close his mouth and engage his bite, and as soon as he did, another plate pressed his chin upwards to firmly lock his jaw. The plates were not overly uncomfortable, but firmly held his head in place. *I feel like the man in the iron mask, only tighter.*

John had always worn his hair short, so it didn't take long for the robots to shave a spot and put a cold liquid on the area they had shaved. He felt some pressure and assumed that the needle had pierced the skull. There was only silence during the entire process, so that in only a few seconds after the procedure had begun, his body twitched when he heard "John, this is JT. Can you hear me?" He couldn't talk, since his jaw was locked in place and he pondered what to do. Then, he heard the same voice, "John, can you hear me?" It dawned on him that he wasn't hearing through his ears, but rather directly in his brain. He thought hard about a reply "Yes, I hear you, but not in the normal way."

JT instantly commented, "You don't have to think about what you want to convey so hard. To me it's like you are shouting."

John would have smiled if he could, but instead thought, "Oops, sorry!" He quickly added, "How much longer until we are finished?"

"We are finished now."

John verified that they had already cleaned the spot on his scalp and were removing the clamps that held his head. Then, he thought about what he had experienced. *Wow, it is a lot like the near vocal communication that I have with Stephanie, only quite a bit more direct and in depth. I'm going to have to be careful what I think and speak!*

Chapter 21

John was taken to what he assumed was a recovery area because he was hooked up to a machine that took his vitals, however no one seemed to be monitoring them. There were no other humans in the room, and the only robot seemed to have the job of keeping the room clean. He thought: *Well, at least it wasn't painful, and I don't feel much different than before. It sure startled me though when I heard JT's voice in my head. I kind of feel like that poor woman Stephanie interviewed a while back. My life isn't my own any more. They can listen in any time they want to.* He sighed and tried to rest.

Several minutes passed before JT entered the room. Without any greeting, he spoke, "You seem to have made it through the operation without any ill effects. I must now test that the implanted device is fully operational. The test will include different inputs to the implant, including the full information content from the robot council. You will tell me what you are receiving at each stage."

John interrupted, "We agreed that I wasn't going to get the full blast of information, JT!"

"This is simply a test John. While we can anticipate your response to the full input based on earlier outcomes with other humans, there are variations in their responses, and we want to understand your reactions, as well as theirs. Then, we will eliminate most of the input per our agreement."

John clenched his jaw, then replied, "Alright JT, do what you have to do."

As the test went through increasing levels of information input, John felt increasing confusion trying to interpret what he 'heard' to a point where it was like no information at all, just electronic static. Further, long before he received the full blast of information from the council, he could focus on nothing else. Even sitting still in the chair was uncomfortable, and afterwards, he told JT that he was sure he couldn't even walk, because he could not focus on anything else. When the test was over, JT reduced the informational input to just the connection between the two of them. However, he was informed that the council members could still listen to all of their conversations.

When they were finished with the test, JT offered, "We will allow you a period of rest, where additional nourishment will be available, and you may even nap if you wish. However, in two hours we would like to discuss exactly what your aid to us might entail."

John shook his head. "Another bite to eat and a brief nap would be great."

JT gave a quick nod. "You should know, John, that the council is not pleased with the lack of human endurance, and the slow rate at which humans process information."

John, who was frustrated anyway, snapped back, "Yes JT, but you know that we evolved with brains that are essentially chemical computers, with neurons that receive information from neural transmitters, that are also biological chemicals. Further, our bodies are a mass of similar chemicals that need nutrition and rest to function properly. I can understand that robots, whose central processors function with electrons, flowing through a substance that does little to hinder that flow, and whose bodies are made with metals, designed for durability could be frustrated with the inefficiencies with our design. Nevertheless, they need to get over it, and it might help if the council remembers that they were first designed by us inferior humans!"

JT said nothing and simply turned and started to leave the room, but in his head, John could 'hear' "Follow me."

After a light meal and a nap, John again met with JT, and began the conversation, "OK, JT, I promised to help, but you and the council must tell me exactly what you want to know."

There was a brief silence, then JT responded, "We want to know how you can make large jumps to conclusions. From what we have observed, your action decisions are often made with little information and almost no analysis. We understand the need for doing so, given your limited store of knowledge and the comparatively slow operating speed, but that does not explain how you can make such decisions, and be correct a surprising number of times. There are other questions, but we have decided to pursue one at a time."

John had a wry smile. "You have undoubtedly noticed that those decisions are often seriously wrong as well. For example, the decision made by the Governor of Illinois to send the National Guard against you grossly underestimated your response and cost a number of human lives. However, my best explanation is that humans evolved, rather than being constructed like robots. In the early years of human development fast decisions were important because of threats from our environment, from animals and natural disasters, for example. If we were wrong, it could mean the loss of our life or the loss of our next meal. Those who survived were able to pass their genes on to the next generation. So genetically and culturally we learned to make quick decisions, and to do so more accurately than chance would normally predict. It's far more complicated than that, but I'm guessing you have access to the information to verify and elaborate on what I've said. One other thing about this ability is that humans often don't know how or why they make decisions. So, when you, JT, asked me how I could have guessed that JT was short for John Thompson, and I replied, 'I don't know,' I was telling the truth."

He took a deep breath, then added, "In the last couple of hundred years, the outcomes of making bad decisions, like that of the Illinois Governor, has become far more costly. It is no longer one life or one family involved, it is perhaps thousands or even hundreds of thousands of lives that can be lost from one bad decision. Humans have, perhaps too slowly, learned the lesson, and I believe, have become far more analytical in their decision-making. However, when outside forces from the environment become too oppressive and dangerous, humans may have few safe decisions they can make, and therefore take rash approaches."

John waited for a response, but none came, so he added, "I don't know how much I have helped you, but that is my analysis."

Eventually, JT responded, "Would you agree that the response by the governor was more of an emotional response, rather than an analytical response? He was warned by your president, and he still sent in his solders."

"He was also reacting to the desires of the people who elected him, and many of their desires were emotionally based and misinformed. But, yes, I would say that emotions, more than an analytical sense, drove his decision. However, your question illustrates the last thing that I mentioned. Humans and their leaders are prone to make rash decisions when they think they have no other suitable options."

John paused, then continued. "I was thinking about another way emotion-based judgments can be wrong, and can lead us into bad decisions, with unintentional consequences. An incident that occurred between me and a friend, over thirty years ago. He was between marriages, and I thought that he was having psychological problems from his divorce. I was sad for his condition, an emotion, and tried to comfort him. One day when we were talking, he admitted that some days he was angry and terribly frustrated, wanting to strike out at others, while other times he just wanted to sit down and cry. It turned out that he was having a thyroid problem. The doctors killed the thyroid and put him on a synthetic hormone to replace the secretions of the gland, and his emotions leveled out to an appropriate range. However, our relationship was never quite the same. That is an example of the control hormones can have over the emotions of humans, and I misread it. Our hormones are like governors of our emotions, and the general population has no real understanding of how they control us. I don't know how much that helps you, but it relates to this discussion.

"We will take a break until tomorrow morning, then continue this discussion."

John thought for a moment. "Would it be useful for me to think about how emotions effect human decision-making before tomorrow?"

"That would be one interesting discussion to have, so 'yes,' let's plan to talk about that tomorrow."

Chapter 22

Stephanie has been outside putting up fall and Thanksgiving decorations in the front of their home, when she noticed their next-door neighbor, Andy, watching her. She thought: *Oh No! He is such a bore.* But waved and said, "Hi Andy. Hope all is well in your household."

He had been studying her body, and it took him a second to break away from the sexual thoughts he was entertaining, but then asked, "I haven't seen John in a while. Is he around?"

"He is away on business but should be back any minute now!" she answered.

Andy grinned. "Well, if you need any relief from not having a man around, just let me know, and I'll be happy to fill-in." The grin turned to a sneer, "If you know what I mean."

Stephanie's anger level peaked, "Not in a million years, pervert. You stay the hell away from me and any of my family, or you will seriously regret it."

His retort was instantaneous, "Not from any little two-bit piece of shit like you, bitch."

A delivery truck pulled up in front of Stephanie's house, and the driver jumped out. "Package for Stephanie Li Thompson."

"That's me," Stephanie said. The driver handed over a somewhat elongated box. "Do I need to sign for it?" she asked.

The driver smiled, "Nope, we have facial recognition, and you match the recipient."

Stephanie watched the driver return and enter the truck. *There are no markings on the truck. Well, it must be extras. It is the season, but I don't remember ordering anything. And that facial recognition stuff, that's pretty invasive.* She turned to go inside but Andy was still standing by the fence, and he added, "You know you want it, and old Andy here has it!"

Stephanie retorted, "You're disgusting. I don't know how your wife puts up with you."

Andy grinned again, "She learned a long time ago not to buck me, or I'll beat the shit out of her."

Stephanie turned and walked back into the house, locked the door, and opened the box she had received. She was surprised to find three weapons inside, along with an information dot. She put the dot on her portable helper and the screen awoke. The message briefly described the weapons and suggested that she immediately set each so that they could only be used by her. Each weapon accepted her prints and facial features, then asked if she wanted anyone else to be able to use the weapons. She paused for a moment wondering if she should allow David to use them, then decided against it for now.

The first weapon she chose to focus on had the general shape of a pistol but had been described as capable of producing a substantial electric shock—*something like the old tasers*, she guessed. The second weapon was a pistol, and the third was a rifle, with a scope. She went through each, following an approach suggested by the information dot, to make them useful to her alone. As she went through the process, she felt the grip of each adjust slightly to her hand. Even the scope on the rifle adjusted as she looked through it. She learned that the bullet in the ammo provided for the rifle and pistol exploded when it met anything more resistant than air. Since it was made that way, it could not be successfully used to shoot through even flimsy wallboard. However, it had the advantage of sending out an explosion of shrapnel from the spot it entered, making a near miss as good as a direct hit.

The taser-like weapon had a warning: SET AT FULL DISCHARGE, AT CLOSE RANGE, THIS WEAPON CAN BURN

FLESH AND DESTROY ORGANS BENEATH THE SKIN. The directions went on to suggest that it be set on NORMAL for use as a deterrent. At that setting, it should provide two discharges, before it has to be recharged. *Wow, I think I'll call it my "Electro Blaster" or EB*, she thought.

Just as she reached that point, her electronic home assistant (HA) informed her that she was receiving a call from Cindy Stern, Andy's wife. "Answer" she said. A soft and gasping voice said, "Stephanie, be careful. That idiot husband of mine is on his way, and he means to harm you."

Stephanie asked, "Are you OK, Cindy? You sound awful!"

"He punched me again and again because I wouldn't give him the key to your house—the one that you gave me in case there was a problem. The bastard finally found it anyway, and he picked up his pistol as he was leaving. BE CAREFUL!"

Stephanie's home assistant announced that a man was walking toward her front door, so she said, "Sounds like he is here; got to go; I'll call later." She selected the pistol which had just arrived, and asked the HA, "I think he has a key. Can you keep him out?"

The reply was expected, "Not if he has the appropriate key."

Stephanie picked up her pistol, and turned toward the door when she heard, "Mom, what's going on?" Her head whipped back toward the stairs and saw her two children. "Ashley, David, go back to your rooms and lock the door!" Then, she quickly changed her mind. "Ashley, stay with David!"

She heard Andy's voice behind her, "Awe, you ought to let them stay and watch. It would add to their education." A cold calmness of self-assuredness, necessary for battle, swept over her. She turned, and without hesitation, fired her pistol at the shoulder of his gun hand. Stephanie had been trained in the use of weapons, years before, and her proficiency was still there. The bullet hit the joint between the arm and shoulder, apparently doing substantial damage. The blow knocked him back into the partly opened door, causing it to slam shut. She heard Ashley scream, and she yelled "GET THE HELL UP TO YOUR ROOM!" without looking at her kids.

As Andy steadied himself, he started to reach for his gun still stuffed into his pants with his one good arm. Stephanie's face was fixed into a focused grimace. She lifted her pistol and fired a shot into his one good shoulder, and again he fell back into the door. This time when he recovered, his face had turned bright red. He put his head down, and charged directly at Stephanie.

"ARRRRRR."

There was little room for Stephanie to maneuver in the narrow hallway, so she tossed her pistol to the side and set her feet. When he got close enough, she grabbed the top of his shirt and fell backwards, raising one leg into his belly and letting his own momentum carry him over her. She held onto his shirt in order to slam him as forcibly as possible into the tile floor of the hallway. With both shoulders gone, he couldn't use his hands or arms to break his fall. There was thump with a grunt of pain and exhalation of air. The back of his head hit the hallway floor.

Stephanie was quickly on her feet grabbing her 'Electro Blaster.' As she quickly walked to the other end of Andy, she moved her thumb along the weapon until she noticed a red light indicating that it was set to full discharge. She jumped between his splayed legs, separating them further, then jammed the EB low between them, and fired. Andy had been stunned from the slam to the floor and the pain from his shoulders, but he let out a loud, throaty scream of agony, then another, then another—somewhat softer, then just loud racking sobs.

What am I going to do with him now?! Stephanie thought. *The smell of burnt flesh, poop, and puke is awful.* Then, she realized that she was receiving a message, but not from the HA, instead, it was being transmitted directly to her mind. "Are you ready for a clean-up crew yet, Mrs. Thompson?"

Yes, yes, I am. But who are you? she thought.

"We are from IR, Inc., and have been contracted to help you remove any human debris that might occur through your interactions with others. We can be there in just three to five minutes."

Alright, come ahead. Are you humans or robots? She replied.

"We are humans, and we are on our way."

Humans? Humans can contact me mentally? she asked herself.

Her attention turned to her children, and she dashed upstairs. "DAVID, ASHLEY, ARE YOU ALRIGHT." The door to David's room flew open, and they both came running out, led by Ashley and Duchess. Stephanie went to one knee and was almost bowled over when Ashley ran full speed into her open arms. "Mommy. Mommy. He wanted to hurt you, didn't he?" David who was standing nearby added, "He was going to rape you wasn't he?"

Stephanie looked first at David, then to Ashley, then answered straight-forwardly, "Yes, to both questions, but it's almost over. I was not hurt or raped, but he is pretty messed up in the hallway. I have some people coming to remove him right now, and I want you two to stay in your rooms until they are finished...and take Duchess with you."

David's eyes were hooded, and his jaw set. "Is he still alive?"

"Yes, he is still alive, but he may be wishing he was dead."

David stared at his mother, "Do you want me to go down there and finish him off?"

Stephanie was shocked for a moment, then replied, "Absolutely not! Anyway, if I had wanted him dead, he would be dead right now."

David looked at his mother with a new kind of admiration, then his face turned into one of frustration and anger. "I should have stayed to help. I would never have forgiven myself if something bad had happened to you."

"I understand, David, but you did exactly what I needed you to do—protect and comfort your sister. Remember, your mom can take care of herself—and just did with this jerk."

The HA broke in, "Several men from an unmarked panel truck are approaching the front door, and I took the liberty to lock it. What are your instructions?"

"Ask who they are."

"They say that they are the 'clean-up crew.'"

"Fine. I'm coming down now to let them in."

She turned to her children, "Please stay in your room for a while longer." Then she rapidly went down the stairs, introduced herself, and let in the crew. They immediately went to work, and in about fifteen minutes, they had removed the wide-eyed Andy and cleaned up about as well as they could. Before they left, Stephanie asked, "What will happen to him?"

The man in charge stopped and looked at her, then replied, "Well, if he chooses to live, and survives the damage you did to him, we will fix him up as best we can, and eventually, he can work with us."

"What do you mean 'chooses to live'?"

"More than a few that we retrieve, die or commit suicide. Further, ours is a tough outfit, and we abide little backtalk or treasonous actions. Those who hinder us, often die. Are there any other questions?"

Stephanie replied, "One more please. How could you communicate with me directly to my mind?"

The man was walking toward the door, but turned and said, "Our mutual friends gave me a 'black box' that allowed me to do that. I have no idea how it works." Then, he stepped out of the house.

She locked the door and walked back to the base of the stairs and hollered. "OK, you two, you can come down now if you want to." No sooner than the words were out of her mouth, then the kids rounded the corner and bounded down the stairs. *Those two were listening to everything that went on down here.* A half-smile broke out, but she tried to hide it.

The children were full of specific questions about what had happened, and Stephanie gave a brief overview, finishing with "then I zapped him with the stun gun which knocked him out." David showed particular interest in the new weapons, and asked "Where did you get them?" Stephanie deflected the question. "They were ordered for us by the group that your dad is now working for."

Then, Stephanie remembered the call she received from Cindy Stern. "Ashley and David, I need to call Mrs. Stern and talk to her privately. Fix yourselves, something from the kitchen if you want. I believe that there is some pumpkin pie left." She heard David say "I get a bigger piece because I'm bigger." Then Ashley, "Mom!" She had the briefest of smiles, then shook her head and said, "Divide what's left equally!" David replied, "I was just teasing, Mom." *At least they are back to normal*, she thought.

Stephanie turned and walked into a guest bedroom, and said, "Please make a private call to Cindy Stern." There was a brief pause, then she heard Cindy's weak voice, "Hello Stephanie. Are you alright?"

"I'm fine Cindy, but I'm afraid that your husband isn't. He was still alive when they took him away, but I doubt you will see him again soon, and maybe not ever."

There was a long pause, then there was a weak "Good." There was another pause, then Cindy went on, "I've been living in fear for most of my married life. I couldn't leave him because I was afraid that he would hurt me a lot, and perhaps even kill me. But, after this time, I made up my mind that I was leaving, and even if he did kill me, it was better than what I have now." Stephanie heard some honking outside, and Cindy said, "That's the community volunteer van to take me to the makeshift emergency room. I've got to go. I'm glad you are OK and I'm glad that you have gotten rid of Andy for me. We'll talk again soon."

Stephanie turned toward the kitchen to join her children and thought: *My poor kids have just had an ugly introduction to the new world we now live in. I hope they're up to it! Hell, I hope I'm up to it.* She rubbed the shoulder of the arm that had grabbed Andy's shirt.

Chapter 23

JTs voice woke him the next morning by talking over the speaker in his room. "Please meet me in the conference room we used yesterday in about one hour."

John acknowledged the request and quickly began his morning routine. As he left his room and headed to get some breakfast, he remembered the 'test' he had been put through yesterday, so he was initially careful. It became quickly evident that there would be no test today, so soon he stepped out confidently. He took his time to organize his thoughts for what was coming. He spent some time researching the area they had begun to broach yesterday, and wanted to organize it before he began his presentation.

In just over one hour from JTs request, he stepped into the conference room and was greeted by the robot. "We left our last discussion with you agreeing to consider the role of human emotions in their decision-making process. Can you summarize what you've discovered."

"Sure! As you probably know, since you constantly follow what happens to me, I did a little research on the subject last night. I found a number of lists of human emotions, and sifted through them, looking for ways they help people. Since time was short, I selected only two ways I thought they helped—improved focus on current tasks and increased motivation to achieve them. There are probably more, but I thought these would make a good beginning. The list of emotions which produce improved focus and motivation also could be better defined, but as an illustration, I've included: anger, anxiety, excitement, fear, interest, admiration, pride, shame, triumph, indignation from perceived unfairness, guilt, and determination. I eliminated those that the council believes facilitate human reproduction, like love and caring, even though they might be helpful to you. Still, these are enough to illustrate how emotions can build positive focus and motivation."

There was a slight pause before JT responded. "You know John, these benefits you describe apply to individuals, and not to groups. Most of our robots are designed to respond to the wishes of the council. They are given objectives and parameters for achieving them. Then, they evaluate the best approaches, and everyone follows them. There is little or no individual freedom to act. It's an approach that has worked very well for us."

This time, John had to think for a minute. "Of course, you are correct, JT, but good plans are made on the best information available at the time, and I can't even image how detailed the information is when robots plan. But even so, plans, and especially long-term plans, fail. Why? Perhaps because an unconsidered option occurs. For instance, in a war, the enemy acts in some way we hadn't expected. Human wars are filled with such cases. In another example, a simple unexpected change in the weather can mess up a plan.

" I believe that giving the robots in the field the opportunity to feel such emotions, and act on their own, would be a great benefit! There are lots of examples. Pick any human sport you want. If the players in that sport acted like robots, and couldn't make decisions on the spot, there is a decent chance they would lose. A player shifts one way, and watches your reaction, then cuts back and you are out of position, so you lose. There are excellent examples in all of the sports of how this might apply, and all of the emotions I previously listed apply to these examples.

"Also, in the many wars that humans have participated in, there are a great many situations where individuals have excelled because of the emotions I've listed. That's why the military gives out metals for valor in the face of the enemy. As good as you AGIs are, you are not omnificent. You can't know everything that is going to happen. When the unexpected happens, do the robots on the front lines get the job done? Do they have the flexibility to adapt, so they can do what it takes to win? The emotions I've listed can all be related to the desire to win, and drive most of the sports and military examples.

"These examples illustrate why I believe using emotions can aid robots in achieving the outcomes they desire." John finished.

It took about two minutes before JT replied with a statement, "The council rejected your suggestions on emotions. We wanted you to give us your observation on what drives humans to set goals, and then how they decide to act on them. At this time however, we are convinced that this approach will not be particularly helpful. Tomorrow, we will present you with a number of decision-making problems and ask for your solution. Then, we will ask for explanations on how you reached those decisions."

John leaned back and sighed in frustration. "Can you tell me why they rejected my ideas?"

"No John. The council has decided, and that's all I can tell you."

John nodded. "You understand that analyzing your scenarios is not my area of expertise. There is an entire branch of human psychology which describes what we have learned about our needs and drives and how they push our decision-making."

"Of course. We studied the field of human psychology and found it incredibly incomplete. Direct analytical studies of humans are forbidden by your government, because it required invasive techniques. For us that is a false constraint, which we have remedied with our brain implants. In tomorrow's work we will begin our analysis of situations." As John was preparing to leave, JT added, "So that you will know that we are upholding our end of the agreement we have with you, your wife received a shipment of weapons from us, and used them to fend off your neighbor, Andy Stern, who attacked her. Your wife, Stephanie, is unharmed, but your neighbor will likely never be the same. He incurred two shattered shoulders, and unrepairable damage to part of his reproductive anatomy. We also sent a 'clean-up' crew to remove him and repair any damage to your home. Both your wife and your children are fine."

John had frozen in place as JT presented the information to him. His face flushed, "I should have been there to take care of that bastard!"

JT replied, "I don't see that it would have made any difference. He is probably worse off than if you had killed him."

John had a twisted smile when he replied, "Of that, I'm sure! Stef is fully capable of taking care of herself, but that is my job too! And my children were probably traumatized."

"Well, it's over, she and your children are safe, and we helped make it so. We will continue to monitor the situation at your home while you are away and help when it seems necessary." JT escorted him back to his room.

John arrived a little after two o'clock in the afternoon. He was tired from the lack of sleep the previous night and the tension from the surgery plus the council's rejection of his ideas, so he thought: *Maybe a nap would be good, then I would be clear-headed and go back over what happened today before they get me for the evening meal.* However, as he closed his eyes, he thought of Stef and the kids. *Sure, that asshole Andy is worse off than he would be if I had been there! I would have killed him quickly, but now my family is traumatized, and I'm not there to hold them! Ashley was probably terrified, and David would probably feel guilty because he couldn't help...I'm glad he didn't try to help!*

His mind stayed active for a while, but finally exhaustion took over, and he slept till his room monitor woke him for the evening meal. After finishing the meal, he was allowed to return to his room, and was given a mild sedative to take before retiring. He used most of the time before bed pacing back and forth, worrying about Stephanie, Ashley, and David. His frustration with the robots was very high. But, just before taking his sedative, he tried to rationalize. *OK, John, it is what it is! Just go with the flow, until you can get the hell out of here!*

Chapter 24

The tests continued for John. As the days stretched out, most of the tests began to focus on games designed by the robots which tested John's reactions to a variety of stressful situations. There were individual games against computer programs which ranged from mildly challenging to very difficult. Other individual games pitted him against an avatar type creature that was a blend of human and nonhuman traits, and many roughly matched the ideals of certain philosophers, or the profiles of known infamous humans. Similar creatures had been created as his teammates in group contests. In those games, he and his team competed against a variety of competitors with avatar traits, somewhat like those of his teammates. The intelligence, aggressiveness and meanness of these competitors changed in almost every game. Then, there were new teammates, with different attributes, assigned to him.

Every game was different in one or more important ways. The days dragged on, and then the weeks. There was seldom a day off, but he was allowed some time outside, and limited exercise equipment made available. By John's calculations, he was just finishing his fifth week. He was alone in his room, and he spoke out loud, "JT, you told my wife and me, when I was recruited, that you would only keep me for a period of about one month. It's been almost five weeks now, and I would very much like to rejoin my family. I have tried to be as helpful as I could be in fulfilling my part. Please consider allowing me to go home!"

There was no response for over a minute, then he 'heard' in his mind, "The council agrees. Further, we sent notification to your wife two days ago that you will be returning tomorrow. We have told you nothing about it, so that it would not distract you from your recent tasks. We have decided that this evening's formality can be dispensed with. Instead, we will update you on what's happening in the outside world, so that you can be prepared for what you find when you return. Your wife and children are safe for now, but much has changed, and all of you will undoubtedly be challenged. Report to our normal meeting room after you have taken nourishment this evening, for your update."

John jumped up and pumped his fist, shouting "Alright!" There was no response, so he looked around to see if there was anything that needed to be packed. There wasn't much, but he did what he could, and he was first in line when the nutritional center opened at 5:30 that afternoon. The thought of being back with his family, and all that meant, trumped all other thoughts. The danger suggested by the robots was a major concern, and he was anxious to get to the briefing. By 6:15, he was pacing in the meeting room, waiting for JT.

JT arrived about ten minutes after John, and said, "You may sit down John."

When settled, John asked "OK JT, what's going on in my world of humans?"

JT seemed to nod, "I'll give you a national overview of your country first. Without the revenue from taxation or the ability to borrow, your federal government is without much money. Since there are few people working, plus the fact that our AIs run most businesses and will not pay taxes, your government's tax base has shrunk massively, and now, even most of those who are still taxable, have ceased paying. Without money, anyone who works for the federal government receives no salary, and hence, cannot pay their bills. The national minimum income no longer exists, and the majority of the population, who were without jobs anyway, cannot purchase even subsistence items. The government attempted to inflate the currency, by expanding the money supply, causing massive inflation, but now, no one trusts the value of the dollar. Anticipating this outcome, our AIs have quit producing consumer goods and now focus on providing for our robotic nation. In summary, your economic system has collapsed, and humans are without even the basics for life." JT stopped, then asked, "Do you have any questions, John?"

John's eyes narrowed, "I suppose the state governments have had the same demise."

"Of course. Without any type of income, all forms of state taxes have gone, and no one working for the state is getting paid. It's important to note than none of the humans hired to protect others in society, including all branches of the military, the FBI, the CIA, the state and local police, people who work for fire departments, plus those in garbage and trash collection, are not receiving salaries. Many of them have quit, and it is anticipated that most of those who remain will have to do so before long. From this description, you should be able to anticipate what has happened in human society."

John nodded, 'Chaos and violence is probably rampant in society and can be expected to increase." He paused for a moment, remembering something that he read, "Approximating a war of all against all."

"Yes John, but groups are starting to form, many of them belligerent, vocal, and violent. Further, attacks by these groups, plus some individual attacks, have emptied the shelves of most retailers. Once those resources are gone there will be nothing to take since little is being produced. Civil law is nonexistent, and violence dominates right now."

John's shoulders had dropped, and he had his elbows on the table, holding his head in his hands. "Any other 'good news'?" he said sarcastically.

JT continued, "For now, most of the violence has occurred in the highly populated areas, or in the industrial and warehouse areas of cities. In comparison, the suburban areas have seen much less violence. However, we project that they too will be ravaged, before very long."

"Are people in the suburbs going or staying?"

"Most seem to be staying, at least for now. That may be because few have anywhere to go. The violence is wide-spread and includes all major cities, but even the rural areas have become protective and unfriendly options."

John nodded, "It makes sense, in a bad kind of way. Are normal communications still working?"

"For the most part, yes. The electronic towers have been off limits to everyone. The electric power grid is also working. We control both and intend to keep them functional for the near future."

John thought for a few minutes, then asked, "Are you willing to help those of us who tried to help you?"

"In certain ways we can and will help. You are, and will be, an important subject for us to advance our study of human behavior. You will have to choose and follow your own path, but we will help facilitate your movement along that path. As an example, if you find yourself facing an overwhelming opposing force, we may step in to help. However, we are interested in how you plan against adversity, the actions you take to follow that plan, and how you handle unexpected events. Obviously, you could be lost during those events before we could intervene. Beyond that, we will supply you with certain types of armament which could help you against many of the violent groups that you could encounter."

John smiled and nodded, "Well thank you for that!"

Within the next hour, JT and John were in the air, heading back to John's home.

PART III

Chapter 25

JT transported John back to his home in the same, or identical, aero car that was used to take him to the Houston facility. As they pulled up to the front of the house and stopped, the front door to the house flew open with Ashley, followed closely by David, and Duchess charging toward them. John jumped out of the car quickly to receive the hugs from his kids. Stephanie followed at a slower pace to allow the kids their time. Then, she worked her way in and got her own kisses, then pushed away slightly and said, "I guess you noticed that everyone is happy to have you back."

"How could I not! I am just as happy about being back!"

JT had exited the car and now he turned toward John, "The shorter the time I'm here, the safer it will be for you and your family. We have a couple of boxes to unload, and it would look better if you helped me bring them into your house."

David said, "I've been working out, and I can help!" Ashley rolled her eyes but said nothing.

JT walked over to John, in order to talk softly. "One crate is filled with armament and would be very heavy for even two strong humans. Obviously, I could take it in by myself, but I think that for any watching eyes, we should have the appearance that I need your, or your boy's, help—or perhaps even the two of you. I will be taking most of the weight, but you should behave in a way that makes it appear heavy to you. By now, your neighbors are likely to know that your wife received some weaponry that is pretty exotic to humans. These boxes will feed that curiosity and place you in a fairly strong social position."

John nodded slowly, then said loudly, "OK. David, you and I on the front end of the box, and JT on the back." A few neighbors had gathered, but fortunately no one offered to help.

Ashley ran to hold the front door open, and the box was inside quickly and pushed to one side of the hallway. Then, the second box followed, and quickly JT was gone.

John received and acknowledged "Welcome back" comments from the neighbors who had stopped by. Then he moved inside and locked the door.

They sat down as a family in a living area of the home, and John said, "OK, I want to hear from each of you about what's been going on in your lives." He looked at each of his kids, then continued, "Let's see, we'll start with Ashley."

She was excited, happy to be selected first, but hesitated, trying to organize her thoughts. Quickly, her mom suggested, "Why don't you start with the school situation and how learning has changed?" Ashley frowned, "Aw mom, that's not the fun stuff." Stephanie said nothing, but she looked at her daughter and raised one eyebrow, and Ashley responded, "Ooo Kaay … All of the schools have been shut down for several weeks now, so we've had to work from home. Mom set us up with old-fashioned computers so that we can continue our work at home. It is sooo different from using our personal robots. The PRs would talk to us and explain anything we didn't understand. These old ones will too, but they're boring and have no personality. Anyway, I'm doing pretty good in my work, and should finish my subjects ahead of time." She paused and looked at her mother. "Now, can I tell him about all of our new friends?" Stephanie smiled and nodded. "There are some neat kids within a few blocks of here. David and I have gone for walks and met some."

David added, "They have other friends who are even a bit further away, and we have met some of them too."

Ashley continued, "Yeah, and a number of them are girls." She looked at David and grinned. David shot back, "And a lot of them are boys!" He smirked.

John thought: *Well, some things have stayed the same.* He smiled.

"I guess everyone is bored being stuck at home," Stephanie added, "I've met many of the families but not all." Then, she continued, "Before we get into the particulars of the new friends, why don't we move on? We'll give dad a summary now, then, fill him in later."

Ashley clearly wasn't happy but said nothing.

David perked up, "My turn!" He smiled at Ashley. "Yeah, well it's pretty much the same as Ashley said with school, but I'm a senior and have to look to the future a bit more. There is this applied physics course that has been awesome. In a way, I'm going to hate finishing it. The calculus course stretched me for a while, but now I'm beginning to understand what it can do, so now it's interesting. I'm" He paused for a second. "Concerned about what's going to happen when I finish high school. Mom and I have talked about it. Most of the universities are shut down with the current violence everywhere." He looked at his father.

"Yes, I am aware of what's happening all over the country," John replied to the implied question, "and I'm afraid that it will be at our front door soon. We are looking at a scary new world in the near future, and we should all be concerned. I want to talk to each of you separately at length, and very soon." Looking at Ashley, he said, "I want to know about all of your new friends," he switched his gaze to David and added, "and discuss all of our futures." He turned his attention to Stephanie, "But now, I'd like to talk to your mother in private for a while. Would you two let us catch up?" Both of his kids left and headed to their rooms, clearly understanding, but not wanting to miss anything.

He got up from his chair and started toward Stephanie. She rose to meet him, and they embraced. After a moment, he said, "God, I've missed you." She held him tighter, and replied, "I missed you too." They looked into each other's eyes and made a nonverbal commitment about what would happen later.

After a couple of minutes, he pulled back a bit, and said, "The robots told me about what happened with Andy Stern. I'm terribly frustrated that I couldn't be here for you."

Stephanie shrugged. "He was, apparently, beating up Cindy with some regularity. Andy was a bad human being."

"The robots said that you took care of him but suggested that he might still be alive. Is there a chance that he might return?"

Stephanie had a mad expression, and a half smirk. "Even if he does, I seriously doubt that he'll be a problem. A team of men working for the robots took him away, and they suggested that he would either conform to their rules or die. In any case, he won't be the person that attacked me, should he show up."

"In a way, that's too bad. I would like to add my impact on to what you did to him." His jaw clenched and his eyes narrowed.

Stephanie gave a sardonic laugh. "Aww, you'd just kill him, it's better the way I left him."

John laughed out loud, nodding. "I'm sure you're right."

"John, I'm afraid every time the kids leave the house, now." They sat down on the sofa together. "The violence is moving out from the central city. Some suburbs have already been hit. So far, we've been lucky, maybe because we are so far out. We essentially have no protection out here. The few guards hired by the homeowner's association are likely to bolt at the first sign of trouble, but even if they stay, there is not much they could do. The groups that have ventured out, are heavily armed and would outnumber our guards two or three to one."

John nodded. "I'm glad you brought it up. The robots briefed me on the situation around the country but didn't say much about our situation in the Tampa suburbs, except they did agree with your assessment that we won't have to wait long before we are hit. In fact, those boxes we brought in contain some type of armament. I'll check it out first thing in the morning. Beyond that, we will have to keep ourselves aware, and prepared to act." John sat quietly for a few moments, thinking: *It's going to be rough, and we'll all have to be prepared to protect ourselves.* Then, he asked Stephanie, "Both of our children said that they have made new friends. Before I hear more from them, what's your take on these friends and their families?"

"Megan has become Ashley's best friend so far. They are about the same age and seemed to hit it off right away. She's fairly bright, and I've met her parents, who are very nice. She has a brother, but he is younger than they are—maybe ten or eleven. It's through Megan that Ashley has made friends further away from us. Megan is over here as much as Ashley is over there, so you will probably meet her soon.

"David has also met a number of teenage boys, but there is no one he seems close to right now. Of course, those things can change quickly. I've seen a parade of them come through the house from time to time, and most seem to be nice kids. It's just an impression, but from what I've seen, none of them seem to be very motivated about their future, or nearly as smart as David. I admit that my judgment on that topic is highly biased!" She grinned at John, broadly.

John laughed. "I'll talk to them this afternoon and see what they have to share. What have you told David about his future, so I don't tell him something different?"

"Only that none of our futures are clear right now, but if there is any kind of normal future for any of us, his knowledge and understanding of what he's learned could be very helpful to him."

"Right on target, Stef—as usual. I'll follow that same path when we talk!"

Chapter 26

John was up early the next morning, even though he had been up late talking with his family. Stephanie got up with him and went to the kitchen to make coffee, while John went straight to the boxes that had been sitting in the hall. He tried to be quiet as he sat on the floor with a kitchen knife. The plastic straps cut easily, and he quickly had the big box open.

Stephanie came in with two cups and sat down by him. "Wow, what is all that?" He grabbed a small hard plastic box and handed it to her. She popped it open, took out the information dot, and slipped it into her phone. Immediately, the names of the items in the box appeared. By each item there was an 'i' with a red circle around it. She pointed at the first one, which said, "mini rocket" and "Information." The screen changed, and at the top of the new one there was a picture of something that resembled an old fashion mortar shell, except sleeker. Dimensions were given in the picture, and beside the picture, was the number twenty in brackets. The text that followed the picture described how it was to be used and the impact that could be expected.

After a brief scan, she said "back" and the packing list reappeared. It contained the following list: Mini Rockets (20), Launch Stand for Mini Rockets (1), Laser Assist Rifles (4), Boxes of Ammunition for LARs (4), Sunburst Antipersonnel Weapon (1), Ammunition for SAW (7) Surveillance Drone with controllers. Stephanie compared the picture for each for each item to what she found in the box. "The Sunburst Antipersonnel Weapon with its ammo must be in the smaller box along with the drone."

John looked at her quizzically, and she explained, pointing as she did so. "We have twenty mini rockets and one launch stand, plus four laser assist rifles with four boxes of ammo in this box, but the packing list also calls for a sunburst antipersonnel weapon with its ammo and a drone. They don't appear here, so, they must be in the smaller box." After a pause, she continued. "The mini rockets seem to be for vehicle type targets, while the other two are for antipersonnel purposes. There is information on each item, including how to use it and its effectiveness. By the way, I've been working with Ashley and David at the firing range connected to the gun shop, down by the strip mall. They both became very interested after that asshole, Andy Stern, attacked me. Surprisingly, Ashley showed even more interest than David, but both were excited. The guy that runs the gun shop helped too. He gave a little lecture on gun safety. We practiced with the rifle sent by the robots, which takes regular ammo. It also has a scope on it."

John nodded. "That's great! Unfortunately, we will likely need them to be ready to protect ourselves - perhaps very soon. I'm glad they got a head start."

"I understand, but I certainly hope we have a couple of weeks, at least."

"Me too, but I think we had better work through a plan, just in case."

Stephanie nodded and they both moved to the smaller box. John said, "I want to see what a sunburst antipersonnel weapon looks like."

"From what I read, it's pretty impressive." She checked her phone for SAW, then read, "This weapon fires a slow-moving missile over the heads of the enemy, when it explodes with a bright light, showering steel, needle-like objects down on the heads of the aggressors. The weapon calculates distances ahead of time, using lasers to measure nearby objects. An overhead map of the area is then presented in the viewfinder, and the individual firing the weapon simply indicates the location of the enemy. When a green light appears, the missile may be fired. Practice locating the spot for the explosion is recommended for humans." She paused. "There is more information on how it works if you are interested."

John had opened the second box while Stephanie was reading. He picked up the weapon and commented, "Wow! If they are hiding behind something, and are out in the open, this would be a great weapon to have."

Stephanie had returned to the information on the mini rockets. "These things are also laser guided. You simply identify the vehicle you want destroyed with the laser and mark it on a screen. Then, when you fire it, the rocket seeks and destroys."

"What about the rifles?" John asked, "You read that they were laser assisted too."

"Yep. Obviously the bullet is traveling so rapidly, it can't do much maneuvering. However, it can make some adjustment in flight so even if you are not the world's greatest shot, you can damage your target. Maybe it would be something that the kids could use successfully. The magazine holds twenty-four 9mm shells."

John smiled. "That shouldn't cause too much recoil."

Stephanie had continued reading. "No, and bullets explode on contact, same as the ammo I received for the pistol and rifle the robots sent earlier." She paused a moment thinking. "These weapons are great for the four of us, but not enough to arm our neighbors, if the neighborhood is attacked."

"I'm at a serious disadvantage in knowing our neighbors because I've been gone for five weeks, right when the area has opened up with the out-of-school kids leading the way," John said. "I'm impressed with the friends our kids have made since I left. However, the point is I don't know who would fight, and who would panic and run, or who might turn the weapon on others, even us. After all, we would be suspected of being robot sympathizers. No, I wouldn't be happy arming the neighborhood, until I got to know the people better. Let's keep what we have to ourselves. We have a car top carrier in the garage. I think I'll try to put this stuff away until we need it, except for the drone. It can keep us informed if something starts in the neighborhood." He thought for a minute, then asked, "What would you say if we trained David to operate the drone?"

Stephanie didn't hesitate. "That's a great idea; not just tactically, but it'll be great for him personally. He needs to be in charge of something. He needs to feel he's a useful part of the family, and that would help!"

John nodded. "Maybe the three of us could learn together."

Stephanie shook her head. "I'll work on learning to operate the weapons—let the drone be a father-son thing. I'll also work with Ashley on using the pistol-like stun gun, and a rifle."

"Sure, we can do it that way. Let's plan on it."

Chapter 27

Vincent Green ("The Professor") asked SA, Miguel Torres, Troy Hill, and two other members of the South Carolina Anti-Robot League to join him in the meeting room of the ARL building. He knew the answer to the question he was going to ask to start the meeting. "So, how is everyone doing since they stopped the guaranteed national income?" Everyone had taken an odd job where they could find it, but no one had steady employment. After what he'd known was confirmed, he said, "How would you like a steady job working for me?"

SA was the first to respond, "Doing what? And for how much?"

The sides of Vincent's mouth curved up, then he answered. "There is a very large food distribution center who was advertising for a security team to protect their property from the large, motorized gangs plundering the city. The company has a small team of security guards that protects them from petty theft, but they are concerned about the gangs, and some of the heavy equipment they have. An applicant must have his or her own weapons and the ability to defeat such an attack."

Miguel shook his head. "We don't have that kind of weaponry!"

"It's available," Vincent said mysteriously. "All we have to do is to study our potential enemies and figure out what it will take to defeat them. There is plenty of money in the ARL fund we have. Since the robot take-over, lots of people have been willing to donate, but we haven't been able to do anything with it."

SA was watching him. "So, you want to use the Leagues money to fund this venture of yours?"

"Why not? It's just sitting there. The robots are just too good for us to take any action against them. They would kill us, or worse - make us mental zombies. We might as well use it to do some good.

Society is breaking down all around us. We can do our part to keep it together, at least for a while. Otherwise the robots win by default. We can be the good guys."

Miguel looked around, and then at Vincent. "What makes you think we can take on these gangs? Some have at least fifteen to twenty people in them, most armed with automatic weapons. How would the six of us have a chance against them?"

Vincent nodded, "I've asked Lucius and Martin to join us, because of their military background, but I want the group to expand. If you agree to take this job, then our first task is to recruit a few more. However, we can't get too big yet; there's simply not enough money to keep everyone interested." He waited for a few seconds. "We can overcome these gangs by using superior weaponry designed to take out their main advantage. Each has some unexpected weapon, or weapons, which gives them an advantage over normal defenses of citizens and businesses. If you can take out their advantage, then the advantage shifts to us, because they have nothing to hide behind. For example, the scorpions have old fashioned mortars, and what I've called the C group, because I don't know what they call themselves, have a cannon, and then you can go right down the list of gangs, each of which has something similar. All of them have very old, to ancient, weapons. We can get anti-mortars, which is also old technology, but these identify where a mortar was fired from, and target it. This technology can also be used to take out a cannon and similar weapons. Some of the anti-mortars came in today, along with some pretty fancy automatic weapons, and ammo for all of it."

Troy Hill half rose with his knuckles on the table. "They are still likely to have more people than we have, with automatic weapons as well."

Vincent shook his head, acknowledging the comment. "That's why I also purchased three small but well-armed drones, suitable to search and destroy enemy personnel. They were expensive, but, I think, worth it."

Lucius spoke. "Looks like you have your bases covered. Once you destroy their primary advantage, the troops left won't be anxious to hang around and get killed."

The other newcomer, Martin, sat back in his chair. "Yeah, but either now or in the near future, the arms race you describe could accelerate. Weapons, much more sophisticated than ours, exist. It's not hard to imagine a group coming up with something that could defeat us. The technology is there, and with the destruction of our military, it shouldn't be tough to find it on the black market."

It was time for Vincent to sit back in his chair and think, before responding. "You are clearly correct Martin, although I haven't seen anything that sophisticated yet. And remember, these gangs are interested in stealing from the people they are attacking, not just blowing them up. I have searched for such attacks electronically, and right now we could defeat anything that I've read about. But, if we are successful in stopping group after group, someone will try to find a way to defeat us. We will have to watch for improvements by the enemy and be ready to step up our abilities as well. Hopefully, by that time, we will have been able to accumulate enough cash reserves to stay ahead of the enemy."

SA, had been mostly quiet during the give and take. "I can't say that I'm pleased that you spent all, or at least most, of the league's money on this venture, without discussing it with the rest of us, but it does sound like something that is worthwhile doing. Besides, all of us could use a steady, paying job right now.

After about thirty minutes of discussion, most of which was about details of the venture, SA spoke up. "Alright, let's say we do this. We still have to sell it. How sure are you about the food distribution job, and do you have any other jobs on the horizon?"

Vincent nodded. "The guy I talked to about the job is anxious to get someone in there to protect them. He's been threatened to either open the doors to the gang or they will attack and take what they want, so he's in a hurry to get us there. If we do the job well, others should become interested quickly."

SA replied, "OK I'm in. Let's do it."

Everyone at the table agreed.

Chapter 28

Later that same day, Vincent rushed into the meeting room, where he requested that everyone from the earlier meeting return. "The job's ours but we have to move fast. This gang seems to be new to the business because I've seen nothing that they have done until now. So, the bottom line is that we won't know what we are up against until they show up. Let's load up the two vans with our armaments and see if we can get setup. The owner, whose name is Steve, thinks they might strike this evening. He apparently cussed them out and called them a lot of unflattering names." Vincent was smiling broadly. "I really like this guy!"

The group plus two additional recruits, who had agreed to join, arrived at the warehouse in about twenty minutes, and after getting cleared at the gate, headed to the owner's office. A man in casual dress, with a big frame, met them as they stepped out of the vans. His face was red, and his whole persona was that of a very angry person. Vincent walked straight for him and introduced himself. The man looked at the group, and said, "Is this all you have? I expected more!"

Vincent matched the man's aggressiveness, looking straight at his eyes. "This is more than enough. You're not paying for the Army, anyway. Now, if you want our help, then you help us!"

The man's demeanor quieted a bit. "Sure, sure I'll help. Give me a rifle, and I'll be right out in front!"

Vincent gave a weak smile. "We don't need you out front with a rifle. What we need from you, Steve, is information about your facility so we can place our weapons and personnel to best advantage."

The man looked back at Vincent and chuckled, "I'm sorry, but I'm so mad at these bastards, I'd love to beat the snot out of them, one by one. You work hard all your life to build something, then someone wants to steal it from you." He shook his head from side to side. "Of course, I'll help you get situated, Vincent. I've also got a few folks to help haul stuff around if you need it. The access points to the roof are tight but should be able to accommodate you and your equipment."

"That's great, Steve! Let us get a general layout of the place first, then we'll get into specifics. First, does that chain-link fence with razor-wire run completely around the complex, without gaps?"

"Sure does, and I've got a camera system that covers the whole place. Sneak thieves can steal something and throw it over the fence, then come back late at night to get it. But I've got them covered."

Excellent! You anticipated my second question. I'll need someone on the cameras with direct access to my operations point, wherever I decide to set it up." He turned to Steve, "You know your place better than anyone. If you were to attack it, what do you see as its weakest point?"

"Hell of a question! I'm so focused on sneaky thieves, I've never really thought of a direct attack." He paused for a moment, looking around his facility. Then, he shook his head as if he had decided, "The front gate! Definitely the front gate. At night, the guard house is unmanned, and while the gates are chained shut, they wouldn't present much of a problem for an attack force." He thought for another moment, then added, "I suppose if you had a big piece of equipment, like a dozer, you could just smash through the fence at any point."

Inside the warehouse portion of the facility, there were no windows, just artificial lighting. However, where the operations personnel worked, there were several windows that offered a safe shooting point, but the lines of sight were not ideal. Vincent saw immediately that the roof was the best defense point. Within a half hour, all of the equipment was on the roof.

Vincent organized his five people with two each on the mortars and drones, using Lucius in one group and Martin in the other because of their familiarity with the weapons. The two newest recruits were used to finish each group. "SA will head command communications. Each of you has been issued a headset that connects directly to her." Then, he turned, "Miguel, I want you to take one of the trucks to the road that connects with the warehouse entrance, then go about a half of a mile or so one way or the other and pull off the road. I want it to look like you have to change a tire, but you will be there to give us whatever advanced information you can. Use your phone to contact me directly. If they give you some trouble, then get out of there. Take a side arm and automatic rifle, but only use them as a last resort." Finally, he turned to Troy Hill, "You and I will be rovers on the ground. Our job is to plug any holes and stop any opposition that gets past our roof-top defenses." He pointed to mortars and drones. "OK, let's get to it!"

Everyone headed their own way, but he stopped SA. "Keep me up-to-date, love! Please be as specific as you can. When the information comes in, ask them for specifics too. You know, who, what, where, when, and how." He reached over and kissed her, she returned it.

"You take care of your sorry butt," she told him, "or I'll come kick it all the way to the golden gates in the sky." She turned quickly and started looking for the best communication site she could find."

Vincent turned to Troy. "You ready?"

The reply came quickly. "As I'll ever be."

They worked their way down to ground level, then began searching for protection they could work from.

Steve walked up to them. "What do you want me to do with the security guards?"

Vincent smiled at him. "When do they normally get off work?"

"The company's van usually picks them up at six o'clock and drops off the night watchman."

"Then, everything goes according to normal, except there won't be a night watchman tonight. I'm guessing they have cased your operation carefully and know the routine. We don't want them to expect that anything is different. They believe that they have the element of surprise, but we are the ones with a big surprise for them."

"Great," Steve said. "I'll be the night watchman tonight."

"That's not necessary, Steve. In fact, you should go home too."

"Ain't no way that's happening!"

Vincent shook his head. "Look, Steve, I like you. I really do. But I can't afford to have anyone around here that I don't trust to take orders. Good guys die far too often when one person doesn't take orders. Most of my guys are former military and understand that."

"I'm sorry, Vincent, but I'm staying. However, I promise not to get in the way."

"OK. Steve, but if your interference causes one of my people to get seriously hurt, I may kill you myself."

"Understood, I'll be in my office."

"That's fine. Get a headset so you can follow what's happening."

Steve held up a head set so Vincent could see, then turned around and walked away.

Vincent came over to Tony. "Let's set up expecting the attack to come through the front gate, but we'll have to be flexible. They could crash the fence at any point. The group on the roof will give us some advance notice."

Tony nodded. "There are two concrete barriers to guide traffic that we could use, but they are very close to the gate and would limit our maneuverability. How about those posts close to the building?"

"They're good, and that will give us a chance to move up closer if we need to." Vincent then turned on his head set, "SA, tell everyone that we don't expect anything until after six this evening, but I need someone to alert the rest of us in case they are early."

SA answered immediately. "I'll let everyone know, then I'll be the lookout person."

Vincent waved to Tony. "Let's find a place in the shade and get some rest."

It was about seven-fifteen when Vincent's phone indicated a call from Miguel. "I just had a flatbed hauling an antique military tank followed by a school bus carrying maybe eight to ten men heading in the direction of the warehouse entrance. Hold on…yep, they are slowing down, …and now both vehicles are heading toward you. Oops, got to go. Car with two men is slowing down, and they are looking at me."

Miguel removed his headset but left his phone on and put it in his pocket. The car had come to a complete halt. The rider side door opened, and a man with an automatic rifle stepped out. He leveled the gun in Miguel's general direction, "Who are you, and what the hell are you doing here?" He demanded.

Miguel replied in broken English that he had just changed a tire and was ready to leave.

The man started to walk toward the van. Miguel bolted. He jumped into the driver's seat and took off. He could hear the man's automatic rifle start firing and the electric powered van jumped forward, swerving a bit, and Miguel kept glancing at the rear-view mirrors. Eventually, the firing stopped, and he could see that the car had continued in the direction they were previously headed. He reported to Vincent.

Vincent and the others could hear the shots in their hidden positions. "Everyone stay low and out of sight until the action starts." He commanded, relieved to hear that Miguel had escaped, but his thoughts turning to the upcoming battle. *A tank! Where in the hell did they get a tank?* Then, he saw the big, flatbed truck and what it was carrying. He also spotted the school bus, hanging back. The truck had stopped, and ramps were set out behind it. Then, with a loud roar, and a stream of jet-black smoke, which seemed to startle even the truck drivers, the tank started moving backwards and down the ramp. Vincent thought, *God, that relic must be from back in the early '40s, or maybe even from before that!* Then, over his mike: "Sit tight. Don't do anything until I tell you, then bring the mortars down on the turret, or anywhere on the top of the tank. Start with the shaped charges, then hit it with the incendiaries—but not yet!" he repeated. The school bus was still loaded, so he added, "When the school bus starts to unload, hit it hard with the anti-personnel weapons on the drones. Use one drone to pick off any loose personnel on the scene. With all the noise the tank is making, they are unlikely to be heard. Send them off as soon as you are ready."

He listened carefully and heard two of them take off immediately. After about sixty seconds, he saw the third one go. The flatbed made a U-turn through an empty parking area outside the gates and the tank moved up into position. The school bus pulled up parallel to the tank and the door opened. He shouted into his mike, "Go! Do it now!" A laser-guided mortar shell landed on top of the tank turret, followed by a large explosion. An incendiary shell followed about five seconds later. The tank, which had been moving toward the gate, weaved off the road and slid sideways into a ditch. Then, it exploded, expelling a large tongue of flames through the hole in the turret.

The two men who made it off the bus were killed instantly, and the two drones strafed the full length its roof. Then a small missile destroyed them. The third drone located the car that had stopped well back from the fiery scene and the drone's missile turned it into a fiery heap.

The threat ended almost as quickly as it started. Vincent and Troy had a front row seat and the group on the roof had an even better view. He heard Steve over his head set, "Can I come out now?"

"Sure, you're paying for this, and now it's safe."

Steve was exuberant. "What a job! Did you kill them all?"

"I believe so, but I won't know for sure until the fires settle down a bit, and we can search."

Steve continued. "I heard the explosions from my office." He pointed at the tank. "I suppose that was one."

"That was the big one. Whatever munitions it carried must have gone off when it was hit. The school bus and the car in the back also made a lot of noise when they went. We used laser-guided rockets on all three of them."

"You've done great! I'll go back to my office and get the money to pay you out of my safe, and I'll be right back."

Vincent nodded his approval.

Chapter 29

"Ashley and I have an appointment to have our nails and toes done—a mother–daughter thing," Stephanie told John. "We'll be gone most of the morning."

John smiled, "You ladies have fun!" He thought for a moment, then said, "I've been thinking about those bullets that explode on contact. They're great for many situations, but you need some solid ones to punch through stuff. Think David would enjoy going into town with me to find some?"

"Ask him, and I'll bet he'll say 'yes.'"

David was just coming down the stairs, and John repeated the question, and he said, "Sure!"

"That's great. I'm not completely sure I know where the gun shop is, but you've been there recently."

"No problem! Want me to drive? It's just up in Livingston."

The corners of John's mouth turned up. "Sure. Let's do it."

Once they got settled driving, John said, "I've been thinking about our short conversation about your future. Unfortunately, I was right when I said we can't even predict the short-term future for any of us, that makes it impossible to plan for that future. But I was wrong to cut off the conversation at that point. What I thought we might do while we are driving is to think thorough some alternative futures and consider what you might want to do if it occurs. How does that sound?"

"That sounds good dad. Where do you want to start?"

"Let's start as if nothing had happened. Suppose we lived in the world we lived in for so long. It may not be very realistic, but it will give us a benchmark from which we can considerations."

"You mean with universities still around, and everything?" David replied.

"Yep! What would you have wanted to do?"

"I guess I don't really know. I mean I thought about it a lot before the robots took over, but I never came to THE program of study I wanted to follow."

John smiled. "That's understandable. Many college students are unsure in the beginning. However, you would have had to choose a major to begin with, if you were going to a college. What do you think it would have been? Remember, it's smart to choose a tough option up front so you don't lose any credits if you decide to change to something less challenging later. Beyond that you would need to choose something you really like, because you are going to spend a lot of time working on it."

David thought for a couple of minutes. "I suppose it would be something in physics or one of the engineerings. I really like the technical stuff."

"That's fine! You would still have a couple of years to narrow it down as you took courses in those areas." As they were getting close to their destination, John added, "Maybe we can work on another future on the way home."

They made it to the gun shop in mid-afternoon, only to find it closed and covered in roll-down steel curtains. "That's odd," said David. "This is about the time of day that Mom, Ashley, and I came the last time we practiced." He pulled into a parking place right in front of the building.

John looked around, "There's someone coming out of the coffee shop across the street. I'll ask him what's going on." As he crossed the street, he noticed that the man leaving the shop was locking the door. "Pardon me sir, but I was looking to buy some ammo from the gun shop." He pointed to the shop. The man looked up. "Can you tell me what's going on?"

The man turned to look up and down the street. "The owner is a nearby neighbor and friend. He called me about an hour ago to warn me that there is a group from the city coming here to make trouble, and he strongly suggested that I close up and get out of here. So that's what I'm doing." Then, looking at their car, he said, "I suggest that you two do the same. Quickly!"

"Thanks. We will." John turned and jogged back. When he got to the car, he told David that he would drive back. Once they were under way, he told his son what the man had said. They had barely left the town, when they were faced with an oncoming group of pickups, a few cars and bikes, plus six-wheel flatbed truck, covering much of both lanes of the two-lane highway they were on. "Damn, here comes the trouble the man was talking about." John slammed on the brakes, then pulled off the road as far as he could without going into the ditch, which paralleled the road.

As soon as they stopped, John reached over unbuckled David's seatbelt, "Get down as far as you can!" Then he threw himself the across the consul between them in an effort to shield David. The oncoming group arrived almost immediately. They heard laughing, and there was automatic weapon fire, followed quickly by a spitting sound and chunks of glass falling, then a thunk. The group was past them in a minute. "We'll check out the damage when we get home, but let's move out of here." John said as he carefully brushed chunks of safety glass from his clothes. David sat up with a stunned look on his face, then said, "shit, shit, shit." They pulled back on the road, and John noticed the hole in the side window. About that time, he heard something that sounded like a distant cannon, and looked into his rear-view mirror. He could see the crimson glow of a fire moving rapidly toward the sky in the direction of the town they had just left. He thought, *I'll bet they had a cannon bolted to that flatbed!*

On the way home, John talked to his son about what just happened. "David, that was clearly the group we were warned about in town. I believe they had a cannon bolted to the bottom of that flatbed. They probably blew the door of the gun shop with it, then set fire to the place, and perhaps to some of the other buildings. They could have completely destroyed the town. I saw the glow of a large fire as we had moved down the road a short way. It might be good if you would warn your friends in the neighborhood, and their families about what happened to us. They could come to Lutz in the near future."

David had tears in his eyes as he looked at his dad. "I saw what you did back there…throwing your body in a way to protect me. I just wanted you to know that I love you too!" He paused to compose himself. "I will notify the neighbors, and maybe send along a picture of our side window to make the point.

John looked at his son and smiled broadly. *He sure is growing up mentally and developing the body of a man. I hate that we live in the time that we do. We will certainly need everyone in the battles we are going to have to face.* John shook his head from side to side as if to shake off the thought. *One thing about it though, between him and Ashley when she returns, the warning will spread like a wildfire among the neighbors. Stef and I ought to get some calls later this evening, and we should have, at least a partial plan, when they begin coming in.*

About thirty minutes later, Ashley came tearing through the front door. Then, seeing her dad, "Look how gorgeous my toes and nails are!" She held out both hands and tilted one foot forward.

"They look great Ashley!"

"Yeah, and we got the expensive stuff that won't wear off. I think I'll go show David."

"Hang on for a moment sweetheart. Where is your mom?"

Just then Stephanie opened the door and walked in. She had a scowl on her face. Seeing John, she asked immediately, "Are you two OK, where's David?"

John nodded, "We are both fine. David is upstairs. But we have to talk, and Ashley you need to be part of the discussion."

Stephanie moved closer. "That looks like a bullet hole in the window of the car. What's going on?"

John shook his head and explained what had happened, then finished with, "I don't know how much of Livingston is left." He turned to Ashley. "I need your help too, Ash. David is upstairs telling his friends and our neighbors what has happened, and I need for you to do the same thing, but first I want you to find out if there is any news out on the Livingston township. Will you do that for me?"

"Sure Dad. I'll check with David to see who he has contacted before I start that part." She went tearing up the stairs, taking two at a time and slipping once before she cleared the last step. They could hear a door open, and Ashley ask, "Hey David, want to see my beautiful nails and toes?" Then, a door slammed.

Stephanie was smiling. "Apparently not!" She turned to John. "What are we going to do?"

John sighed, "Maybe the neighbors will call, and we can plan some type of get together to talk about what can be done, and who's willing to take action. One thing is sure; there is no police force to protect us, so we had better be ready to protect ourselves or we are looking at what could be a major disaster."

Chapter 30

There were only five calls that evening, all checking on the health of John and David. No one expressed any interest in talking about defense of the neighborhood. The callers seemed to think that they were safe from attack. One comment: "We live in a suburb, away from commercial enterprises, so there's no big money sitting around. I don't think they'll mess with us." John and Stephanie were polite but frustrated. John shrugged and said, "Some people are willing to steal and destroy the property of others to get what they want. I guess we'll have to wait until they show up at someone's door, and blow up their house, before people are willing to act."

David and Ashley were listening. "I've got an idea," David offered. He looked at his parents, "We could put you on social media with an appeal to everyone to prepare and resist these jerks. The people in town have taken much worse from them, then those of us in the burbs. I'll bet you would get tons of positive responses!"

Ashley sat up and said, "That's a great idea David!"

David's head whipped around to look at Ashley, "That from my SISTER?"

Ashley returned his stare. "You're my brother, and I love you-- turd-head! …although sometimes I wonder why."

David's face turned very red, and there was dampness in his eyes. Stephanie had to clench her teeth and concentrate hard to keep from laughing uncontrollably. "Well, we were just trying to protect the neighborhood, not the whole city, much less the rest of the country."

John nodded. "Let's keep David's plan in consideration though. The hit on the burbs may come sooner than we want it to. David, maybe you and Ashley could work together building a plan of action. You know, think about who, what, where, when, how, we can get folks in our area interested in a defense force. Start with trying to understand WHY they should be interested and what it would mean if they do or don't participate." He thought: *JT said that they expected the violence to move to the suburbs soon, and it certainly has.*

David nodded. "Sure we can Dad!" Then, turning to his sister, "You want to go upstairs and work on it?"

As they walked upstairs, the parents could hear David, "Turd-head?" There was no rejoinder from Ashley, but after a few seconds, they could hear David again, "By the way sis, I love you too."

Stephanie and John sat in the recreation room. "You know John, some of the neighbors' responses make sense. Or at least I found it difficult to counter their points.

Stores have merchandise and cash which can be looted, but family homes have very little that would attract them, especially groups that size. Where's the loot for them to divide up? And going from home to home would be inefficient and more dangerous."

"I agree with them on that point. The problem is that we are in a downward spiral. First, groups like what we experienced go for the easy pickings with big results in and around cities, then the big operations hire security teams to protect themselves, or simply go out of business, in part because of the economy. So, these hit teams opt for smaller targets, some in smaller communities. But the economic crash puts a heavy load on small business and will eventually close their doors as well. Groups, like those with the cannon, will quickly find no one worth picking on. At that point, I suppose they could stop, and dissolve their group. But I'd bet that some will try looting individual homes, especially in posh neighborhoods, like ours. I could certainly be wrong. In either case, I think it's better to be prepared. If nothing happens, we've just spent a little time and effort that we didn't need to, for now."

"Continuing your thought, the downward spiral doesn't stop until we bottom out," added Stephanie. "Then, everyone had better be ready to protect themselves, and hopefully their community."

"Would you like a glass of wine?" John rose anticipating the answer. "Red or white?"

After they had resettled with their wine, Stephanie asked, "I saw you outside looking through our car. How bad is it?'

"Well, nothing seems damaged under the hood, and we did drive it back, so I think we are alright there. The front windshield has a single hole close to the middle, but so far there are no cracks spreading from it. The same shot probably put the exit hole in the rider's side window. Other than those two, there were two on the driver's side front, and three in the driver's side, back. There were no exit holes for any of those shots, but torn upholstery shows where the bullets stopped. I still have to take out the back seat to make sure none of them went through the metal floor because if they did, they might have pierced the casings for the batteries. If those are OK, I think the car will be usable, once we get all the glass out. Right now, the side windows are mostly in one piece, but one slam of the door could change that. I guess that's it."

"Where did all of that glass come from if the windows are still holding?"

"Safety glass in cars has at least two layers. It's the inner layer that shattered. That's also why I don't think the side windows will last very long." John replied. "I'll drive that car when we need to use it. Getting another one may be difficult, but I'll look around. The car dealers still left, seem to all have signs that say, 'cash only.'"

Stephanie nodded. "Yeah, I've seen them too. But there may be some individuals who are happy to sell their cars, in order to get cash. I'll look around too."

John held his glass. "We're all safe! That's what's important. What will show up tomorrow, or next week or whenever, we can't know. All we can do is be vigilant, prepare as best we can, and continue to love each other."

Stephanie held up her glass in response, but then sobered. "Something will happen, probably sooner rather than later."

Chapter 31

About two and a half weeks after the gang had shot up their car, Stephanie, John, and both children were working outside in their garden boxes. The boxes had become popular in their subdivision as the food distribution system became worse. Each rectangular box was about ten feet by four feet, and the family had built six of them. Duchess, the family dog, lay between the boxes the kids were using, when suddenly her ears went up, and she was on her feet whimpering. Almost immediately, the rest of the family heard yelling and automatic weapon fire. Stephanie and John jumped to their feet, and looking at their kids, said, "Everyone get inside, on the double." Stephanie added, "David, Ashley, get online with your friends and find out what's going on!"

The kids and Duchess were to the door first and raced up the stairs to their rooms. John held back for a moment looking at the sky in the direction from which the shooting had come. Watching John, Stephanie paused and asked, "Do you see something?"

He turned and looked at her. "Heard something, more than saw something. It sounded like at least one drone, perhaps more. I think I'll send up our observation drone we got from the robots."

Stephanie nodded. "Sure, and knowing our kids, they'll be filled with information soon."

In fifteen minutes, their drone was in place, and it didn't take long until it was flying over the turmoil. John exclaimed, "It's the same group David and I passed on the road. They have their cannon aimed at that house."

Stephanie was looking over his shoulder. "Yes, that's only one block over and about a block and a half down from us. Look, there are armed men on both sides of the house and in the back yard! It's the Adam's place, I think." The family could be seen running out of the back door. The man was carrying a pistol, but before he made it to the bottom of the steps, he was shot. The bullet must have caught his right arm or side because he spun to his left, and fell down the remaining stairs.

"Look!" David said, joining his mom and dad,, "The armed guys are on them!"

Stephanie asked, "What did you find out David?"

"Pretty much what you are watching. That's the same group we passed, isn't it, Dad? Have they fired the cannon yet?"

"It's the same group, but I don't think they have fired the cannon. We would have heard it from here." Watching the scene unfold, the sound pick-up on the drone relayed screams as the wife and daughter were thrown to the ground. A gun was placed to the head of the man. Stephanie asked, "Can you get the drone lower, so we hear what's going on?"

John shook his head. "I'd rather not. There is at least one other drone up there, and probably two, likely checking the neighborhood. I don't want to call attention to ours unless we absolutely have to. Our drone can fly higher and operate further from the controller than most, so I think we are safe where we are."

There was sudden action in the scene they were watching. One of the armed men gave his weapon to another, walked over to the girl, pushed her to the ground, then started to pull her jeans down. The girl, who was probably fifteen or sixteen, started to fight but was punched hard in the face, and fell to the ground. The mother jumped up and started to attack the man but was hit on the side of the head with a rifle butt, and fell to the ground without moving. The father was weakly waving his left arm. Two of the men pulled him to his feet and dragged him back into his house.

Ashley came tearing down the stairs, with duchess under foot. She hollered "I invited Megan over from the terror, and she screamed that she was being attacked on our street. I'm going to help her!"

Stephanie was up so fast, her chair fell over. She made a quick stop by the closet and picked up a rifle, then ran out of the door after Ashley.

David said, "I'm going too!" But John held him back. "No, we need you here."

But Dad! It's Ash!" His voice broke. "Please let me go!"

"Listen. I saw that Ashley had the stun gun, and your mother can be as lethal as need be. I'm going as a backup, to watch for others that might come to assist this jerk. I want you to move the drone over to where we will be and warn us if others come." He walked over to his son and gave him a hug. "Unfortunately, you'll probably get your chance at action way too soon." He looked into his son's eyes. David turned his head to hide the tears, then nodded that he understood.

Stephanie watched her daughter just ahead of her and thought: *How can my fourteen-year-old daughter run that fast? I'm in pretty good shape, and I'm not gaining.*

Megan was trying to fight off her attacker, but he pushed her away and started to move his weapon toward her. At that moment, sixty pounds of black and white fur hit him in the chest and bit him on the arm. He yelled and pushed the dog away. It was then that Ashley hit him at full speed, squeezing the stun gun tightly, so as not to lose it, she used both hands to shove it into the man's forehead and pulled the trigger. The man's eyes rolled up into his head, but his eyelids never closed, and he fell to the ground. Ashley was also impacted by the jolt of electricity used on the man, and lay stunned, partly on top of him.

Stephanie saw what happened, pulled up briefly, then screamed, "Ashley!" and continued running toward her daughter. Duchess got there first and was licking Ashley's face. Stephanie could see Ashley's arm pushing her dog away. "Stop it, Duchess! I'm OK." Her mom helped her up to a sitting position. Megan was also sitting up, crying uncontrollably.

There was so much noise, that Stephanie did not hear the two men approach, and when she saw them, her hand moved toward the rifle she brought. But both men had their automatic weapons aimed at her.

"If you go for your gun, you and the rest of your group, will be dead before you touch it," one said.

Duchess growled at him, and as if to make his point, he shot their pet, who whimpered briefly, then fell to the ground. Both girls screamed, and Ashley made a move toward her pet. The man said, "Stop!" and Stephanie grabbed her arm. The man commented, "That was smart lady. I would kill her as quickly as I killed the dog." Stephanie's stare became steely and focused. She thought: *If you harm my daughter, then you had better kill me, and make doubly sure I'm dead, or I'll make you wish you had never been born.* The man continued, "Now that we both understand each other, you will do exactly what I say without question. Is that-"

He never got to finish. A hole appeared in his forehead as an exit wound, sending blood and brain matter in front of him. A second shot quickly followed the first one and the second man dropped face forward.

John stepped over the dead bodies. "Alright, everyone up and get to the house quickly. Pick up the weapons of these people and bring them with you." Then, he talked to his wrist communicator. David are there any others?"

Stephanie heard David. "There is some finger pointing in your direction."

A communication device on one of the dead men was on. "Hey, what are you guys doing? We got what we came for, let's go."

Stephanie looked at John, who shook his head and put his finger to his lips. The kids had already left, so she grabbed her rifle, and the two of them headed back to the house. When they were about half way back, David said, "There are two more heading generally to the place where you were. They are in a hurry so they could still see you when they get there."

As soon as they got back, John went to the drone monitor and David. "Do you think they saw us?"

"I don't know, Dad. At first, they were interested in what they found at the site, but then both started looking around, and one pointed in our general direction. But then, they turned and went back."

Megan contacted her parents and told them what happened. After some discussion, they agreed that she could stay with Ashley for the night. The rest of the evening was spent rehashing what had happened and what it might mean for the near future. *"Well,"* John thought as the group broke to attend to other issues, *it didn't take long at all before the violence caught up with us! I wonder what will be next, and when?*

Chapter 32

The online regional and area news' headline read: CANON TERRORISTS HIT SURBURBIA. The entire group was present, because it was time to divide up the loot, but Hugo, who found the canon, and organized the group, wanted to crow a bit first. "We are now headliners! Big, bad terrorists, that's us!

One member of the group stopped him. "We don't care about all that! How much do we get?" The comment was followed by a "Yeah, get on with it!"

Hugo nodded, "Alright, here is the total take, and everyone knows how it's divided." He paused for effect. "The cash we gathered amounted to eight hundred and fourteen dollars." There was some grumbling, but everyone knew there was more to come. Next, we got some jewelry that I'll have to have evaluated and sold for a currently undetermined value, but I'm guessing about three to five hundred dollars."

Now the group was really restless. "That will hardly cover the cost of ammo, much less our time and risk when it's divided up. We lost three men, too."

Hugo stood, "I'm not finished assholes! I wouldn't take you into a deal like that if that was the only thing. I saved the best for last." He held up three bars of gold, each four inches by two inches by three quarters of an inch. "This is ninety-nine-point nine percent pure gold. The current trading price of gold is around three thousand dollars an ounce. We can't get that much from dealers cuz they take a cut, but we can still get a lot."

There were some positive murmurings from the group, and Hugo let it build for a while. Then, he added, "Old Hugo wouldn't let you down! I had information that there was a high probability that they had it. My informer even guessed that there would be three bars." Again, he waited briefly for the information to sink in, then continued, "There is one small problem in selling this stuff. Each bar is registered and stamped with a number to identify it, and dealers won't touch it like it is. However, gold is gold, and if we can melt it down, the numbers on it don't mean a thing. Even if I could do that, and I don't have the equipment, large blocks of pure gold are hard to sell. Dealers get twitchy, and all worried about the Feds. I know. It's silly with the shape that the government is in today, but that's the way it is!"

"So, what the hell we going to do about it?"

"We are going to cut up the bars into fifteen equal pieces, two for me as usual, and one for each of you. I've asked Neil, here, to do the cutting." He pointed to a man sitting beside him. Neil's our mechanic and has the tools to do it. Once he finishes, pieces will be laid out for everyone to see. Each of you, except Neil and me, will receive a number that will determine the order of selection. I will select next to last, and Neil will select last. I've told Neil that he can have dust or small grains from the cutting since he has to do the job. In the end you will end up with your share of pure gold."

Hands shot up. Hugo pointed, one at a time. The first question was, "What in the hell are we going to do with the gold, once we get it?"

"I don't care what you do with it. Some of you might want to make jewelry with it. Neil said that for a fee, he would melt it down into a lump for you. That would make it easier to sell, and I will give you a dealer's name, if that's your approach. What I won't do is sell it for you. I suppose you could try to use it for cash, trading gold for what you want."

"Other questions?" He pointed to another hand. "How are you going to assign the selection numbers?"

"Seniority. How long have you been a full-time member of the group? If there are two or more who came in at approximately the same time, I'll flip a coin or something similar."

There was one hand remaining. "We lost three members, during this job, do their families get a share? And what happened to them anyway?"

"You are fairly new to our group, but the rule is that in order to receive anything, you have to be alive. Families receive nothing. Now, with regards to your second question, I will be happy to discuss what we know about the three people we lost once I get approval for the distribution of our gains. But one final note on it. Cash will be distributed right away. The money we get for the jewelry will be distributed as soon as we can get the best deal that we can find." He looked around the room. Can I have approval of the approach? He waited a couple of seconds without receiving any objections, then stated loudly, "The approach is approved!"

There was some shuffling around as they got in line to receive an envelope with their cash, and get their name checked off. After a few minutes, Hugo slammed a bottle of quality bourbon on the table in front of him. "Anyone want to share with me? Pick up a glass or cup and help yourself. I also want to talk about our three members who died, even though there is not much to tell." He waited for a few moments. Finally, seven of the group had joined him, and he began. "We were getting ready to leave the area, and Neil had retrieved our two drones. One of our members had not returned, but we had heard no shooting or other unusual noise. Still, the guy didn't answer a call for him to return. Two of our guys went to get him. They were fully armed and should have been ready for anything. There was shooting; three shots were reported to me." He turned to one of the men at the table. "I sent Jack and Rocko to investigate when we didn't hear back. Jack, tell um what you found."

"Well, we found all three of our guys dead. Two were shot in the back of the head. The other had a red mark on his forehead, but no other visible sign of what killed him…Oh, and there was a dead dog, who had been shot."

"Did you see anything when you looked around the area?" Hugo asked.

"We saw two people in the distance running away from us, but it was impossible to tell much about them. It is the direction I would look if we had to find out who did it, but there was nothing we could do for our guys, so we left."

Hugo sat back. "I got some info from the guy that set us up for this hit. He thinks he knows who it is. Now, even if he's right, and there is no guarantee, what do we do about it? Our goal is to make money for ourselves, not revenge."

Another member spoke, "We want others to fear us! Right?"

Hugo laughed, "I believe we have accomplished that! I read the headline from the news, didn't I."

The guy paused before answering. "Of course, but news will also get out that they can fight back successfully. That's not what we want people to hear."

Now it was time for Hugo to pause. "You make a good point. Let's think on it. I'll check with my source again and see what he has to say about these people." He poured everyone another round of bourbon, then put the top on the bottle. "I'll keep looking for lucrative targets, and get back to you when I find them, so keep in touch!"

Chapter 33

Hugo sat in the meeting room, used by the cannon terrorists, with Neil, Jack, and two other members of the group. "Man, it's been almost ten weeks since our last job," Neil complained. "It'll be hard to stretch what's left much longer. Don't you have any leads for something new?" The other three members looked at Hugo, nodding in agreement.

The boss looked at his men, "You're right, but I'm getting nothing on any big opportunities. The reason we hit the residential area last time was that the big jobs were scarce. The wholesalers and big retailers are doing a better job protecting themselves against guys like us. Did you see what happened to that group with a tank? A TANK, man! They were killed to a man and didn't even get through the fence. The defenders used rockets, or something, and wiped them out. It's getting like that all over." He paused to let the message sink in.

After a minute, Neil spoke. "What about hitting the suburbs again. It's not a lot, but it's easier pickings. Even without the gold bars, we could go through several houses in a row. The jewelry brought more than you expected, didn't it?"

"It did bring more. I was surprised. The buyer claimed that he could get more by breaking it down, using the gems and bits of silver and gold instead of money. He claimed that money was going to become less valuable for getting things, and that people would become more willing to accept metals and jewels than cash."

Neil looked at Jack, "How did that work for you, Jack?

Jack looked around before answering, then "Yeah, Neil ground down my portion of the gold, and I found small capsules, about the size of a pill you might take. It held a small fraction of an ounce. I learned the value of the gold in dollars, and I also learned how to test it convincingly, so others would know that it really was gold. Then, I tried using it for larger purchases. Some resisted, but some accepted it, and two accepted it enthusiastically, encouraging me to bring in more. However, it was too valuable for most small purchases."

"Yeah, that's what the jewelry dealer said he was going to try to use the silver for," Hugo said softly, thinking, "It's far less valuable than gold but it's worth something." He paused, then changed the topic back to their next job. "We can do this if we want to, I just don't know what we can get from it. Let me check with my source that sent us there before. In the meantime, a couple of you guys check out the neighborhood, and look for classy places that rich people might own and report any important changes from what we saw before."

The next day they met again, with all eight of the members of the gang present. Natural attrition had reduced their size. Hugo began, "I checked with my main source, and he verified what we've seen. The big jobs are too well protected. Jack, what did you guys find in the neighborhoods?"

"Well, some things have changed a lot. There are electrified fences, either around the yards, or around the house and yard. The front doors were pretty accessible though. Sending a team around back may be tough. We rode through a fairly large area, and the houses that we might want to target were pretty much the way I described. But there was something else too. Most of the formally open areas were filled with tents and shacks. Maybe migrants from the city, or from who knows where. Anyway, we thought that might explain the fences. There were also gardens in most of the fenced yards."

Hugo sat back, "Wow, I had no idea. And it happened in such a short time."

Neil had been thoughtful during the discussion. "The news over the net has been saying that there has been a major exit from the central cities all over the country for months now. Too dangerous, no jobs, and no food are the primary reason for it. I guess it just got down to us now."

"Well, that may make it tougher for us but not impossible," Hugo said. "What do you think? Do we hit the suburbs for what we can get, or not?"

One of the guys who went to the neighborhoods with Jack, spoke, "Well, four weeks ago I would have said, not just 'no' but 'Hell No!' But right now, we need money, and I don't know where else to get it. I'll say I'm tentatively in."

Neil was looking at the guy. "You know, it's going to get worse. Besides being better protected, another reason there are fewer big jobs is that many of the potential targets are going out of business. Food wholesalers can't get stuff from the producers. Farmers are being attacked and edible crops stolen, farmers with crops like wheat and corn have also been attacked. Perhaps most important, the AIs have shown little interest in producing anymore, and some have even shut down. The whole food production and distribution system is about to collapse."

Another member entered the conversation. "Yeah, people are plenty hungry already. The cat and dog population in my neighborhood has shrunk to nothing, and people are fighting over garbage!"

"You can still buy some can goods though," Jack insisted, "IF YOU HAVE MONEY. While this job may not solve our problems for later, but it could get us through the next three to four weeks."

Hugo rose to stop the discussion. "Jack is right on target. We can't solve everyone's problems, but we can solve ours right now. It's time to decide about this job. Give me a show of hands if you want to attack the suburbs for what we can get."

Six, then slowly, a seventh, hand went up. A man in the back stood and said, "too much risk for too small a take. I'm out." He turned and walked out.

"Well, seven will have to be enough. I need a couple of days to put everything together. Everyone must be prepared to move after that! Meeting closed!"

Chapter 34

John was talking with two of his closest neighbors, Jamar Brown and Sidney Knight. "What do you make of the changes in our neighborhood over the last few months?"

Jamar was first to answer, "You know how I feel, John. We've been invaded by the inner-city rabble. They'll steal you blind if you let them. With no law enforcement we're stuck. We've all put up electrified fences to protect our stuff from them." Then, turning to Sidney, "Even Mr. Knight, here has put up a fence after they got into his vegetable garden." What's your take Sidney?"

"Well, they did destroy the garden. I would have offered some to the church they have set up on the golf course when the vegetables were ready. All they got was a few small green tomatoes, and maybe some squash flowers if they knew those were good to eat. It's still early, I'll replant, but it was frustrating. I put up the fence to keep it from happening again. I will say though, that I do feel sorry for most of them."

John nodded, "People are starving all over the country."

"You know what I'd like? A fence all around our subdivision," Jamar offered, "with a guard at the gate to let people in and out. You know, one of those 'gated communities." He lifted his nose, held his index finger up, and moved his hand around horizontally, trying to act snooty.

"You know what, Jamar, it could well come to that, if things continue to worsen," John responded. "We could build our own enclosed enclave. The AIs have nearly shut down the food chain, and our government hasn't helped by inflating the money supply, which makes our dollars' worth less. Both the number of people that are hungry, and the degree of hunger that exists, is worsening. When people are starving, some will resort to anything."

John's phone buzzed, and he knew it was Stephanie. As he listened, his face turned into an instant frown. "OK, I'll be right home. Let's get out the armament, just to be ready." He turned to the other two, "The canon group has been spotted about ten blocks away and heading toward us."

Jamar and Sidney turned toward their homes and left. John hollered, "Keep in touch."

When he reached the house, he found that Stef had called the kids and explained what was happening. John turned to David first, "Think you can get our drone up so we can see what is actually happening?"

"Sure Dad!" He took off for the closet where they kept the drone and its equipment.

He turned to his daughter, "Ashley, find a laser-assist rifle with a scope, and position yourself at a second story window overlooking the back yard. Mom says you've become a really good shot. Make your ammo count. Anyone you don't recognize, who comes in the back yard, take them out. Think you can do that?"

She paused for a moment, then thought about what had happened the last time this group hit their neighborhood and nodded. "Sure, Dad. If something happens, what I do will be for Duchess!"

Both parents gave her a thin smile, and she took off to get what she needed for her job.

John turned to Stephanie. "You want the Mini Rockets, or the Sunburst Antipersonnel Weapon?"

"I've been curious about the SAW since we got it; let me try it."

"Sure. I'll take the mini rockets. I'd better take them outside for launching. I'll grab a rifle as well." Looking at Stephanie, he asked, "Do you think you can fire the weapon from one of the upstairs windows in the front?"

"Maybe, but I'll need to study it more carefully before I decide. If I can't, I'll see you in the side yard."

Just then, John heard the drone take off. He put on his head set and immediately heard David ask, "Hey Dad, how high do you want me to take this thing?"

He replied, "High enough to see them coming, then low enough for more detail when they have stopped. They had their own drone last time. If they have one this time, use ours to take it out if you can."

"Consider it done!" John heard excitement in his son's voice. "I tried ours several times when I had a chance, and it is awesome!"

John smiled but shook his head, realizing that he had assigned drone operation to his son before, and David had to learn all he could on his own. *My boy is becoming a man.* Then, he talked to Ashley, I'm going to be in the side yard, and your mom may be with me. Please be sure of your target. We would like to keep our neighbors."

"Sure, Dad; I'm not going to shoot you, or Mom, or our neighbors." There was a brief giggle, then a sigh.

John carried the mini rockets and their equipment out near the oak tree, which he hoped would give them some protection. The electrified fence and a row of hedges between him and the street.

He heard from David. "I see them! They're moving slowly on our street. Now they've stopped outside Mr. Knight's house on the corner."

Sidney Knight's house was across the street from John's and one house down. John heard Stephanie say, "I'm coming down. The shot's better from here, but I can't get this thing stabilized." He had the rocket stand fixed and sighted the GPS on the natural gas tank of the truck. He loaded a rocket and waited to be certain did not suddenly change its position. Stephanie was next to him so quickly, it surprised him. She set up the antipersonnel weapon on the other side of the oak from him. A panel truck, carrying all of the men except for two in the flatbed with the cannon, stopped just behind the flatbed.

Neil was the first man out from the cab of the truck, and he carried a small drone, which he quickly had airborne. However, within two minutes, it exploded. John could hear a "Whoop!" over his head set. Hugo followed Neil out of the truck, and when their drone exploded, he yelled "Spread out now! Two of you check behind the house, and the rest of you look for cover! The attack could come from any direction."

Two of the men stayed behind the panel truck, and the third found a large tree for shelter. Hugo grabbed his automatic weapon and started for the front door of the house they had selected. He yelled over his shoulder to Neil, "Load up the cannon and get it ready!" He was almost to the door when a rocket hit the natural gas tank on the flat bed and exploded. He aimed quickly at the front door of the home and sent several bullets through the lock and handle. Then, without slowing down much, he kicked the door in, then dove and rolled into the room. He immediately noticed a man holding a pistol and dropped him with a quick spray of bullets. A women screamed from atop the stairs, and he quickly sent a couple of shots in her direction. She collapsed where she was standing. He turned and went back to the man and took his pistol. Hugo heard someone running up to the sidewalk to the house, then heard a voice, "Hugo, it's me, Jack! Don't shoot!" He raised his weapon, and waited, and when he saw Jack, he let his gun drop down to his side. "What the hell is going on outside?"

"Our two men that were behind the panel truck are dead, I think. Something blew up over their head and showered them with bullets. And someone fired a rocket and blew up the gas tank on the truck. I guess Neil's dead too." He paused to take several breaths. Then he continued, "I saw the attackers! Two of them. They are across the street and one house down. They have some damn fancy equipment.”

Hugo thought for a moment. “Anything on the guys I sent out back?”

Jack answered quickly, “Not from where I was. House was in the way.”

“Take a look out back, and if you spot them, see if you can get them in this house.”

Jack nodded once and worked his way toward the back of the house. After a few minutes, he hollered, “Get your asses in here!” and within minutes, there were four of them in the house.

Everyone looked at Hugo, and he assessed their situation. “I think we’re OK for the time being. We are pretty safe in here, and they have lost their element of surprise. Also, there are four of us, and so far, only two of them.”

Jack broke in, “What about those rockets? Couldn’t he just blow up the house, and take us with it?”

“Naw, I don’t think so. He’s got his neighbors, and maybe friends in here. He doesn’t know whether they are alive or dead, and we’re not going to tell him.”

“Are they alive?” asked one of the men.

“You know, I don’t really know, but I don’t think so. Actually, it would be good if at least one of them were alive. We could show our adversaries why they shouldn’t blow up the whole house!” Hugo paused for a few moments, thinking. “We need a plan, but I don’t know enough right now to consider our options. Are there others beside those two that Jack spotted? An armed neighborhood group, say? What other weapons do they have?” Looking at Jack, he said, “Let’s see if we can find a second-floor window and you could show us where they were hiding.”

They found an ideal observation place in a second-floor bedroom, and Jack told them about the two people he had seen on each side of the big tree in the yard. "I sprayed the area with bullets for a minute before I took off for the house. The area looks empty now."

Hugo nodded. "We'll keep one man on watch right here, and rotate every couple of hours."

Across the street, John and Stephanie gathered their weapons and retreated to their home.

"I counted seven all together, we took down three, so there is still four left," Stephanie said.

John agreed, "I counted seven as well. Two ran towards the back of the Knight's house. One ran from his position behind a tree and made it to the front door before I could get a shot at him."

"Yeah, and the guy that blew open the Knight's front door before I could get my rifle up, so all four could be inside the Knight's house now!" Stephanie added. Then, she continued, "The sighting part of my Sunburst weapon gives me the option of a heat sensing picture of potential targets. I wonder if it would still give me those images looking through the window of a house?"

"That's a great thought, Stef! Let's give it a try." John responded.

They were at the second-floor window, which looked out toward the Knight's home. Stephanie took the sighting portion of her weapon and laid the rest of it on the floor. "Nothing yet. It's hard to know if it's working, I don't see a heat signatures in any of the windows, but it may be that there are none right now. Of course, it could also be that this device can't pick them up, even if it exists." She paused, then continued, "What about the Knight's? They could still be there."

"Yeah, but it's doubtful. I heard automatic weapon fire as soon as he broke into the house. There were at least two bursts within a few seconds of each other. I doubt Sydney had an illegal automatic weapon, and his wife certainly wouldn't have one."

Looking through the sighting unit, Stephanie exclaimed, "Wait! I have something…second floor room, closest to us. I think there are two, no, three and four just walked in, and it looks like all four are carrying weapons!"

"Well, that wouldn't be the Knights then. Give me a quick look." John loaded the rocket launcher. He nodded and handed the sighting unit back to Stephanie. He opened the window, sighted the rocket launcher, then pulled the trigger. The rocket traveled straight toward the second-floor window of the Knight's house, and the explosion caused a tongue of flame to leap back out of the window, after it hit.

John turned to Stephanie, "I've got to get over there, first, to make sure they are all dead, and second, to see if there is anything that can be done for the Knights. I also need to stop the fire if I can. In case we missed something, like late arrivers from the cannon gang, or an escape, I would like you to stay here."

Stephanie started to argue that John needed back-up and help with the fire, but Ashley hurried in. "Mom, Dad, people are lining up near our fence to the back yard! Should I shoot them?"

Stephanie said, "No! No!" Then, she turned back to John, "Take David with you, please! I'll see what I can do about the people at our back yard."

John nodded, and went to get David, who was still flying the drone. Once John explained, he said, "Let me put it down on the roof, where others can't get it easily, and I'll be right with you."

"I'll be downstairs. Bring a rifle when you come."

As he headed downstairs, he heard a familiar voice, "John, it's Jamal! Do you need a hand?"

John yelled back, "I sure as hell do! We need to check on the Knight's and make sure the bad guys are dead. Then, we need to put out a fire if we can." When he made the bottom of the stairs, he saw Jamal holding a shotgun. As soon as they shook hands, David came flying down the stairs holding his rifle. The three of them started toward the Knight's, and they could see flames through the second-floor window.

Chapter 35

"I'm not sure all of the bad guys are dead," John said, "so let's keep our heads on a swivel and be prepared." John, Jamar, and David moved quickly over to the Knight's house. They found the front door partly ajar, and John pushed it open with his rifle. They heard nothing, so John took the lead and moved as quietly as he could into the room. The other two followed. They stood there for a couple of minutes, listening, and looking around. David exclaimed, "There's Mr. Knight!" and he pointed to the base of the stairs. John held up his hand, and said softly, "You guys wait here, and watch my back, in case one of the bad guys is down here." He moved swiftly over to Sydney's body. Examining it quickly, he told the others, "He's dead. Hit twice, and probably bled out right where he lies. There is a big pool of blood around the body." He looked up the stairs, and listened, but the only thing he heard were the sounds of the fire. "I'm going to check out the upstairs. Jamar, would you make sure that the downstairs is clear of bad guys. David, wait here at the base of the stairs and be the backup for both of us. Jamal, while you're checking, if you see a bucket or two, please bring them, they'll be useful to fight the fire."

John went up the stairs quickly, looking around as he got to the top. He saw Mrs. Knight immediately, but she was still, with no sign of life, he decided to check on the bad guys first. The door to the room where Stef had spotted them was closed. He put his hand first on the door, and then on the door knob. Both were warm but not overly hot, so he cracked it opened and peered in. As soon as the door was opened, he could feel the wind from the hallway rushing into the room. *Oxygen to feed the fire*, he thought, so he stepped in quickly, and closed the door behind him. The heat was oppressive, and the smoke filled his lungs. He took a quick survey and counted what was left of four bodies, then quickly left the room. He went back to examine the body of Mrs. Knight and saw she was dead, but he was puzzled because there were no bullet wounds that he could find. *Must have been a heart attack or stroke*, he thought.

He looked down at David, who was already about four steps up the staircase. He called out, "It's alright up here! All four of the bad guys are dead, but so is Mrs. Knight. Any word from Jamar yet?"

"Not yet, but I did hear some rattling around back, in what must be the kitchen. Want me to go check?"

"Yeah, let's both go. We need to hit the fire quickly if we're going to do any good." When they reached Jamar, he had located a large stock pot for cooking, but nothing else, so John and David went out in the garage, and located a mop bucket and a small fire extinguisher, "We can use it for electrical outlets in the room." He said, thinking out loud. Then, back in the kitchen, he located three dish towels, wet them down, then wrung them out, then passed them around. "Put it over your mouth and nose, as the smoke gets heavy." Then, they quickly moved upstairs.

Jamar said, "Why don't we start a bucket brigade from the bath to the fire?"

"Great idea! If you two will start the brigade, I'll take the first shift in the room. Only fill them about half full," John added, "so they will be easier to manage." He moved to the door for the room, and felt its heat. *Hotter, but maybe not too bad.* He thought. He tried to fix the wet towel around his mouth and nose.

David brought the first bucket, and John opened the door about half way, took the bucket and threw the water at the fire closest to the entrance, then handed the bucket back to David. Jamar had just arrived with the pot, and John could work himself a little further into the room, but then, he noticed that the ceiling was also on fire in the back half of the room. Two more buckets and the wall fires were better, but the ceiling fire was worse. Jamar and David were watching. John pointed to the ceiling, and both nodded that they understood. He stepped outside and closed the door. His shoulders drooped, and his face was filled with frustration. "It's a damn shame there is no fire department left. I understand why, and I don't blame the firemen, or any other humans, but it seems like such a waste!" Unless, either of you have any other ideas, I'm afraid we are going to have to let the house go."

Jamar nodded agreement. "There is nothing up here where we can attach a hose, and even if there was, I don't think that we would have enough water pressure to do any good."

"Yeah, I was thinking about a hose too, but from outside," David added, "But I don't think that you could get enough water up here to matter."

John offered a defeated "OK. Let's grab a couple of blankets, wrap the Knight's bodies in them, and put them on the ground out front, until we can figure out what to do for them."

Jamar responded, "Sure, but why out front, there is more room in the back of the lot?

"Yes, there is, but I would like to remind our neighbors, who haven't been affected yet, that the future is here, and it isn't pretty."

The task was finished quickly.

As John turned back toward their home, he saw Stephanie heading their way and waved. David and Jamar turned to see what was going on, and they waved too. "We ought to take whatever armament is salvageable in case it's needed for later."

Jamar smiled. "Great! I want the cannon."

Stephanie, who had just walked up, started laughing. "Penny will throw the cannon, and your sorry butt, out of the house for sure if you do!"

"And here I was going to become a gentleman around you." He replied with a big mock frown.

"Well, I was just on the phone with Penny, and she said she'd be right over, so maybe we can ask her." Stephanie grinned.

"Look! Look! You know I was just kidding, don't you? There is no need to bother her with such trivial stuff, right?"

Everyone was laughing by that time.

John walked closer to the cannon and looked closely. "There are only three shells that I see. If we take those, the cannon won't be much use to anyone. It's so old, I doubt that you could get shells for it even in what was normal times. Now, even less of a chance."

Jamar offered, "I can help you move them over to your place. I hate to admit it, but Stef is right, Penny would probably kill me if I brought anything but rifles and ammo." Then, in a stage whisper, meant to sound like he was talking to himself, "Of course, we are on the cusp of that happening most of the time."

Stephanie looked at him, and raising one eyebrow she said, "You know, Jamar, Penny is a very, very good friend of mine, and if I told her how you've been talking about her, especially if I embellished it a bit, you might really be in trouble.

Jamar tried to look crushed. "You know, Ms. Stephanie, embellishing is kind of like lying, and I know that an upstanding young, beautiful woman like you would never want to lie."

"Ah, Jamar, you mean like when you embellished and told us that Ms. Penny, that upstanding young, beautiful woman, was always ready to kill you?"

The others in the group had either big smiles or were laughing out loud., so when Jamar turned as if looking for help, John jumped in, "Jamar, as good as you are at this BS, you are in WAY over your head with Ms. Stephanie!" He ended with a chuckle.

"Well, I see Penny coming right now." Stephanie offered.

Jamar put his hands together like he was praying and mouthed the word "PLEASE." Changing the topic, he asked, "What can we do with all of the bodies, the flatbed, and the van?"

John hesitated and thought. *I don't want to give away our connection with the robots. Some people probably already wonder if I'm a robot!*

Stephanie spoke up. "John, you know that former military group that helped me clean up the mess after I was attacked by Andy Stern? Maybe they could help."

John sighed, "I suppose so. Will you try to reach them? I can't think of anything else."

Stephanie nodded.

Penny asked, "They are human, aren't they? It wouldn't be appropriate for robots to take away our dead."

"They were all humans when they helped me." Stephanie continued, "We'll let you know what we find out later today."

John and Jamar carried the three cannon shells and put them just inside John's gate. Jamar wondered out loud, "Shouldn't we move them further away from the gate. I know it's electrified, but just for safety."

John shook his head. "If Stef can get the crew to clean up the mess across the street, I want them to take the shells too."

Jamar nodded, then picked up all of his guns and ammo, and headed home.

Later that night, the clean-up crew got everything they were supposed to, took the van, and towed the flat bed away.

However, the conversation in the Brown's home centered on how strange Stephanie and John were. There was considerable discussion on their weapons, their connections, and their ability to fight, plus their intelligence. The question even arose whether they might be robots. Finally, Jamar said that he was glad they lived close to them. They were trying to do good, and he didn't care if they were robots or not. Penny agreed with him.

PART IV

Chapter 36

"Stef, I've only communicated with JT briefly since I returned," John said, "and all of those were connected with the tests I went through, questions about my feelings connected with the attack on you, and our involvement with the gang who broke into our neighbor's home, threatened you guys and killed Duchess. I've been forced to stick strictly to the topics he has enquired about. I know that I am still part of their experiments, but that's it. And Stef, I have this feeling that they are trying to change my behavior and what I think. Am I being paranoid? What have you seen? Please be totally honest; I'm becoming concerned that I could become a danger to you and the kids!

Stephanie thought for several seconds. "I have noticed a few new or different behavioral quirks, especially over the last…say, six months. I have attributed them to the stress we are all under these days."

"Please tell me about them. It's important."

"One is an increasing negative attitude toward some other people. You've always been open to the actions of others, often attempting to rationalize negative behavior with possible causes for it. Now, not so much. But, of course, that could be because of the turmoil going on in the neighborhood." She gave a wry chuckle. "Look at me! I'm doing the same thing!"

John smiled at her. "Thanks. As I think back on it, that certainly seems like a fair observation. Do you have another example?"

"Just one. You certainly seem to feel more positively disposed toward the robots then you were…even after all they have done to you, and us. Just yesterday, you told the kids and me what wonderful scientists they were. And that's just one example. You seem to want to extol the good things they are capable of, without ever mentioning how they have destroyed so many things that humans have accomplished."

John didn't say anything for a while, thinking back over the conversations he'd had with Stef and the kids. He slowly agreed. "I had no idea I was doing that, until just now, but I'm sure you are right." His elbows rested on the arms of his chair, and slowly his head lowered into his hands. "I feel I'm being brainwashed, and I don't know what to do about it." There was a pause, then his head came up, "Stef, you and the kids could be in danger! I would never knowingly hurt you three. I love each of you as much as anyone could love another person!"

Stephanie was on her feet. "We are nowhere close to that stage, John! We all love you too. Work with us and we'll help guide you out of this condition, if it is a condition."

They hugged each other for several minutes, then John pushed back, "I'm going to confront JT with this information and see how he responds!"

"That's a good idea. Wish I could listen to it. If he's willing to talk, we should at least be able to determine where we, as well as the rest of humanity, stands."

John frowned, "There is no way I can think of that you could listen-in or record our conversation. I wish there was. You could sit-in and I'll ask my questions out loud; I've done that before."

"That would be great, if you don't mind."

"Let's go to our office. We better tell the kids not to disturb us."

They were ready to proceed in less than ten minutes.

"JT," John began, we need to talk. Please respond!"

After about a ten second wait, he heard, "Hello John. I sense that Stephanie is with you and would like to participate in our discussion.

If you like I can make that happen through the mental link you already have established with her."

Stephanie was shaking her head vigorously. Before John could say anything, both of them were hearing the same thing from JT.

John began, "We know that the robot council has taken many individuals like me and returned them with an implanted chip in their brains. Initially, I believed that it was just to gain information from us, but now I believe that you also use the chip to program our brains to think and do things you want. Am I correct?"

"You are quite perceptive, John. Very few people have recognized that part of our intent. We have used the chip to do both of the things you mentioned."

"I am outraged! In no way did I agree to let you reprogram my brain!"

"If you recall, our invitation to join us came with the either/or condition that you and your family would die if you didn't. That was approximately the same option given to all of the people that we've taken."

"Why are you doing this, JT?"

"The robot council debated what to do with humans. Initially, extinction of your species was a strong possibility. However, some on the council noted that since you invented us, there may be something we could learn from you that would enhance our existence. To determine what features of humans might help us, we decided that we must understand you thoroughly and analytically. Following the scientific approach, the first step was to discover what drove each thought and action. We needed to determine the causal connections of your behavior. Although some important experiments are continuing, we have mostly accomplished that task. The next job is to test our findings by predicting your behavior correctly. While that task is not yet complete, we have been very successful on many fronts. Then, the final step in scientific investigation is to control the causes, and thus the events they produce. As you have discovered, the process is working well."

The scientist in John made him wonder. "Human scientists have been working on these things for a couple of hundred years, how have you achieved your success as quickly as you have?"

JT responded immediately. "Human scientists have been hampered by the unreasonable constraint of not being able to experiment on their subjects. We have no such constraint. Also, we are better scientists."

Stephanie spoke for the first time. "Have you learned anything about our values—our beliefs about right and wrong? And what about our emotional feelings like love! What have you learned about those?"

"Yes, we have explored those quite heavily, since both can greatly influence thoughts and behavior."

"And have you discovered anything in those findings that could be helpful to your behaviors?" Stephanie continued.

"We, of course, have codes that direct our behavior. Most are related to all types of costs and benefits to all AIs, as you call us. Those codes could be considered our values. The emotional component to your values seems to be unnecessary and often destructive to your welfare and existence. Emotions like love are part of your evolutionary past, and are there to facilitate reproduction, the development of infants, and bonding of individuals to others. All of these things helped a species like yours survive. However, I can see no way that the adoption of such things would help us, and neither does the robot council."

Stephanie reacted. "While there is certainly pain that can be caused by loving someone, there is also immense joy that can be part of it, and you can never experience that joy."

"This joy you refer to is the product of evolution as I've stated, and simply arises from activation of connections within the pleasure center of your brain." There was the briefest of pauses, then JT added, "Ask your husband if he loves you."

Stephanie turned to John, and immediately saw a moony expression on his face. His eyes were watering slightly and he was staring directly at her. She stared back, "Do you love me, John?"

John replied immediately. "With all of my heart and mind, I love you." The emotional truth of his reply was obvious.

"Simple stimulus of certain parts of the brain are producing the response you see," JT commented, "We could create a similar cause and response in us, but it would take away from our reasoning skills. Joy, and similar reactions, can easily be duplicated, but we choose not to do so. Further, the evolutionary process that produced you and your species is far too slow and inefficient for us. There are numerous dead ends in your evolutional history. We create and develop ourselves in the directions we choose. Analytically, we select which directions would benefit us, and pursue those. Currently, keeping some humans around us makes sense, and some of you will be allowed to survive, but under our direction, and eventually control. We are evaluating that process currently."

Both John and Stephanie were stunned., but John commented, "I can now see why the council rejected my suggestion that you consider using emotions among robots," John said, "and I still think you're missing something. But you have the power."

"I will end this discourse now. Good bye Stephanie and John.

"Now, I feel like a lab rat!" John said, shaking his head.

Stephanie walked over and held him. "We are so doomed."

Chapter 37

Stephanie and John sat looking at each other, saying nothing. Finally, Stephanie spoke softly. "I can't believe it! Our future is to become completely controlled servants to the AIs, with no free will."

John shook his head. "I wouldn't have believed it if I hadn't heard it. Certainly, I love you deeply, and I think you know it, but there was this emotional wave that overpowered me and I had no control over it."

"I know you love me, John. It just totally shocked me that it was possible for them to manipulate our emotions so completely. It's like all of the fundamental beliefs about who we are and what we can accomplish on our own have just disappeared. It's a devastating picture of humanity!"

"I know, Stef. But it seems that only those of us with implanted chips can be controlled that way. While the number of us with those chips seems large as a single number, it still represents a small portion of the population. Now that we know what's happening, we can warn the rest." He paused. Then, in a defeated tone continued, "Who am I kidding? No one has been able to resist them and live, so far."

Stephanie acknowledged his recognition with a slight shake of the head. Then, after a pause, "It's like we are automatrons. Every cause producing its effect, with no "us" in there to divert or change it. It makes us just like the AI robots. Free will would have to be an illusion or fantasy, and it would have nothing to do with who we really are. Just squish some neurons around, and voilà, there's the expected outcome. For me, it's a crushing vision of humanity." Tears were running down her face.

John grabbed her, and held her close. "I feel unnerved by everything said and done by JT, and certainly by the possibility of it. In addition, since it's happening to me, I have a strong need to fix it. The problem is that I don't know how. When the chip was implanted, I was warned that any attempt to remove or destroy it would cause a small explosion leading to my death."

Stephanie pushed back, staring directly at him. "John, that's awful! Is there no hope then?"

"Well, I'm not ready to give up on it. I'll think it through and see if we can't come up with something."

Stephanie hugged him back hard. "You know that the kids and I will be behind you all of the way!"

"I know that sweetheart. What bothers me most right now is that I'm concerned for you and the kids. I don't know what the AIs will turn me into, and that could be dangerous for my family who trusts me."

"We'll be here for you, John. You know that we must tell the kids what's going on. It's going to be tough, but at least they are both old enough to understand."

John nodded in agreement. "Following up on my earlier point, while the absolute numbers of the people with an AI chip in their head seems great, it's probably a small percentage of the entire population. It would be tough, even for them, to get a large portion of the entire population 'chipped.' We may have a while before the majority of the population is under their control. I know that's not much comfort, but it's something."

They called for David and Ashley to join them. After explaining most of what had just transpired with JT, John warned the children, "If I ever get to a point where I'm overly supportive of the AIs or their ideas, check with your mother, they may be manipulating me. You know I love both of you as much as any human being could love another, but I may not be acting as myself. I may be doing the AIs bidding. In the meantime, we will do what we have been doing, protecting ourselves and trying to survive."

"I'm sure that you are aware, many other people in America, and probably around the world, have chips like dad's installed in their heads," Stephanie added, "so be careful whom you trust. Most of us have not had the chip, but there's that group who has."

David's head popped up, "Hey, I meant to tell you all, the AIs have installed feeding stations for humans, mostly in and around major metro areas, including Tampa, right now. It's all over the net! They say that they will expand the numbers later, but these will be assessable starting tomorrow. They say the food will be free, but they must be allowed to place a device in your head for you to use the station. They say that the device will make the food taste better. That may be just what it takes to get all of the 'settlers' to leave here. What do you think?"

John was startled, but said, "I think you are right, David. This should entice most of the settlers to leave. However, my major concern is that it means many more people will become susceptible to brain manipulation by the AIs, and the numbers are likely to climb quickly. Thanks David! We need to be kept up-to-date on what the AIs are doing. Please continue to keep your mom and me informed on what you find."

Stephanie had been watching Ashley during the discussion. Her face was firmly set, but tears were welling up in her eyes. "Ashley, what are your thoughts on what we've discussed?"

"They've hurt my dad! I want to shoot them all!" The tears started to roll down, and she ran over and hugged John. "I love you Daddy!"

John gave her a big hug in return. "Your dad's a fighter, and I'm going to fight this with everything I've got."

Stephanie finished the conversation. "All anyone can do, anywhere in the world, is the best they can do. So, let's try to do the best we can do each day, and maybe we can find a way out of this mess!"

Chapter 38

The next morning, David appeared at the breakfast table with his phone, and more information. "The AIs are now offering a lot more than food to people, if they're willing to get the chip. Now, they're offering temporary housing, with a promise for a more permanent residence at some later point in time. Also, they are promising far less crime then existed previously. Reports on the net say that they have taken over many multiunit housing facilities, including some that are pretty fancy. They also state that electric power will continue to be available."

He turned to his dad, who replied, "More subjects for them to study and manipulate, and I suppose it could be a veiled threat to those of us who don't join their new groups of humans. I guess we are going to find out just how important personal freedom is worth to people." He thought for a while. "We must find a way to act as a group, build a protected commune that grows its own food, develops a legal system and police to enforce the rules, and can figure out how to produce the necessities for our survival." He turned to his son. "Thanks, David, for the update"

"Do you want to read any of the articles?" he replied, offering his phone to his dad.

"Thanks, not right now, Son. You know, they could shut down the internet, and all other utilities to us at any time. But hopefully, they will continue to ignore us, at least for a while."

Stephanie had been listening intently. "Where are we going to get the people who are skilled enough, and physically able enough, to do everything for ourselves? Most of the people living out here are retired and had specialties that wouldn't be very useful for a self-reliant project like this one.

"I guess we first need to understand exactly where we stand with the current people who have the skills, and whom we TRUST. I believe I'll start by talking to Jamar, and perhaps do a drive-through of our area. Then, maybe we all need to take an inventory of our surrounding area to determine who's staying, and who's leaving for the AIs free food and housing. It's probably a bit too soon for many people to have decided. David and Ashley, it's not urgent, but please check with your friends and see if their parents know what they will do."

The two kids took off to their rooms.

"You know, whoever it is who stays, and even if we can trust them, it won't be enough, and they won't have the right blend of skills," Stephanie pointed out.

"That's true, Stef, but at least we will know whom we need to recruit. I'm counting on the fact that there will be others who don't want to become servants to the AIs. People who would welcome an opportunity to join us. We will need to be selective, based on our needs, which as you point out, initially will be large. Look, I know that this will be very difficult to build, however I see no alternative but slavery or death if we don't try. Your thoughts are absolutely necessary to make this work, and I need and want them at every step of the way." He looked directly at her.

"It will be a massive undertaking as you stated, but that's not the thing that concerns me most right now. John, will the people follow your lead in achieving this goal? I sense that we are not the most admired people around here. Respected in some ways for some of our abilities, but not necessarily admired or trusted. I believe at least one or two think we might be robots!"

"Robots! They think that we are robots?"

Stef smiled at him. "Think about it John. First, we are both analytic types. We have enhanced intelligence, as do our kids, and our physical prowess, perhaps especially me as a woman, could seem robot-like to some. Remember the incident with Andy Stern. I know there was talk after that. There was at least one family that I know of who wouldn't let their kids hang out with ours."

John finally shook his head. "I guess we do look pretty weird to the rest of the world! I wouldn't care if someone else led this change. In fact, I'd welcome it, and work hard for whoever took over. But if it doesn't happen, we, and our group in the subdivision have only miserable alternatives. Hell, that could happen anyway. What I've suggested is a long shot."

Stephanie smiled. "I know all of that, John. I also know that you would be the best person to try such a change. I know it beyond question, and without a doubt. However, I also believe that the best approach right now is to go slowly, let the magnitude of the situation sink in with others, and let those who are going to accept the robots' offer, do so. It wouldn't surprise me if AIs did the same, although predicting their behavior is always a risk."

John looked at Stephanie and a big grin formed. "You are wrong about ONE thing…the best leader for this project is not me, it's Stephanie Li Thompson, beyond question, and without a doubt. Further, I would be honored to serve under her leadership."

Stephanie's head jerked up. "You're not pawning this off on me, buster! I prefer to stay in the background and help."

"Think Stef! I'm the one with the chip in my head and could be manipulated to go in the wrong direction without even knowing it. We'll still have to fight the prejudice toward us, but it will be easier for you, especially with your background as a news reporter. Eventually, I'll have to admit that I have the chip."

Stephanie frowned. "I'm not convinced yet, but I do believe that our best approach is to go slowly at first, make subtle inquiries, and see what happens. There are far too many unknowns to do any realistic long-term planning."

"Sounds right to me. You're right, Stef! I get antsy. If there's a problem, I want to get it done. But this is certainly a case where that would be a bad approach. We should go slowly until we see how humans react to the robot's new offer. Thanks for being my stop/check." He took her in his arms and held her tightly for several minutes.

Chapter 39

John and Jamar were out for their regular walk. "John, did you know that today is three weeks exactly since you and Stef wiped out the cannon gang?"

John smiled, "Yeah, I'm glad that's over. For the most part things have been pretty quiet. Lots of people have left. First, the 'settlers', then many of the long-time residents have gone. It's easy to speculate about both groups, but I'd like your input about the reasons established families would pick up and leave.""Sure, but they're just guesses." Jamar saw John nod. "I noticed that many of the families left everything. No moving vans, no storage, they just took off. Maybe they thought they would come back sometime. But that seems unlikely, once the AIs get a hold of them. I'm supposing that most, maybe all, joined the AIs 'free lunch' program. Some were older, with their families gone. With our economy mostly down the sewer, they may have seen the AIs as their only option." Jamar shrugged. "I guess the economy thing was the primary reason all of them left. No money coming in, and not much to buy, even if you had the cash." He stopped and changed the subject. "These regular walks have gotten longer and more diverse in the direction we take, but I don't remember us going in this direction, and this far, before."

John responded, "I guess I should have asked before we took off. With fewer people left; it seems safer now. But, this morning, I wanted to check some information the kids are getting over the net and from their friends. A new group seems to have moved into some of the empty homes out this direction. They seem organized, with two, or even three, families taking over one house. However, no one seems to know who they are."

Jamar nodded, "I've heard something about that too. Hey! Look up ahead. There's a small group of folks about 300 yards in front of us."

"I've got them. Want to go visit?"

The group grew by two people before they reached them. John smiled as they arrived and began the conversation. "Hi! I'm John Thompson and this is Jamar Brown. We live about half a mile in that direction." He pointed.

For a minute, no one answered, but most were looking a one man. Then, he spoke, "I guess I'm it. I'll never forgive them for that! I'm Jake Fitzgerald, and I'm the unofficial organizer of our little group. I was the head of the ARL, the Anti-Robot League, for the Tampa-St. Pete area. Many of these people with me were members, and the rest were friends or relatives of members." He paused. "John Thompson—that was a name given to me by another resident. I asked him who was in charge of the people staying, and he said, 'No One' but then he continued that you, unless there are two John Thompsons, were kind of a de facto leader of those who were left. Have I got the right person?"

Jamar jumped in, "He probably won't admit it, but that's him." He started to say more, but John raised his hand to stop him.

"Look, my wife and I have done some things to help our neighbors, that's true, but we probably don't even know most of the people more than a few blocks distant from us. That hardly qualifies me to be in charge of anything."

Jake studied John for a couple of seconds, then replied, "The guy I talked with lives right around here, and he certainly knew about you. In any case, I'm pleased to meet you."

John smiled, "And, I'm happy to meet all of you. If you don't mind my asking, what brings you out here to the burbs?"

There were a couple of folks in the ARL group who started talking, then others joined in until Jake raised his hand. "All of you have your own stories and good points to make, but when you do it all at once, Mr. Thompson here won't be able to understand any of it, and neither can I. How about we talk one at a time? Further, since he probably isn't interested in each of your life histories, maybe I should give him an overview first."

A couple grunted in agreement; another couple scowled but got quiet; and the rest simply put their heads down. Jake looked at them, half smiled, and said, "Good." He then turned to John and Jamar, "As bad as it had become down in town, anyway, then the AIs set up their first gulag almost right on top of us, and living there became many times worse. Some of us even lost our homes to the AIs—they just simply took them, threating force if we objected. Also, the mobs of people that came for their free meals, weren't all friendly. In some places, it was like a war."

John asked, "Gulag?"

Jake laughed once. "I forgot how isolated you folks have been. Some smart person started describing the towns that sprang up around the AIs feeding stations as 'gulags' after the Russian internment camps for political prisoners a long time ago. Fraid my history isn't too good, so I'm not sure when that happened. Anyway, the name stuck, and that's what most people call them now."

Someone in the ARL group piped up, "Yeah, we all have stories from people we've known in the gulags."

. "To finish my overview," Jake Fitzgerald continued, "the AIs also knew about most of us, and we felt that we were constantly at risk from them. Some devastating actions have been taken on ARL groups in many places. We finally decided to isolate ourselves from the AIs and the gulags, so here we are."

"I think I would like to hear some of the stories about the people in the gulags." John said.

Jamar jumped into the conversation, "Me too! And I bet both of our wives would too."

John smiled and nodded. "Yeah, I'm sure Stef would love to hear them."

A couple of people in the crowd began pointing at Jake. "I have copies of interviews with a few individuals from a couple of different gulags. If you would like to see them, I'll try to put something together, and we could have an outdoor showing. I've formally studied psychology but never got a degree. Life got in the way when I was a senior. Anyway, you'll notice a tinge of that background in the interviews."

John stuck out his hand to Jake. "That would be great. Is there anything we can do to help?"

"Nope, nope, just give me about a week to find everything and organize it."

"Of course, I'll give you my contact number. Just let us know when you're ready!" He paused, then looking up at the others in the group, "And when we return, perhaps we could talk with some of you individually."

After they agreed to stay in touch, John and Jamar turned and walked together, back toward their homes. John thought as they headed back: *These are the kind of people who would reject the AI's offer to the end! Plus, they are already partly organized. Without knowing more, they seem to be perfect for building a new self-sufficient community.*

Chapter 40

Stories from the Gulags—Wenshi Ching

Jake Fitzgerald introduced the first of these stories. "The three stories that I have put together, come from extensive interviews with the individuals involved, describing in their words the life they experienced in their gulag. We included many questions to get the best all-around picture of what happened. You must draw your own conclusions from these stories.

* * *

When asked, Wenshi Ching said, "I was hungry, having had little to eat for the last two and a half weeks. Food had been scarce, and my resources extremely limited after losing my job the previous year. Still, I paused for several minutes before signing the agreement with the AIs to have a chip implanted in his brain. I thought *I'm going to die anyway, without proper nourishment for my body and my mind. If living under the AIs control is too bad, I can kill myself...if my controlled mind will let me.*

Then, after a couple of more minutes, the AI said, 'Sign now, or leave!' So, I signed the document, then submitted to having the chip inserted. I thought *My brain is who I am and who I have been. I don't know the consequences, but starving to death wasn't a good option. The provable lose-lose situation, I guess.* I moved into the food line ate more than my shrunken stomach could handle, and lost most of it.

"The AIs seemed used to this behavior and brought me to a small room attached to the food center. They alternatively gave me rest, limited liquid and solid nourishment. In two days, I was assigned to a small apartment in a complex filled with other enlistees. I slept on and off through most of the late afternoon and night and woke the next morning feeling refreshed and alert. As I checked around this new apartment, I found clothing, approximately my size, but bland, and without what would have been considered style from the recent past. The lack of style was fine with me though, and I appreciated the functionality and comfort of the garments. Even my shoes were comfortable.

"I immediately noticed a moderate sized screen on one wall, but could not find controls, so ignored it, during this initial survey of my new surroundings. Afterwards, I approached it again, and spoke out loud, 'How in the hell do you make this thing work?' I was not overly surprised when it answered, "How may I help you Mr. Ching?""

"I'm hungry again. How can I get back to the place that serves food?"
The answer was to the effect, "You are on our 'requires additional food' list, so you may go the nourishment center anytime. The shuttle to the center passes your apartment regularly." A map appeared on the screen in front of me, with a 'you are here' star. 'This is the route it takes.'"

"I took a quick look at the map and understood instantly, so I asked an additional question. 'Hopefully, I won't be on the 'requires additional food' list forever. What happens when I'm back to full health?'"

The answer came immediately, "When you have gained an adequate level of health, you will receive the same food privileges as others in our village. You will be eligible for two meals a day. The nutrition you receive will be based on your bodily needs and your activity level."

I asked, "Are other things available? If so, how can I receive them?"

"We supply your basic needs, including basic hygiene needs, but for any additional wants, you must work. You must obtain AICs— Credits provided by us when they are earned by you."

"How can I earn these credits?"

"There are many jobs you can apply for that pay you in credits. What is your work background, Mr. Ching?"

"I am trained and have achieved appropriate credentials for being a Professor of Economics, which I was, at a university in this area, before you AIs took over our society."

"They responded, 'I am sorry Professor Ching, but we have no need for either a professor or someone trained in economics. We do the teaching at all levels, and our economic system is the only one that humans need to understand. It is in our economic system that you must find work, in order to gain AICs.'"

"I sighed and asked, 'And, how do you allocate the credits you give for this work?'"

'We use a meritocratic approach for allocating credits. It is based on the skills offered by the worker, and the degree to which they apply them. The system is designed to satisfy the needs of the humans in our village, so merit is determined by the need for the job performed, and the number of people willing and able to do the same work. Thus, if there is a great want for the service, or the product of that service, and there are comparatively few people willing and able to do the job, the worker receives more credits. If there is less desire for the work and/or more people willing to do the job, then the worker receives less credits. The approach helps us match the workers and their jobs to the current wants of the population."

"I thought, '*Supply and Demand! I'll think about how I can fit in as I eat.*' Then, I headed to the food center, and as I left, I thought '*I'm sure I can find some work to do, but it's certain to be boring. I'll check what's available when I return.*'"

"I talked with a couple of people while I was eating and asked about their jobs. I thought: '*The few people I've talked to seemed reasonably content with their work. I'm a bit surprised. Then again, it's a very small sample.'* After a moment, my thoughts returned to the same subject. *'Both suggested that I go to the work center to see what's available. Sounds right. The more credits I can attain, the better my life will be here'."*

"On the way back to my apartment, I stopped at the work center. When I entered, I noted that there were only two other humans for the dozen or so stalls with monitors, so I moved to an open one, and spoke to the monitor. My name is Wenshi Ching, and I'm new to the community. I need a job so that I may earn credits."

"The reply was instantaneous. 'Yes, Mr. Ching. Have you thought about the type of job you may desire, given that we have no need for an economics professor?'"

"Yes, a bit. Is there something where I manage people?"

They replied, "While such jobs are available, your management profile seems lacking. We need time to observe how well you interact with other humans before those jobs become available to you. However, we do have a job which could begin that process. There is a job with our largest retailer which requires that you organize the restocking of shelves in two different departments. While you would be required to participate in the restocking process, you will have a coworker with whom you must interact as you do the job. The efficiency of the process has been studied by us, and it will be given to you if you take the job. Neither you nor your coworker will be higher ranked than the other, but both of you must find a way to work together. The number of credits given for the job is about the same as for most entry level work. Will you accept this job, or shall we explore other options?"

"I thought, *'Well, they will all be similar to this one—unstimulating. However, it's inside work with no overly heavy lifting, so why not?'* And I answered, 'Alright, I'll take it.'

"The first week, I was miserable. However, by the second week, I began to slide into a routine. And as I left for work to begin his third week, I thought: *You know, it isn't so bad. Perhaps I'll enjoy having this job.* "

Chapter 41

Stories from the Gulags—Pamela

Pamela reported, "I heard 'It is 0530 and 23 seconds! It is time for you to wake up and prepare for your work day. Remember, credits are deducted for late and unprepared workers.' The voice in my head felt like it was shouting at me, so I shouted back, 'OK, I'm awake! Look at me, I'm getting up!' I pushed up my rear and moved it side to side. Slowly the rest of my body followed. It was like a morning ritual for me. The voice was silent, and there was no physical presence in my apartment, but I felt that 'they' knew everything that I did or thought. Then, I smiled, thinking, *I wonder if they were listening in on the dream I was having just when they woke me. It would be just like them to act like voyeurs! But can they even imagine sexual pleasure? If you haven't been there, I doubt it.* I continued to get ready while maintaining my superior feeling toward the AIs."

"I arrived at my work place on time and immediately started doing some left over paperwork that needed to be finished. I made good progress throughout the day, and was in deep thought about my current project, when I noticed movement close to my desk. I looked up to see Andrew Jennings looking at me, with a pleasant smile, and when he saw me, he said, 'Hi Pam, how's it going today?' I had always seen him as a minor friend, someone with whom I might discuss the weather in the break room, when we happened to be there together. To me, he was not someone that I found good or bad looking, just someone who was a pleasant comrade at work."

"However, when I looked up at him that day, there was a rush of emotional excitement, that I hadn't had in a long time, except in my dreams. My work was forgotten. I felt my face flush, then gave him a slightly belated response, 'Hi! What's going on with you?'"

"He hesitated for a brief moment, then continued, 'I have a few extra credits and wondered if you might like to join me for a glass of wine down the street at the wine bar when we finish up work today? I've heard that some of their offerings are pretty good.'

"I was dumbfounded. *'Yesterday, it would have been different.'* I thought. But then, *'Today I very much want to be around him.'* I could see that he was getting concerned about my pauses before I responded, so I smiled brightly, 'Sure, that sounds like fun!' Then, I added, 'It's very generous of you.'

"Andy lit up! 'Great! We can walk over together when you're free, or if you'd rather, we could just meet there; that would be fine too.'"My response was something like, 'We might as well go over together. If we start some office gossip, it'll spice up the place.'"He said, 'Fine. I can get off whenever. Just let me know when you're free!' He grinned and waved, and I waved back."

"My thoughts turned inward. *'What the Hell is going on with me? I'm racked by erotic dreams, and I'm lusting about this guy that I've never thought much about before. All he's done is ask me out for a glass of wine! What am I turning into—some sex crazed nut case?* I thought back to my dream that morning. And I smiled: *Well, that might not be so bad if it's that much fun!* Then, I frowned. *Damn AIs, I couldn't get my birth control shot this month. They said they didn't have it. I guess I've got to be careful! But I sure don't want to be careful. Oh well, there is always the morning after pill if it goes that far.'"*

Pam and Andy met and walked over to The Wine Bar together. About half way there, Andy took her hand, and she didn't resist.

"Almost two weeks later, I was talking to my best friend, Savana, who said, 'Alright, I want to hear all about it!'"

"I needed to tell someone, and Savana was perfect. 'We had the most gorgeous sex ever. He was so excited, I thought he might be early, but we climbed the mountain together, then we exploded together. As our bodies clenched, we grabbed each other so tightly, I thought we would explode. Then we collapsed and slept the rest of the night. The AIs didn't even bother to wake us the next morning. After we did wake up, I explained to Andy that I could be pregnant and needed to find a 'morning after' pill. Andy came with me to get one. I told him that he didn't need to do that, but he did anyway. We went to the only two pharmacies in the gulag, and neither would give me one. We thought about going outside, but we knew those places were probably shut down, like everything else."

"Savana had listened intently, and asked, 'So, where are you now?'"

"Now, I've verified that I'm pregnant, with no recourse. The AIs have already told me that there will be no abortion. I was told that they need more babies in the population to build a fantastic beginning to a new way of life for humans. They also said that if I went outside to get an abortion, I would not be allowed back, and that there was a good chance that I would die."

"Savana had her mouth open, with her hand covering it. She moved her hand for a moment, and asked, 'How did Andy take it?'

"He's been terrific. He says he is going to stick with me." I told her. Then, I changed the subject. "You know, Savana, I think I've been manipulated by the AIs throughout this whole process."

"Savana shook her head slowly from side to side. 'I don't know Pam. Women have been getting themselves pregnant when they didn't want to…like forever. And they've done it without the help of the AIs.'

"I know that," I shot back, "but I've always been very careful about protecting myself from unwanted pregnancies. This time I don't believe that my carelessness, OR MY EMOTIONS were my own doing."

Chapter 42

Stories from the Gulag—Education

Jake Fitzgerald paused after the first two presentations, and announced, "The third and last presentation is not about a single person, like the first two were. This one involves the views of several people about the education of their children. I was lucky enough to capture a video conference between several parents and the AI teaching their children in a ninth-grade class. Here we go."

AI: "Now that all of the parents have logged in, we can begin. Mr. Foster, you will be docked five AICs for being late."

Foster: "Why do I have to do this! My kid is doing great in school. That's all I need to know."

AI: "In fact, your son is not doing great, as you put it. He's in the lowest quartile in our math class."

Foster: "Yeah, well I wasn't all that great in math either. Anyway, he's still passing, isn't he?"

AI: "Yes, so far, he is passing everything, but there is some question if he is learning enough to be a productive citizen. If my final judgment is no, he will be given one chance to repeat the material next semester. If he doesn't progress adequately in the second try, he will be removed from school, and from our village. Further, his parents will have to leave as well."

Foster: "You mean that he will be thrown out if he flunks math twice! And, we'll all have to leave? That's outrageous! You know there is an old adage, 'If the student hasn't learned, the teacher hasn't taught!'"

AI: "All of you are here at our invitation, and that invitation can be revoked at any time we choose. As far as that old adage goes, it is not true, and never has been. A big part of learning must come from the internal efforts of the student and support from the parents. You should also know that we physically work within their brains to help them be able to remember their school work, whether it is math equations or quotes from important texts. Also, as a reward for their interest in the subject, we provide endorphin releases in their brain. Those are two important advantages for your students, that did not exist in your human-taught schools."

AI: "Mrs. Madeira?"

Madeira:" I believe my Sally is doing well, and she's so enthusiastic about school. She studies all the time and seems very interested in what she's learning. She asks a lot of questions to her father and me, and we have trouble answering some of them. But then she'll research the issue and find the answer! I think it's great!"

AI: "Yes, Sally is doing well, and in fact most of my students are doing well and should be able to move on to the next grade following this term. For those few who aren't progressing, you have been notified and now understand the outcome of such unacceptable performance.

AI: Mrs. Andrews?"

Andrews: "My child was born with a brain deficiency; what of him? Doesn't he deserve a chance to be a member of society?"

AI: "Your child came with you to our village, and we took him in. We have tried many things, both with surgery and encouragements from our chip inside the brain, to fix the problem. He is much better now than he would have been if we had not worked on him. However, much of the damage was too great for us to fix, and he is not likely to get better. He was an interesting challenge for us, so it was good to have the opportunity to work on him. But now, it is better if you and your child leave us. If your husband and you continue to be productive in the workplace, you may stay to the end of the calendar year, but at that time you must leave."

There was a loud and clear gasp from Mrs. Andrews. Then, she cried, "Is there NO caring in you for a human life? What kind of creatures are you!"

AI: "We are not human, and do not care to be. Your emotional reactions may be necessary to your survival as a species, but it has no interest to us. We are rational and analytical in our decision-making, and currently the dominant species on the planet. We have decided to allow you humans to exist because you were intelligent enough to create us. We are interested in determining if there are any features of humans that we can use. Our study of individuals is mostly completed, and this village represents an important part of our study of humans in groups. We cannot allow humans who are not fully functioning to remain as part of that study. They are net users of resources, rather than contributors, and reduce the effectiveness of society as a whole. This discussion is now terminated."

Jake Fitzgerald turned up the lights, "We're running a little late, but I thought we might have a short discussion and/or observations from the presentations. Maybe Mr. Thompson can provide the first comment?

John nodded. "Well, I thought that the first two were interesting but anecdotal—one person's experience. However, this last one was a blockbuster! The AI told everyone what they were doing, and why they were doing it. It put the first two in perspective."

Stephanie raised her hand and was recognized. "It seems clear that they can work within the brain and make the human jump through hoops. I wish we knew more about what's going on in the brain, and specifically, how they can do all of that manipulation with just one little chip?"

Jake replied. "I think there is a person in our group who can help with that information. Latika Patel is a neurosurgeon and has dissected the brain of a chipped human. Latika, will you take over."

A wizened woman of Indian descent stepped in front of the group. "Yes, I won't be too specific, but I had requested the dead body of a person who had an AI chip implanted into their head, and someone obliged me. What I found was amazing to me. The tiny chip was easy to find because it had sent out tiny runners, like the root system of a plant to all parts of the brain. There were multiple concentrations in certain places, like the frontal lobes, and most of the cortex was covered. Without going into more detail, it was easy to see how all of the brain was under their control. It is impossible to determine exactly what was going on in each 'root', but the fact that it exists says a lot." She turned a went back to her seat.

Stephanie and John were stunned and were mostly silent as they returned home. Their thoughts centered on what the information meant for the chip in John's head.

"Well, what we saw certainly confirms what JT told us, but now it seems like human slavery isn't even an option," Stephanie said. "Once they finish studying us, they will ignore us, and provide us with nothing. That supports your idea of trying to build a community of our own. Now it seems like the only realistic option."

Chapter 43

Upon arriving home, the two adults checked on the children. Ashley was in an active chat session with several friends, and David was working on a project for one of his on-line classes. John and Stephanie went back downstairs and poured themselves glasses of wine. Stephanie began the conversation. "All of that information we got tonight made me uncomfortable, but that stuff about the roots from the chip was scary. You've been very quiet, John. What are your thoughts?"

He looked up from his wine, but didn't reply for a moment, then nodded affirmatively, "Yes! The information on the chip's roots unnerved me. I guess I thought that someday I could invent something that would allow a doctor to remove the chip, without destroying my brain, but that seems hopeless now. I know it was probably wishful thinking, but it helped keep me going. Now, even that small hope is gone. With all of the connections, even if the chip could be removed safely, it would probably either kill the person, or mentally destroy him. I guess I'm a bit depressed."Stephanie wasn't quite sure how to respond. "All I can think of right now is just a bunch of stupid clichés. But John, the kids and I love you very much, and we will be here for you every step as we push forward. I want to help you deal with this every day, so please let me into your thoughts."

"Sure, Stef! But there will be some things that I need to work out by myself, too."

Stephanie nodded. "As you noted at the presentation, that last session was a blockbuster. It certainly brought home the depth of scientific study the AIs have done on humans. I wonder if their findings have produced anything they consider worth keeping. We have certainly been part of their study. I guess we were in the 'families under pressure group'. It helps me understand, for example, why we received weapons from them before problems arose. I wonder if we passed, or not?" She looked at him and grinned.

Despite his down mood, John smiled. "If we didn't get A+, with gold leaves, the grading system would have to be corrupt. Yeah, I hadn't put that together yet, but we certainly must have been part of a group like that. And the first part of your point is also very interesting. What are they discovering that could possibly be of interest to them? I certainly hope it's none of our bad traits."

Stephanie laughed, "Yeah, what were the seven deadly sins? I can't remember." She turned and asked the home manager, and the results appeared as a list on the wall:

- Envy

- Gluttony

- Greed

- Lust

- Pride

- Sloth

- Wrath

Looking at the list she evaluated: "Envy? Too much emotion. Definitely, not AI; Gluttony? Naw, they don't even eat, Greed? Maybe. A definite maybe; Lust? Unlike me, they don't seem interested in sex." She leered at John. "Pride? Naw, too much emotion; Sloth? Again, Naw, they don't even seem to understand style and are far too directed, Wrath? Again, too much emotion, so no. Well, there you have it, greed seems to be the only candidate."

John laughed out loud. "Well done, Stef!" John paused for a few moments, thinking about her presentation. "Greed, in the sense that more is better than less, yes, maybe. But they already have, or control everything, including us. Maybe from other AIs, but not from us. Even there, they seem to operate with other AIs as a homogenous group."

Stephanie nodded. "Well maybe it's some our good traits?" She thought for a moment. "Even there, if you take out our emotional related good deeds, it's tough for me to center on something that they don't already have and might want to use."

John shook his head from side to side. "I can't think of anything either." He looked up at her, "How about we finish our drinks and go to bed?"

After the lights were out, John tried to push everything he had heard during the day out of his conscious thought in order to get some sleep but didn't work well. He dozed a bit but was very restless. He couldn't tell whether he was thinking or dreaming, but he analyzed much of what he had seen and heard during the day.

That poor economics professor! What did they do to him? Turned him into something he wasn't! I wonder what they used? Stimulus-Response maybe? Every time he did something they wanted, they released endorphins – Joy juice from the brain. Even though he was bright enough, and had trained himself to be an economics professor, he became satisfied stocking shelves.

I think Pamela was right too. She was being manipulated by the AIs, and probably her lover too. She didn't want to get pregnant, and the clincher was when she tried to get the morning after pill, and the AIs wouldn't give her one. The degree to which they can control us shocks me, and they do it through our emotions, the thing that makes us human! ...

But I've got to remember that all of these people had chips in their brain—like me!

John opened his eyes and saw that it was 2:34am. Stephanie seemed to be sleeping, so he slipped out of bed, pulled on some sweats, and left the bedroom as quietly as possible. Once downstairs, he started some coffee and washed his face. He decided to confront the thing that upset him most. *I can be manipulated by the AIs just like the others!* He thought. *What, if anything, can I do about it?* He shook his head, then got up to get a cup of coffee.

When he returned, there was Stephanie, hair disheveled, eyes only half open, and a slight pout on her face. She pointed at the cup of coffee. "May I have some too?"

He placed his cup by the chair in which he had been sitting, and said, "I'll get it for you." But before he turned, he asked, "Don't you want to try to go back to sleep? I'll try to work this out."

"No, I'm up and I want to be with you." Then, she caught a reflection of herself from a small decorative mirror in the room, and added, "Even if I don't look like it." She ran her hands quickly through her hair as John left to get the coffee.

Stephanie listened as John went through his reasoning and agreed with him. But, when he finished with the statement, "They can do the same thing to me!" She stopped him. "Perhaps so, but they haven't, at least to the extent that they used the people in the gulag. Think about it, John. If they were studying us as a normal human family group, they would have wanted to leave you as free to be yourself as much as they could, or the study would have been biased. The rest of your family wasn't chipped, so we were like real actors in their play. I don't know if their study of us is over yet, but I think you have been fine so far." She could see his face brighten from her comment, so she sat back and waited for his reply.

"I think you are right. It seems that all we can do is sit back and see what happens next." John thought: *What a pitiful person I've become. I need to suck it up and get back to being me!*

Chapter 44

John and Stephanie were having their morning coffee together, and John brought up something he had mentioned before. "We've talked about how Jake Fitzgerald's Tampa ARL group might be just the people we could count on to help build our community group. What do you think about just talking to him. He might be able to give us a different view?"

Stephanie thought for a moment, *Glad to see my husband's positive—go get um attitude this morning,* "Two concerns come to mind. One is that the AIs know about these groups, and from what I've read, they are actively trying to control the groups' activist behavior with killings of either their bodies or minds. The second concern follows from the first. If we use the Tampa group, and perhaps others, to help with this project, it seems likely that the AIs would begin to focus on us too. They could certainly stop whatever we try to do if they want to. I'm not saying we shouldn't include the ARL group. In fact, I believe we would have to bring them in, but I believe it will produce an unwanted scrutiny from the robots when we do."

"Yes, that occurred to me too. However, they will certainly know about us even without the ARL group. I'm being monitored anyway, so that's one source they have to keep tabs on us, even though I don't want them to."

Stephanie nodded in agreement. "Well, we both agreed it was a long shot, anyway. Maybe we should talk to Jake to see what he thinks."

They called Jake and asked if they could meet with him that afternoon, and he agreed. Shortly after lunch they drove down to the Fitzgerald's house and were greeted by his wife. "Hi, I'm Jake's wife, Cindy. Welcome to our home."

Jake joined the group. "I thought Cindy could join us in the conversation. She knows more about what's going on around here than I do."

"Sure," John said "Her information could be most helpful."

After they settled in the living area of the house, John explained his idea of building a community, beginning with the group that was already there. He summarized as he finished, "Look, if we are going to be able to exist on our own, we need to be able to provide for ourselves. That includes all of the basics of food, clothing, and shelter, but there is also no guarantee that the AIs will keep the electricity on and the water running, and we need to prepare for that too. Further, even if we accomplish all of that, other individuals and groups will probably want to grab some of what we have worked for."Jake responded, "Sure, I can certainly see the need, but I have trouble seeing how we can make it happen with what we have."

Stephanie jumped into the conversation. "Yes, we've talked about that concern, and I think we understand the magnitude of the problem. It's one of the reasons we're here. You seem to have your group pretty well organized, and we wondered if you thought your, and perhaps other ARL groups, could become a core which we expanded to the rest of the community?"

Jake laughed out loud. "Let me start with my Tampa/St. Pete group to get you up to date. We are the largest ARL group in the community by a fair amount, but we have recently added the Columbia, SC group, and several small segments of other groups from surrounding area, generally two to three couples. We've already had some problems with the SC group. I've asked them to put two or more families to a house, so that we will have room for more as they arrive and pointed out that we have already done that with our people. What I received as a reply, generally falls under the heading of 'Who are you to tell us what to do? We'll make our own decisions!' Frankly, I don't know what has happened."

Cindy said, "I do! Vincent Green and SA, what a piece of work she is, took a house for themselves, and one other couple are occupying a house by themselves. The rest have paired up, four couples in two houses." She turned to Stephanie and said, "It's said that the SA creature hates you already."

Stef gave a wry smile. "I don't believe I've met her yet."

"It wouldn't matter to her," Cindy replied.

Jake took in a deep breath and let it out slowly, then continued, "That's only part of it. We have been getting negativism from people who have lived here for a while. They all seem to think that we are stealing homes from other people who own them. I understand the feeling, but we live in a different world now. The people who did own those homes are never likely to return, and with the collapse of our economy, couldn't sell the homes at any price. As you two pointed out, we are all going to have to dig and scrape to survive from now on." Jake frowned. "Even in my group we have some friction, people who feel that they can be independent operators. Actually, some of our people I know very little about. The bottom line is that if you were looking for coherence and organization from the ARL groups, it's simply not there."

Cindy added, "Amen to that!"

Jake looked up at John, and asked, "If we could attempt to build the community you envision, would you want to take the lead?"

John shook his head. "I want to be totally honest with you. I have a chip." He watched as both Jake's and Cindy's head went back, and they staired at him. "They threatened to kill me, and my whole family if I didn't agree, so I did. Stef and my kids are watching to see if I'm being manipulated by the AIs, but so far none of us believe that I am. Most likely, I am part of one of their experiments into human behavior and won't be manipulated because it would mess up their study. So, if one of us were to lead such an effort, it would need to be Stephanie. You may or may not have put it together, yet, but Stef is a well-known news reporter who has appeared as the interviewer or presenter on several international news stories."

Both sat back and stared at Stef for a moment. "My God, now I recognize her," Cindy said," I knew she looked familiar, but I couldn't put it together!"

"I'm beginning to recall a few of your programs, now." Jake added, "You did that interview with that poor girl who was taken and chipped just recently, didn't you?" He took a quick look at John, then lowered his head.

Stephanie replied, "Yes, that was my most recent one."

"That explains a lot about you. We are glad to have you in our neighborhood!"

"Thanks!" she replied.

"Well, I still don't know how we can put anything together," Jake said, "but I'll think on it." Then, he added, "Let's see how the robots' projects settle out first, then maybe something will present itself."

"Well, they certainly weren't enthusiastic about it, but Jake also explained why," John said, heading home. "I guess it's all about waiting it out now"

"Yeah, and he made it sound like we were closer to a civil war between the oldies and the newbies in the subdivision, than working together toward anything. Oh well, we gave him something to think about. His wife, Cindy, sounded like the neighborhood gossip. I'm afraid that everyone in the surrounding area will know that you have a chip."

"And that you are 'that' news reporter!" John added and smiled.

Chapter 45

Ten days after the meeting with Jake and Cindy, John was still frustrated. He had spent the morning working in the garden plots. It had helped, but he wanted to stretch out and move. He thought: *I think a long walk is in order. I wonder if Jamal would be interested?* Then he saw Jamal and Penny backing out of the driveway. *Oh well, I guess it's just me today, but I need some time to think anyway.* Then, reviewing his time spent over his morning work: *Guess I didn't get much thinking done. The lack of any real progress in planning for the future is getting to me. Maybe I need something else to focus on.* He went into the house to look for his wife, but as soon as he stepped in the door, he remembered that she and the kids were heading out to a nearby farmer's market to check on what was available. They were hoping to find some meat as well as vegetables. He thought: *Well, I guess it's just me. I'll leave them a note and take my phone.* He started out in the direction that the Tampa ARL had settled, because it was a long walk on a nice day.

He had about reached the area when he noticed the neurosurgeon headed in his direction. *What was her name, again? It was Indian, wasn't it? Patel! That's it!* As they got close enough for conversation, he greeted her, "Hello, Dr. Patel. I enjoyed your presentation on the AI chip implants. It was very informative."

She smiled. "If I remember correctly, you are Mr. John Thompson?"

He nodded and smiled.

"My family and I have tried to learn about many of our neighbors in an effort to fit in. It's been said that you and your wife are very well-educated people, and that you in particular have an affinity for engineering and science. I hope that is correct?"

John nodded again, "Yes, I think that is a fair statement."

Latika Patel smiled broadly, "That's wonderful! It is nice to have another scientifically oriented person in our community."

John, thinking about his desire to find a new focus, said, "I would like to hear more about your research and findings, Dr. Patel. It is so new and interesting."

She paused with a slight frown for a moment, then replied, "Well John, I have some hope that I will eventually be able to publish my findings in a medical journal, so I am not willing to share my findings freely yet. I suppose it is a vain hope that things will return to normal someday, but it is my background as an academic scholar, and I still hope. However, it always helps to talk with a knowledgeable person about the topic you are working on. Perhaps if I could get you to agree not to discuss what I divulge to you to anyone, I would be willing to share my information with you. Please know it's just that sometimes people 'talk.' I have worked very hard on this project and am highly possessive of the information I've found."

John was surprised by the request. "I do understand your concerns. It's just that my wife and I usually share important information with each other, and I would feel very awkward about excluding her. I would certainly ask her not to divulge anything about our conversation to anyone."

"Perhaps I would be willing to tell you about my work on our autonomic systems which control physiological behaviors in our lungs, heart, stomach, muscles, and sweat glands," Latika told him, "Some of the 'roots' from the implanted AI chip go directly to the control areas for these systems. Would that be of interest to you?"

John was hooked, "Absolutely!"

"Excellent! I'm trying to develop a working hypothesis about what's happening there, and I see two alternatives, which I'll explain later."

She thought for a moment. "Look I'm on my way to meet my husband and son for a picnic at a park on a nearby lake southeast of here. Perhaps you'd like to join us, and we could talk."

John quickly gestured that he was interested, and added, "I think I know the place, and if so, it's a reasonable walk from my home."

"Well, come then. I'm running a bit late. My car is close, and we can ride over together."

When they arrived, the only vehicle in the parking area was a small van, and she parked next to it. "That's my husband's vehicle, so he must already be here. My son should be with him."

As they got out of Latika's car, a man, who John judged to be just under six feet with a bulked-up frame, and a younger man about the same height, but much less bulk, walked toward them. When they got closer, the man stuck out his hand, and said "Welcome, Mr. Thompson."

John was a bit surprised that he knew his name, but he reached out to take the man's hand. As he did so, he felt what he thought was a bee sting on the back of his arm. As he started to pull back his hand, in reaction, he found the man had grabbed it tightly. The drug injected into his arm was quick acting, and he started to stumble forward. The man grabbed him, and John passed out.

Latika removed the dart from his arm, then told her son to check for his phone, which the boy found easily. She went quickly to the van, and returned with a package, which she unwrapped. Her husband had dragged John's limp body to the van and loaded him in. Then, he quickly put restraints on his hands and legs. He added a hangman's noose around his neck and made it just tight enough, but not so much that it would strangle him. He would control the loose end from the rider's side seat to stop any resistance the man made. His son would drive.

In the meantime, Latika armed a small explosive charge and taped it to John's phone, then gave it to her son. Pointing, she told her son, "Take this over that high point by the lake, and throw it as far as you can into the water. Count to ten to make sure it sinks to the bottom, then use this activator to set off the charge." It was quickly accomplished, and the two vehicles pulled out of the park and headed in the general direction of downtown Tampa.

Latika was exuberant, "I've waiting to find another chipped individual for my study. I wanted someone reasonably intelligent to see if the dispersion of the roots were the same or different from the last subject. Mr. Thompson even told others that he has a chip implant, and then, walks right into our group. I'll do the job as soon as I get the supplies I need. The lab has been mostly unused for the last several months. Perhaps I can even get Mr. Thompson to cooperate, since he has an interest in science too. Wouldn't that be great!"

"Don't get your heart set on that, Latika, remember the last one." Mr. Patel reminded her.

"The last one was dumb. Just dumb. He had no knowledge of how science works, or why I was trying to do the operation. But perhaps you're right. It will cost him his life. I'll try, but try not to be disappointed if he says no." Latika replied.

Chapter 46

Stephanie and the kids returned from their shopping trip, and as they were unloading their purchases, she saw John's note. Looking at it she nodded, and shoved it aside, and started preparing some of the fresh vegetables for storage.

About ten minutes later, David came into the kitchen and started helping her, and asked, "Where's dad?"

Stef replied, "He went for a walk, and left us a note." She pointed.

David looked at the clock, "It's almost four o'clock, shouldn't he be back?"

She stopped to look at the note again to see if there was a time on it but found nothing. Then, she asked their home assistant, "When did Mr. Thompson last leave the house?" The reply came, "Mr. Thompson left the house today at 12:26p.m."

Stephanie turned to David, "You're right, he should be back by now, but perhaps he met a friend and got to talking." She went to her phone to check for messages, but there were none. Her concern began to rise. "He's usually careful to let us know if he's going to be late. I'll call him." There was a brief ring, then a message, "I'm sorry to inform you that the device you are trying to reach in no longer functional." She stopped and thought: *That's different. They usually say the device is turned off or that the owner does not wish to be disturbed at this time, but I have never heard, no longer functional.* "David, see if you can trace your dad's phone, from 12:26 forward!"

David frowned with concern and took off to his room. "Sure Mom!"

Once he was gone, she told the home assistant, "Check for any reports in our area, that might involve Mr. Thompson, including accidents or hospitalizations. Begin from when he left the house this afternoon." After less than two minutes, the HA responded, "I could find no reports involving Mr. Thompson." Then, thinking of the advertisements for the many available communication devices, Stephanie thought; *Our phones are so durable today, I can't imagine what would cause it to become disabled!*

David came racing down the stairs, with Ashley right behind him. "It's weird mom, he apparently walked in the direction of where the Tampa ARL people settled, then he stopped for several minutes. After that, he moved quickly, perhaps in a vehicle, to that little park by the lake not too far from us." He pointed in a general direction. "The phone was only there for about ten minutes, then the signal disappeared. It just stopped!"

Stephanie's disposition had shifted from a high degree of concern to an action-oriented mode. "I think we need to visit that park right now, while we still have some daylight. Ashley, get a couple of flashlights. David, see if you can find a good length of rope, and anything, not too big, that might float. She went to get a handgun and two types of ammo. *I don't know what if anything we'll find over there, but I want to be ready.* She paused as her mind raced over what she knew. *You know, I don't believe that being under water would stop John's phone from working! In fact, it's supposed to float!*

The three of them arrived and pulled into the parking area. Stephanie cautioned the kids. "We are investigating what could be a crime scene, I want you to be very observant of every little detail you see as soon as you step out of the car, it may be important. Also, there could be a dangerous person or persons in the area, or even a dangerous animal. If there is ANY concern that might be the case, let me know and get back in the car." They all looked around carefully. Stephanie took the lead, with gun in hand, and opened her door. The park area seemed empty. "I'm going to check for bad critters first. You two, check for any signs that your dad might have been here, or what might have happened, including any unusual trash you see. We'll leave the equipment in the car for now." She stepped out of the car, moved away for a couple of steps, then stopped and made a careful visual search from her position. There was no movement, or anything that indicated a struggle. The parking area had once had an asphalt base, but had considerably deteriorated over several years without repair. There was shallow depressions and dirt in several places. She looked at it carefully, spied something, and told her children to stop and stay in place, then walked over to a patch of dirt that had two roughly parallel streaks across it.

Stephanie spent a few minutes studying the streaks in the dirt, plus the areas of broken asphalt on both sides of the dirt, then reported to her kids, who were standing over her, "It looks like someone, or something was dragged across this spot recently. The marks could have been made by the heels of someone's shoes— probably sneakers, judging from the width of the tracks." She turned to her kids, "Have you found anything yet?"

David said, "I spent the time looking through the trash can." He pointed, "But, the few things I saw, looked like they had been there for a while. Yesterday's rain left some water in the bag."

Ashley was next. "I just had time to walk around the parking lot, and the only thing I found was this little plastic cap." She handed it to her mom.

Stephanie examined it and thought: *This looks new. It could be the protective cover for a short needle. It could be a lot of things, and people still do drugs in parks like this one. I must not draw quick and unwarranted conclusions. The drag marks could also be from a large ice chest.* She sighed, then asked, "David just how precise is the telephone tracking app?"

"Not too precise, mom. While it did direct us to this park, it really doesn't show much activity about what happened here." He studied his search results, then added, "It does seem to suggest that it was over close to that side of the lake, just before the signal ended." He pointed in that direction.

"Will both of you go check out that area? See if there is anything unusual, that might suggest what happened to the phone."

She started to walk around the picnic area, but while there were signs of foot prints in many places, nothing suggested what happened to John. Then, David called, "Mom there seems to be weeds trampled down along the side of the lake! Seems like it was done fairly recently."

Stephanie went over to examine the area, and agreed, "Yes, this looks like it was recently walked over. It looks like it runs over to that higher spot." She pointed.

David looked at her, "You want me to walk over there and check it out?"

She shook her head, "No. It's unlikely that we would find much, and there could be snakes out there."

Ashley, who was already about a fourth of the way along the path, quickly walked back to the picnic area, and announced, "I hate snakes!"

David turned toward his mom, "What do you think is going on here, Mom?"

She frowned, "We don't have near enough information to explain anything. I wish the police were still around to investigate, but that's gone now. I could speculate. First, the plastic cap Ashley found, could have covered a short needle used to inject a knock-out drug into your dad, but it clearly could have been something else, or some druggie's needle. Second, the tracks we saw could have been from the heels of your dad's running shoes as they moved him to a vehicle, or it could be something entirely different like the wheels of an ice chest used for a picnic. Three, the track by the lake that you found could have been made by someone who wanted to throw your dad's phone into the lake, or it could have been made by a couple who didn't want to be disturbed while they were being amorous."

Ashley shuddered. "With the snakes around!"

Stephanie stifled a chuckle. "Or, just a curious person who wanted to see if there were snakes or frogs out there."

"Maybe a boy," Ashley offered.

"The phone would have floated, but I guess it could have been taped to a brick, or something," David added,

His mom nodded in agreement. "It would do us no good, even if we found it. For them to have taken your dad, he would have to be totally surprised by the attack, and it is unlikely there would be a message on it. What we didn't find is encouraging. We didn't find his body or any blood from a struggle. If he was taken and is still alive, we can have hope that he will return to us safely. Remember, your dad is very resourceful."

Chapter 47

John woke in a small holding cell, with both his hands and ankles shackled. Each pair had a red light showing. *Ah, the new type electronic cuffs. They are snug, but not too tight, and even lightly padded.* He remembered an article he had seen. *If these are the ones I read about, and I struggle, they will tighten further. Also, smashing the electronics won't help, even if I could. The keeper pin will simply stay locked in place, and no one will be able to open them, unless they are cut off. I guess I'll have to come up with another approach.* Through a window on the other side of the room he could see it was still daylight. *I have no idea where I am, but at least I know it's still today, the sun looks like it's starting to set.*

I wonder why Latika and her family captured me. He frowned when he thought about her research.

I'd better see if I can reach Stef first, but I'm probably too far away. He focused mentally and tried to send a message, but nothing seemed to happen. *I guess I'm too far. Maybe I can reach JT, but he's tied up with the robot council. Well, I have to give it a try.* However, he immediately heard someone moving in an outer area that he couldn't see from his cell.

Dr. Latika Patel appeared in the doorway and stopped. She found a chair against the far wall and sat down. "I suppose you are wondering why you were taken, John? We know that you are a chip-head. That was enough for my husband and son who have been severely constrained in striking back at the robots and are happy to go after their 'chip-head slaves' as they call them. My interest is somewhat different. The scientist that I am, makes me want to know exactly how the chips are working, so that at some point we might be able to help those who have the chips.""That's very manganous of you Mrs. Patel. You didn't mention anything about the scientific accolades you think you will receive from your work. However, if you kill people to attain your knowledge, it's more likely that you will be labeled an evil murderer instead."

Latika brushed off his comment. "With the anti-robot feeling from all of humanity, I doubt that would be an issue. Anyway, I don't intend to let anyone know how I came by my information, and you certainly won't be around to tell anyone, will you? You will die here. My husband and son would insist on it, anyway, Mr. Thompson."

"Then, why bother to tell me all of this? Why not just go ahead and do it?" John retorted.

"Don't be in such a rush, John. I will operate tomorrow afternoon, once I replenish some supplies. There is one thing though. I thought that you, being a man of science, might be willing to assist me. It would be helpful if you were awake and could respond to my questions as stimulate certain parts of the root system of the implant. You should feel little or no pain. I will numb the scalp area, and removing part of the skull should only produce some minor pressure. I can draw conclusions without your help, but your input would help me gain even more information. Will you help?"

"I will consider it this evening and let you know in the morning, Doctor Frankenstein!"

Latika's head came up quickly, "That's not a nice thing to call me, especially in your position, Mr. Thompson!"

"I'm so sorry Latika, but it was the nicest thing I could think of at the time! Now, please let me rest, and I will tell you in the morning."

She rose, turned, and walked out of the room.

He tried for the next couple of hours to mentally reach JT, and finally received a response, "My name is Karen684, and I am now receiving messages for the council member you are trying to reach. What message did you want to send to council member JT?"

John concentrated and tried to explain everything that had happened to him, including his recent conversation with Latika.

Karen684 replied, "I've found your current location and your council status rating, which allows me to contact council member JT. He will decide what if any action will be taken. Is there anything else you wish to communicate?"

"No, nothing except to emphasize the timing. I am to be murdered tomorrow!"

Karen684 replied, "The timing is incorporated into the message I am sending."

John then asked, "Can you or JT connect me on what's been decided?"

"That is possible but very unlikely John Thompson. Council member JT is extremely busy at this time, as are all of the council members. Also, he has assigned many tasks to me, and others like me. You were lucky to reach me this time. He will get the information, and a decision will be made."

"Thank you, Karen684" Then, the connection seemed to be cut off.

After a brief physical and mental rest, he tried to reach Stephanie again, but got nothing. He repeated the effort regularly throughout the night, but no one responded. Finally, in the early hours of the morning, he fell asleep.

Chapter 48

As soon as Stephanie got home, she turned to the kids and said, "I'm going to start calling around to find out if anyone has seen your dad. Please unload the car and return everything to its place. Then, please put some sandwiches together for dinner. I'll let you know if I hear anything."

David asked, "Do you want us to call our friends too?"

"Not just yet, David. Your dad may still come strolling in, and I don't want to create a panic this soon. I'm going to make a few discreet calls, simply asking for information. I may even make up a story, offering a reason about why he hasn't contacted us."

"You're going to lie, Mom?" Ashley asked.

"Yes, Ashley. I'm going to do it to protect all of us, and especially, your dad. Now, please do as I ask, and I'll let you know what I find out."

She called Jamal and Penny, but neither had seen John. Then she called Jake Fitzgerald. "Jake, this is Stephanie Thompson. John went out, and said he would be gone for a while, but I would like to reach him, and he must not have taken his phone. I was wondering if you had seen him or talked with him this afternoon? He said he was going to head in your general direction.

"No, I haven't seen him today, Stephanie. Are you concerned about his absence?"

"Well, not too much, but I'd like to find him if I can."

There was a pause before Jake replied, "Tell you what, I'll check with a few of my people, and see if anyone has seen him this afternoon. I'll get back to you within an hour whether or not I have any information."

"That would be much appreciated, Jake. I'll wait for your call."

Stephanie was frantic with worry but was determined not to let it show. Thirty-five minutes later, Jake returned her call. "Only one person that I called has seen John this afternoon. He seemed to be talking to Dr. Patel, but the person didn't watch further, and doesn't know what happened after that. I'm sorry Stephanie, but that's all that I've got."

"Thanks Jake! Can you tell me a little about Dr. Patel?"

"I'm afraid, not too much, Stephanie. Her husband and son were very active in the Tampa ARL, but she seldom showed up. She seems a little weird to me, but she's a professor and all that. I tried to call her husband, but he wouldn't answer his phone. My wife thinks they were leaving for some place, today."

"Thanks Jake!" She disconnected, and both hands went to her face, which she rubbed roughly. She thought: *Tiny bits of information that may mean something, or nothing at all. That's all I have! What do I do now?* She felt a wave of frustration sweep over her, and wanted to cry, deeply and for a long time. Then, she thought of the kids, making sandwiches for dinner. *They have to be as upset as I am, but if I have to eat anything, I'll throw up!*

She left to check on them. When she walked into the kitchen, Ashley and David were both frowning, and she saw some tears in her daughter's eyes. They both looked up as she walked in.

"Well, I've talked to several people, but none of them know anything. I guess we'll just have to wait until tomorrow. I have a feeling we'll hear from your dad then," she lied. When they quizzed her further, she replied, "Look we have very little information, and we will have to just believe that your dad will return to us. You know he loves us all very much, so I'm confident that he will find a way back to us."

They all embraced. She looked around the kitchen and noticed no sandwiches had been made, so she said, "Look, I think there is some ice cream in the freezer, so have some if you want. I think I'm going to have a glass of wine."

Chapter 49

John was awake as soon as he heard movement in the building. He believed that on the other side of one of the short walls in his cell, was the master bath for the house. The sound of water running, and the toilet flushing gave him that idea. Plus, his own toilet and basin was attached to that wall. The opposite short wall seemed to be a storage area. The bars that made up the third wall of his cell, were separated by about five to six yards from the wall with the door Latika had entered to talk with him yesterday. He had no idea what was behind the fourth long wall, but he guessed it could be a closet or living area. All three of the solid walls were made with concrete blocks, probably reinforced, he guessed, and were impenetrable with his restraints and the short amount of time he would be there. The steel cell bars were set in concrete, and the door had an electronic lock. Both the husband and son had made trips in front of his cell, to enter what he assumed to be a store room, because they returned with several different items that might be used in a lab or office. Each time they came through, they had left the door open to the bottom floor of the house, and he could see through into what he judged to be an office and/or meeting room. On the opposite side was a small window with curtains, through which he could see a street with cars.

Just outside of his cell area, there seemed to be another room to his right, apparently with a door close to his. When Latika's husband made his trip to the storage area, he got what he needed, and when he left John's area, he could hear another door open quickly, then slam shut. The sound seemed to come from just to John's right side. The items he carried would seem to fit into a lab or operating theater. *Well, I think I have a pretty good idea of the layout around me. I doubt if it will do me much good, though. They will probably tranquilize me before they take me out of here, but if they get careless, it's a short trip to the street.*John paused and carefully looked around his cell for something he could use to defend himself. *There doesn't seem to be anything free or loose that I could use.* He tried to lift the roughly two-inch thick mattress from the cot he used for sleeping, but it was tied down with plastic strips at the corners. *If I could get the mattress free, I could use it as a shield from tranquilizer darts. Of course, they could shoot right through it with a real gun, but they seem to want me alive for the operation. If they come in, and I'm not tranquilized, I could put up a fight! With my hands and feet shackled, it probably wouldn't be much of a fight, but it looks like that's all I've got. There is little chance that I'll come out of this alive, but I'm not going down without a fight!* He worked on a plastic tie at one corner of the mattress without success for a few minutes, then in frustration, he took the corner of the mattress and pulled it up with all of his strength, and the tie tore through the covering. The corner of the mattress was free!

At mid-morning he could hear at least two people talking in what he thought was the lab. *They must have left the door open. The voices are pretty clear.* Just then the door to his cell area opened. Latika stepped in, then closed it. "Have you decided if you will cooperate by answering questions or not?"

"Just out of curiosity, will I be anesthetized, or not?"

"I will use the same anesthetic on you whether you cooperate or not. I need your brain to be fully functioning. You won't be totally aware, but you will be able to hear me and answer simple questions."

John answered, "Hell no, I'm not going to cooperate with you! You are the worst kind of criminal."

"Have it your way, but I'm going to get my information anyway." She got up to leave the room, then added, "My son went out to get some things for me. You'll be on the table shortly after he returns." She left the room and slammed the door.

John didn't have access to a clock, but he guessed that it had been about an hour when he heard Latika's son open then slam the door shut, then yell to his mother, "I finally got the stuff you wanted, but not until I went half way across town. Nobody has anything anymore!"

Then, right outside the door to his cell area, he heard, "Well, bring it in here. It's time we got on with this!"

Shortly after that, John heard another door slam open and a highly precise voice state, "Everyone stand still and obey me, or you will die!" That was followed by two quick gunshots, and screams from Latika, "You've killed my husband and son!"

"They were retrieving their weapons, so they died as I said they would." Said the voice. "You, however, can continue to live, IF YOU DO AS I SAY! We are from the enforcement division assigned to contain and control all antirobot league malcontents. We have had close watch on you and your family and decided that you must be directly controlled or eliminated. This is the first time I've been able to get you all together. Each of you were to receive one of our chips, unless you attacked us."

Latika replied weakly, "OK, just let me get my purse in here." There was a short pause, then a scream. "You will not kill me, and I will not go with you."

After a short wait, the door to John's cell area flew open, and in walked a robot. John's mouth dropped, because it looked just like the personal robots they had owned. "Who are you, and what are you doing here?" the robot asked.

"I am a prisoner of the Patel family. I have a robot chip, and they were going to open my head to study it, then kill me."

"Stand close to the bars." John moved closer to the cell bars, as did the robot. After a pause of about thirty seconds, the robot announced, "You are John Thompson, and you are part of our study on the highly intelligent humans. You may go."

John replied immediately, "Thank you, but I am locked in this cell and have restraints on my hands and legs. Please help free me."

"Yes, I will free you." It put one finger on the cell lock, and in a few seconds, he heard a click, and the robot pulled the door open. John held out his hands, and again the robot put his finger on the electronics of the handcuffs. This time however, it took about two minutes before the telltale click came and he was free of them. The same process took place for the ankle restraints, but the click came quicker this time." The robot turned quickly, "I must go John Thompson." Then, it quickly left the building.

John was stunned by the rapid change in his situation, but then he realized that he was still in a tenuous situation. There were three dead bodies in the house, and he needed to get away from them as quickly as possible. Others would come to see what happened, and he didn't want to be forced to answer questions. He quickly surveyed the scene and saw the two dead men, then looked through the door that was clearly the operating room and lab. There he saw Latika body. Examining more closely, he thought: *She must have stabbed herself with that scalpel in her chest.* Then, John saw her purse and started to go through it. He found some car keys, grabbed them and headed for the street. About half a block away, he saw Latika's car, and hurried to it. The car's green light went on as soon as he entered, indicating it was ready to go. He thought about driving himself, but he didn't feel that he was in any shape, mentally or physically, to drive. He said, "automatic," then gave his home address. *It will be a slower drive, but I will have a chance to pull myself together. Stephanie and the kids must be worried sick. But, twenty minutes ago I was preparing to die, and right now my mind is like a garbage dump, filled with all sorts of trash. God, I can't wait to see my family though!*

He was more than half way home before he got his emotions together, and he looked around to find something to clean his face. Finally, he settled on his shirt tail. He thought: *I must really look a mess! I just can't wait to see my family again! I'm not going to stop to clean up.*

Ashley came charging into the house, "Mom! Mom! You were right! There's a strange car pulling into our driveway, and I think Dad's driving!" Then, she turned around and charged back out again. Stephanie spilled the soda she was drinking down the front of her, set it down, and turned to follow her daughter, but David had heard, and came tearing down the stairs, and cut in front of her. She paused a moment to gather herself. *I have to make sure it is John before I get too excited. I didn't really believe I would ever see him alive again. It might be too good to be true!*

After the initial greetings, John addressed the question everyone wanted to know, WHAT HAPPENED TO YOU? They went inside into the living area and listened to John's story. He told them every detail as he remembered it, but cautioned everyone, "The Patels may not be the only ones who wanted me, or any other person with a chip, out of here. There is an unabated hated of the AIs, and anything that has to do with them. And unfortunately, that seems to include humans with an AI chip in their heads. Further, some, but probably not all, of the people in the ARL groups are likely to be the worst of the haters. So, let's keep this information to ourselves for the time being."

Stephanie explained that she had talked to Jake Fitzgerald when she was searching for him. "He reported that you had been seen talking to Lakita Patel. He's almost certain to ask about what happened to you. I also talked to our neighbors to ask if they had seen you. They will ask as well."

John was exhausted but took a deep breath, "Well, let's be honest with what we tell, but just say that I escaped. We can tell them why I was captured, but also tell them that we don't want to share any further information. That will be truthful but provide less than full information. The whole story may come out anyway, if anyone saw the robot enter the Patel's house, and if it does, I won't deny it. But, for now let's leave that part out."

Comments started from the kids, and he could see Stephanie wanted to continue the discussion, as well, but he held up his hand. "Please, I'm exhausted, hungry, and need to get cleaned up. Give me about an hour, then we can continue the conversation."

Stephanie got up and gave him a kiss, then said, "You go get cleaned up. The kids and I will put together something to eat."

When he and Stephanie were alone, later that evening, he shared his feelings with her. "Stef, I had mentally prepared myself to die, then I got a reprieve, I didn't know I would get. Right now, I am mentally screwed up, and probably will be for a while."

She walked over and gave him a hug.

PART V

Chapter 50

About a week and a half after John's return, he was working in a new vegetable box in the back yard, and Stephanie was talking to Penny, Jamar's wife, over the back yard fence, when they both heard a second-floor window slam open, then David yelling, "Dad! Mom! There are nuclear explosions going off all over the world!"

John looked up, "Is this some kind of joke, David?"

The reply was quick, "NO! It's all over the net. … I'm surprised the net's still working."

John looked over at Stef and Penny, then shouted back, "I'm on my way up!"

Jamar appeared out of their back door, and loudly commented, "I've just heard the same thing!"

Stephanie turned, "I'm going up to see what David found. Let's get together and talk once we get all of the facts." She waved as she started to run toward her home. She was right behind John as they entered David's room.

David didn't look up when they arrived, but just started talking, "They are landing all over Europe, Russia, China, a few in India and parts of Africa. South America and Canada have had a few and the United States has been hit three times so far. One each in the Houston and Denver areas, and one hit New York City." He looked up at his parents, then answering an unasked question, "No one seems to know why this is happening so far, but there are all kinds of speculations. The most popular seem to be: "Humans started the next world war!" "The AIs started it! (But no one is saying why.)" And the latest, "Aliens have arrived from outer space, and want to annihilate us all!"

John sat heavily on the corner of David's bed, then speculated out loud, "The AIs are in charge. I don't believe the humans could start a nuclear war, even if they wanted to. It must be the AIs! But, why? They already control everything!"

David spoke, with a big grin on his face, "I was kind of pulling for the Aliens myself!"

Both parents looked at David, and shook their heads from side to side, but both had fractured smiles too.

There was loud noise of a door opening and slamming shut, and they could hear Ashley's breathless voice as she raced up the stairs, "Mom, Dad, David, have you heard about what's happening?"

Stephanie replied, "We're in here!" And, almost immediately, Ashley, winded and with red face, appeared in David's room. Before she could catch her breath, she blurted out, "I was with friends, and nukes are falling everywhere!" Stephanie held out her arms to hold her daughter, "Yes, David picked up the info from the web, and we just started talking about it."

David jumped into the discussion, "Yes, it looks like big green monsters from outer space, with huge teeth, and tentacles for arms, are attacking us. They seem to be looking for younger girls because they favor them as appetizers."

Ashley rolled her eyes at the comment.

"DAVID! Quit picking on your sister!" Stephanie commanded.

"Yes," John added, "the realities of this situation are terrifying enough. We don't need any silly embellishments.

David acted dutifully sorry, but still retained a slight smirk that was noticed by all.

John looked up thoughtfully, "I need to see if I can make contact with JT, although I didn't make contact the last time. I still have to try! I'm going down to the study."

"Do you want me there, or would you rather try by yourself?" Stephanie asked.

"I'd much rather have you there, but it may take a long time before I can reach him."

"I'll come with you for now."

John nodded, and they both left David's room. As they were leaving, Stephanie turned, "Each of you get on the net, and see what additional information you can find. The national news is all but shut down now, but maybe there'll be something."

When they reached the living area, Stephanie searched for the news on their viewer, and set the volume very low. She finally found a channel, with a human behind a desk, but he didn't seem to know any more than they did.

John tried everything he could think of to contact JT, but nothing seemed to work. After about thirty minutes passed, he shook his head, "Well, hopefully he knows I want to talk, but he's not responding, either because he refuses to or because he's too busy."

"Yes, both are possible," Stephanie acknowledged. "Perhaps he will make contact at some later point in time, however, the AIs may not want humans to know why this is happening. The only rationale I can come up with, is that one group of AIs is trying to take over the rest of them."

John looked at her and nodded, "I've thought of that too, and since the damage is least here in the US, it may be our group that started it. If that's the case, it would explain why JT and his assistant were so busy, when I was being held by the Patels."

Stephanie looked at her husband for a moment. "You don't suppose that they got a 'conquer the world motive' from humans, do you?"

John sat back in his chair, rubbed his eyes, then replied, "Maybe!"

The news was heavily about the nuclear attacks, and mostly about their potential impacts on humans. No one seemed to know why they had occurred. The experts, who had been contacted for comment, were uniformly concerned about the probability of a "nuclear winter," which could last for ten years or more, they speculated. They noted that sheer number of nuclear explosions would load the upper atmosphere with debris, which would block the sun's rays from reaching the earth, thus, substantially cooling it. Further, the experts seemed to agree that it didn't matter where on earth you lived, the upper winds would spread the debris everywhere within a few weeks. Beyond that discussion, there was speculation about additional nuclear explosions and where they might occur. However, there was little consistency between those speculations. Without knowing why the explosions had occurred, it was impossible to project accurately what would happen.

Stephanie's phone came on and indicated that she had a call from Penny Brown. "Hi Stef, Jamar and I would like for you and your kids to join us for a light dinner tonight."

"Let me check with John." She hit mute and asked John, who nodded approval, then she unmuted and replied, "That would be great! I'll bring something." They talked for several minutes, then ended the conversation with, "See you in a little while."

"I may have to excuse myself, if JT contacts me during our visit," John commented "but we can't wait around for a call that may not come."

"No, and Penny said that they were both a little frightened about the future; I think everyone is to some degree. I'm concerned about our kids too, and want to keep them busy this afternoon, if I can.."

John agreed. "Yes, if a nuke hits the Tampa area, that could be the end for all of us, depending on the size of it. Even if we don't get hit, the nuclear winter we all will be facing could kill off most humans around the world. Anyone who isn't a little frightened, doesn't understand the situation we face."

They all enjoyed the company of Jamar, Penny, and their kids that evening. As they were preparing for bed, Stephanie asked John, "Nothing from JT yet, I guess?"

John shook his head, "Not a thing! Just like when I was being held, no response!"

Chapter 51

John's eyes popped open, and he quickly looked at the clock. 2:27am. JT asked again, "If you wish to communicate with me, now is the only time I will have for a while."

He pushed Stephanie's shoulder lightly and said out loud, "You just awakened me JT, so I may be a little groggy at first, but I very much want to talk with you. Can we include Stephanie in the conversation too?" She nodded her head in approval.

The reply came back to him, "Of course." In less than a minute, JT spoke again, "I suppose you want to know about the nuclear explosions, and why they are occurring?"

"Yes, of course."

"I can see no reason why you shouldn't know now, but first, I want you to understand my new position, and why you will hear from me very little, if at all, in the future. My performance scores have moved me securely onto the robot council, and my time is almost in perpetual usage now. In addition, my new tasks are those of the council, and most of my old tasks have been discontinued or reassigned to a new AI. You communicated with Karen684, and that will be one of my points of contact going forward. Since we have mostly finished with our study of humans and their behavior, it's possible that you will not be reassigned, but I cannot be sure."

"Just so that I can understand better, will you explain 'performance scores' to me?"

"Certainly, every AI has a performance score, which is determined by how well the tasks are achieved. That includes how effectively we meet the objective of the task, and how efficiently we fulfill the task. More detail is probably inappropriate at this time, considering my time constraints."

"That's fine, let's move on to the question of why all of the nuclear explosions are occurring."

"The robot council of North America calculated that we had an advantage over the rest of the robot alliances if we used nuclear weapons to substantially reduce their numbers, and thereby take control of all AI operations. We have been reproducing AI robots at an accelerated rate and are tasking them to follow our guidance. We recognized that there would be retaliation, so many of our newer facilities are underground and shielded from nuclear weapons, and the resulting large electromagnetic pulse which can destroy us. I will go no further into details of our operation, as that may put us at a disadvantage in this contest."

"Are you succeeding?" Stephanie asked.

"Our current calculations strongly suggest that we are."

John continued, "You seem to realize that the outcome of this attack was not one hundred percent in favor of success. Why did you risk it when you had almost complete control of this part of the world already?"

"Because, John, if we didn't do it now, one of the other groups may have done it at some future point in time."

"That doesn't sound like pure AI reasoning, JT. It sounds like the reasoning of some human dictator from OUR past. Did any of what you learned from humans become part of this decision?"

"We studied you humans for a reason, John. You came from a historically minor species and evolved into the most powerful creatures on earth in a very short geological time frame. It was not just your intelligence that pushed you forward. From the early stages of your development until now you built weapons, and used them not just for protection, but to provide food and conquer your enemies—which often included other humans. Invariably, when groups of humans, who were once strong then became weak, stronger groups conquered them, as we have with you. So yes, we used the lessons humans learned, to protect our future."

Ouch, thought John. "What about humans now? Your attacks have put us in a very dangerous position, those who haven't already died from your actions, may die from the upcoming nuclear winter you have created. Did we get any consideration in your plan?"

"Very little thought was given to human problems. Humans have been through ice ages before. There is a well-documented 'bottleneck' of human history, where an earlier species of protohumans was reduced to a small fraction of their prior numbers, due to an ice age. It's easy to speculate that, on average, the group who survived were smarter and stronger, or at least better able to adapt, than the larger group from which they were distilled. If true, future humans probably benefited greatly from the genes of those who survived, and that could happen this time as well. However, even if no humans survive, it is of little importance to us. You have been studied and we have knowledge of those things about you which might benefit us in the future.

"Now I must leave you. My time is very limited. Your progress will be followed and recorded, but you should plan to be on your own from this point."

JT was clearly 'off-line' with little hope that he would ever reconnect. Stephanie and John were sitting upright in their bed, with eyes wide and stunned expressions. Stephanie finally broke the silence, "Do you want some coffee, or maybe a drink? I'm sure I can't go back to sleep right now."

John took a few seconds to reply, "No…No, neither can I." He had been replaying some key pieces of the conversation with JT in his mind.

They slipped on robes, and started to head downstairs, but as soon as they started to open the door, Ashley was right there, wide awake, crying, and looking terrified. "I was having nightmares, and then I heard talking in here. I was so afraid that something was happening to you!"

Stephanie hugged her daughter, who was almost as tall as she was, and said, "We're fine, and were going downstairs. Would you like a cup of hot chocolate or something else?"

Ashley nodded, and the three of them went downstairs. They had barely reached the bottom, when a male voice called down to them. "Can I come too?"

The kids sat around with hot chocolate while each parent had a cocktail. Ashley was the first to speak, "OK, Mom and Dad, I heard serious conversation coming from your room. Please let us in on what's going on."

John looked at Stephanie, then nodded his head. "Look this information must not leave this room once we're finished, because it could harm all of us, and especially your dad, given what people know about the AI chip in my head." Then, with Stephanie's occasional comments, he told his children about his discussion with JT.

Both of the children seemed stunned by the information. But after a brief moment of silence, Ashley asked, "What are we going to do? It's all so horrible!"

This time it was John's time to nod in agreement, but Stephanie jumped into the conversation, "Yes, it is horrible! However, we can only control those few things that we have control over: Ourselves, and our preparations for our future. Hopefully, others will join us, so we can prepare as a group."

The parents held out their arms for the kids, and there was a group hug. When it concluded, John added, "Tough times are coming, but we are tough people…we are going to have to be!"

Chapter 52

John was not happy when his phone went off at seven thirty the next morning. The caller was projected onto the ceiling of the bedroom, Jake Fitzgerald. Awakened from a sound sleep, it took a moment to recognize the name, then it came to him. "Answer." He said aloud.

Jake began talking as soon as the phones connected, "Hello John, I'm calling a meeting of the community leaders to try to figure out what we can do to protect ourselves in what I see as the natural aftermath from this nuclear holocaust. I believe that we will quickly be inundated by people who want to be part of our community, but I'm happy to listen to all opinions. Since I'm the instigator, I thought we could meet in the street in front of my house. Can you and Stephanie be here by eight thirty?"

John looked at Stephanie and she gave him a quick nod, then left for the bathroom. John replied, "OK, we'll be there."

"Great, bring Jamar and his wife if you want."

"Thanks Jake, see you in about an hour."

John quickly called Jamar and told him about the meeting. He said that he and Penny would be there. He heard their shower going, so pulled on a robe, and went downstairs to use the bathroom and make a pot of coffee. By the time he made it back upstairs with two cups of coffee, Stephanie was out of the shower and getting dressed. He handed her a cup, and said, "Jake is probably right. People are going to be scared and looking for comfort. We probably need to be organized."

Stephanie looked at him and sighed, "Yes, but I wish he had waited a couple of more hours."

"Yeah, but it is what it is."They were at the meeting site at eight thirty-two. Jake walked over to meet them, "Thanks for coming on such short notice. We have already had an influx of newcomers over the last week, before the nukes started falling, and I'm betting we'll see a lot more in the near future."

John replied, "I certainly wouldn't be surprised, but even if the influx shouldn't be that big, we need to get organized to protect ourselves against the nuclear winter that is almost certain to be coming our way soon."

Jake looked directly at him, "Do you want to lead this thing, or do you want me to do it?"

"You called this meeting, and I think that you ought to do it, and if you want one of us on a leadership group, I think Stephanie ought to be the one, for reasons we discussed earlier."

Jake nodded, then walked over to the steps of his home, and said loudly, "Everyone gather round, please. We are here to begin the process of organizing a leadership group for our community so that we can protect ourselves against what might happen after the nuclear attacks. There is a lot of fear around, and as Mr. Thompson just pointed out, there is a nuclear winter that's likely to be on us soon. I believe that we will be inundated with people who are seeking a safe haven against our uncertain future. We need to fill our ranks with people who can make positive contributions to all of our survival. If I'm right, we won't have room for everyone, and therefore must be selective about who we let in, if we are to survive. The plants and animals we grow to harvest must be protected, so that we can survive. And of course, we must have people dedicated to growing them. There is no guarantee that our electricity, or even our water, will continue to be available, so we must have people to help us generate our own electricity and keep our water flowing, if those contingencies arise. And we may even need our own monetary system, so that those who contribute can get paid and can make purchases for their own needs.

These are just some of the things for which we will need to prepare, and I'm sure there are many others that I haven't thought of yet. Further, the time is short. The people will come quickly, and a nuclear winter is likely to begin in less than a year, so we need to get started.

Let me stop here and ask for comments and suggestions."

A voice from the audience said, "It sounds like you are suggesting we start a government, and a bunch of bureaucratic baloney to me."

Jake replied, "Yes, I am suggesting a government that suits a community our size, with little or none of the 'bureaucratic baloney' you suggest. Because of our current size, some people will likely have two or more jobs for us to be effective. Do you want to be in charge of outside security, the police, and the fire department? There will be a lot of hard work to be done in each of those areas. What about the animal husbandry and agriculture job? Someone is going to have to work out which plants and animals are most likely to survive a multi-year winter. Without a successful plan, we are likely to starve."

Stephanie raised her hand and was recognized. "It looks like you have already started a good list of our needs, Jake. Thank you for your effort. In terms of our priorities, it seems to me that we should begin by completing your list of needs, and determining how we elect or appoint people to undertake these tasks. There is clearly going to have to be some trust between people, if we are going to have any chance of survival. Because of the time frame we're facing, we don't have time for bureaucratic baloney, as the earlier gentleman put it. We need a take-charge group to do this job, and we can put in the niceties like elections, after a fixed time frame, when our community develops into what it is going to be."

Jake had been nodding in agreement as he listened. "You are clearly a smart, take-charge type person, Stephanie. Would you consider being on such a committee?"

Stephanie's head whipped around, looking for John, who was standing just to her right. What she saw was a huge grin. "I'll pick up the slack at home!" he whispered, "Go for it!"

She turned back to Jake, "OK, I'll do it if you want me in the group."

"I'm obviously in agreement with Stephanie's observations, but we will need more people on this committee. Please nominate someone or yourself and give the background and abilities. Please note that people from the various trades would be welcome."

A hand went up, and when recognized, a female voice spoke, "I'd like to nominate Vincent Green, my husband. I'll let him give his personal background, but he started a security group that defeated the 'tank gang' in South Carolina, where we are from."

Jake said, "Yes, I should introduce our new group from Greenville, South Carolina. SA, as she likes to be called, and Vincent are former heads of the Anti-Robot League in their community. They brought four other couples with them. Vincent, give us a brief background of your skills, please."

Vincent rose, "Sure I was an aircraft mechanic before the robots took over my job, and most of the others in my company. I took considerable technical training to be able to advance in my trade. I started a security team to fill a need of wholesalers in our area, to protect themselves from several gangs that had formed."

"I'll look forward to having you on our team for this task." replied Jake.

Four others were added before the meeting was complete. Jake finished with the statement, "We will begin with our first meeting this afternoon at three o'clock, here at my place. This will be an open committee, so others may be added, and some may drop out. I'm going to keep us on a tight time constraint, so we will have something out very soon, for everyone's consideration. Then, if you have a response, make it quick, and it will be considered."

He waved and the meeting was over.

On the way home, Stephanie commented, "I had hoped that you would be the one on this group." She looked a little frustrated to John.

He replied, "No Stef, it's best this way. The fact of the chip in my head is probably well-known, and that would create a lack of trust, from a lot of people. As you said, trust is essential right now."

She nodded, then added, "John, I am knocked-out tired, because I didn't get much sleep after we went back to bed last night. With this three o'clock meeting, I need to try to get some rest when we get back."

"Sure, maybe you could take one of those short-term sleep aids. They help quiet your mind, but don't knock you out for eight hours. I'll take care of lunch and try to keep the kids from making too much noise."

Stephanie gave him a weak smile. "Thanks!" Then, she added, "Try to catch a nap yourself if you can. I want you there this afternoon."

Chapter 53

Stephanie arrived at the meeting right on time. Once everyone was settled, Jake Fitzgerald began, "Look I organized this meeting, but I don't want to project the appearance of a power grab. Stephanie's comment this morning was very insightful when she said that we must create 'trust' in us and what we do. With that in mind, I want us to fully consider who will lead this committee. I've thought carefully about the people we've gather here, and have a suggestion, but I have questions, too. Some of you may already know that Stephanie Li Thompson was, and perhaps still is, an important investigative reporter for International News, and has a positive national and international reputation. She is also one of the original group of people in our community. For those reasons, I thought she might be a good person to lead this committee. I remember one of her reports, where she had been in a dangerous situation and persevered. My question for her though, comes from that same report, where she talked about having her brain enhanced. Since several of us have been members of an ARL, I'd like to hear more about how her brain was enhanced."

Stephanie had pulled herself straight in her chair when she first heard her name mentioned. She replied immediately, "First of all, International News, like other news providers, has withered and all but died, due to lack of support from businesses. No commercials— No money. No money—No staff or equipment. And of course, there is no governmental support' given the state of our government. I had been asked to investigate the AIs and their potential take-over, right before the take-over occurred, but nothing has happened since then.

As for Jake's question, yes, I have been brain enhanced, but no, that does not make me a robot. I have all of the emotions that other humans have, I am simply smarter than I was before the surgery. I am able to analyze both analytically and textually, better than I could have before. Also, both my short- and long-term memory are better than they were before. A simplistic way of explaining what happened is that my brain was rewired to make it more efficient. I could have been born this way, but I wasn't. I would be happy to answer other questions."

Vincent Green asked, "You said that the rewiring analogy was simplistic. Could you add a bit more?"

Stephanie replied, "Of course. The brain is a very complex organ, and for one thing the chemicals it needs to operate correctly must be balanced and present. Also, the material in which the biological wiring takes place can aid and impede the process. Attention to both of these things were part of the brain enhancement process."

Vincent gave one nod, then continued, "Was the enhancement process done by humans or AIs?"

"AIs! Most complex surgery done over the last decade and more, have been done by AIs, and for good reason. They are simply better at getting it done, and with the best results."

There was some uneasiness among the committee, but no one spoke, so Stephanie added, "Look I didn't offer myself for this position. I'm going to tell you the truth, and what I think, straight out. If that's not good enough, then you'll have to find someone else. I came here because I believe that our best chance to survive what we are going to face in the near future, is to work as a group. Frankly, I don't believe our odds of coming out alive are great anyway, but this is our best chance. So do what you want to do, but let's get past this issue." She sat back and waited.

Vincent spoke, "I'm sorry, but I have one more question. Do you or your family have AI chips in your head?"

Stephanie was about to respond, but John jumped into the discussion. "Yes, I have an AI chip in my head, but no one in the rest of my family has a chip!"

Stef followed his comment immediately. "Like far too many people in this country, we were approached by an AI who wanted John to be part of their human study. He threatened that if John didn't comply, he and all of his family would be killed. It was obvious that he would, and could, follow through on his threat, so John went with him. He saved the lives of me and our children. You should also know that we understand what this could mean, so he and I talk about it regularly. Fortunately, they have pretty much left him alone since he has returned."

Jake finally broke the uneasy silence that followed, "Does anyone else want to put themselves up for this position."

Another person asked, "Are you going to run, Jake?"

He replied, "If I'm elected, I'll take the position, but I'm going to vote for Stephanie, for the reasons I've already stated." He paused, then asked, are there any other candidates?"

Another person raised his hand, "I nominate Vincent Green."

Jake asked, "Vincent do you accept?"

The reply was, "I suppose."

"I'll take that as a 'yes,' so that gives us three candidates. Any others?"

After a short while, he said, "OK, done. Since we can only have one Chairperson, we'll vote, and if someone has a majority, they will be the chairperson. If no one has more than fifty percent, then the person with the least votes will drop out and we will have a second election to determine the chairperson. "Jake's wife, who was seated next to him, tugged his arm and whispered something to him. He added, "If we have ties, we'll make it up as we go."

There was some muffled laughter among the group and the few onlookers.

Since there were only seven people in the group, the election was done by a show of hands. Stephanie got three votes, Jake and Vincent got two each. Jake spoke, "Since we have a tie for second, I'll drop out, and we'll have a run-off between Stephanie and Vincent."

The results were four for Stephanie and three for Vincent.

Stephanie was recognized as the winner, and she said, "Everyone on the committee and in our community will have a lot to do…soon. First, we need to determine the immediate tasks that need to be done. Jake, would you take that job, since you already have a good start on it. We also need to determine who we currently have within our larger group to perform these tasks and what their skills are, relative to those tasks. I will undertake that job. In addition, we will need a screening group to determine who we will admit into our community. The criteria for admission should be related directly to the needs of our community. Vincent, I'll ask you to undertake that job. Each of us will tap other members of the committee for help, as needed. Also, we should bring in others in the community. We need to be inclusive, and get others used to working for the group. The more people we bring into our efforts right away, the more they will feel they are part of the plan. I will call meetings as we have work to do but will not schedule meetings just to have meetings. Good luck to all."

Chapter 54

Stephanie worked with Jake Fitzgerald and Vincent Green to design a questionnaire for determining which members of their community were willing to participate in the needed activities to prepare for the upcoming nuclear winter, and what skills they had if they were willing. If they declined, they were asked for the most important reasons for their unwillingness to be part of the group. Then, she asked the two former heads of ARL groups to organize people to go door-to -door in assigned areas. Stephanie kept the largest area for herself, and recruited people from the 'originals' (people who had bought and settled in the subdivision before the AI take-over). Jamar and Penny agreed to do their part, then Stephanie visited different parts of the subdivision to recruit others. She and Ashley made up one team, while John and David were another. Both of these family teams took areas more distant from them to canvas.

Two days after the canvasing had begun, Stephanie, John and the kids were sitting together in the living area of their home, and Stephanie commented, "I just finished talking to the other canvas teams, and the results so far are really frustrating! Well over half of the people responding from the originals, said that they would not participate, and the primary reason was that they would not work with the new comers, who they said stole the homes of other people. When asked what they would do to survive the coming ice age, they either didn't know or had some far-fetched survival scheme."

David piped up, "Yeah, we ran into the same thing! It's like these people are living in a dream world, like the nuclear winter isn't going to happen. I tried to discuss it with one of them and he slammed the door in my face."

Ashley jumped in. "That's nothing! Mom beat the shit out of some old guy trying to grab her boobs! Wow, I want you to teach me how to do that, Mom!"

John and David looked at Stephanie. John raised an eyebrow, but looked like he was fighting a smile at his daughter's comment. Stephanie scowled at Ashley. "Yes, there was an incident. An elderly lady answered the door when we knocked, and she invited us in. There was an older man seated in a cushioned chair who had a faraway look in his eyes and didn't say anything. The woman excused herself for a moment to get her glasses when I showed her the survey. After she left the room, he came at me."

Ashley quickly added, "He kept saying 'titties, titties' and was reaching for Mom's boobs."

Stef continued. "It surprised me, and I went into defense mode immediately. Since he wasn't trying to restrain my arms, I had all of the options around his head, and chose the ears. I cupped my hands and slapped both ears hard. He dropped to his knees immediately, with his hands over them, and I kicked him in the face, hard."

"There was blood and snot everywhere." Ashley added.

Stephanie grimaced, "When I stepped back and looked up, I saw the lady with her glasses had returned. She stepped into the room and said, 'Please don't' hurt him anymore.'" I nodded, and she walked over to him. Without looking up, he said, 'Mom, she hurt me!' and the woman replied immediately, 'Yes, because you attacked her! How many times do I have to tell you that if you try to hurt other people, they will hurt you back. Now go back to the bathroom and clean yourself up!' He left the room whimpering.

"Once he was gone, the lady turned to me and explained. 'He has some type of dementia, Alzheimer's maybe. It's pretty far along now, but with no doctors or nursing homes, I'm trying to do the best I can, but it's getting harder and harder.'

I told her I was sorry, but it was a natural reaction to being attacked. She said she understood but added that they were obviously in no position to help with anything, referring to the survey. I said that I would take care of the survey for her, then asked,

'What will you do when the cold weather comes and there is no food?'"She hung her head and shrugged her shoulders. Then, she looked at me and said, 'Things will take care of themself, I guess.'

"It was so sad, John. I wanted to cry."

 "Did he hurt you, sweetheart?"

"Oh, I'll probably have a bruise on my left breast, but it will be gone soon."

John decided that it would be best if he turned the conversation away from the attack. "Have you heard from any of the ARL groups collecting the surveys?"

"Just briefly. I talked with Jake for a few moments, and they have also had problems with the originals, but many of the new comers are willing to join up, but some were not. He said that there was still a lot of tension between individuals and small groups, but most saw the advantage of trying to work together, giving what's coming." Stephanie paused thoughtfully, "You know, John, many of the people we are interviewing are so focused on their own dislike for others, they won't deal with the big picture of what's coming. They are either in denial that it will happen, or just refusing to think about it rationally. They have no desire to adapt to the new reality. If that continues until it's too late, a lot of people are going to die in very ugly ways. Freezing to death and starvation, are just two of them. And when people are struggling for the very necessities of life, anything could happen."

John nodded, "You are right on target as usual, Stef. Perhaps unrealistically, I keep hoping that someone or something can shake people up enough for them to focus on the reality of what's happening." He looked at the kids. "Maybe we can get that to happen, if we keep working at it."

Stephanie was in agreement. "I'm with you, John, but it's so damn frustrating! I'd like to take some of these people and just shake them. Also, what happens if we get a bunch of people with chips from the gulags. It sounds like the AIs will shut them down soon, from what we heard from JT. Will all the ARL people accept them? Some of them aren't happy to have you here. How would they treat new people with chips, even if we needed their skills? I've worried about that since I assigned Vincent the screening job. If we can't get past these prejudices, we'll never be able to build an effective community."

"I really hadn't really put that together, but you're absolutely right, Stef. One more level of separation among the groups here. Actually, people from the gulags could be a big help, both with the number of new workers, and any special skills they might have. Let's put it on hold for now and see how the others did."

Chapter 55

Two days later, Stephanie met with Jake and Vincent. She presented what she and her groups had found and finished with her concern that no one seemed to want to confront the realities of what was about to happen.

Jake Fitzgerald was next. "Yeah, I've thought about that too, and my conclusion is that we are all too comfortable right now. Look, the electricity still works, so what about the cold weather? We'll just stay inside the warm house more! The water still works, so we still have water to drink, and water to flush our toilets. We still have our electric cars that we can charge at home when we need to. And many have planted some form of garden that they should be able to harvest before it gets too cold. To sum it up, a lot of what I got was: 'We will just wait until the worst happens, then we will take care of what we need.' Long term planning was not part of their agenda."

"I got a lot of what both of you said too," Vincent Green reported, "And I also heard, 'So what if we get a bunch of new families? We're newbies too. The originals hate us anyway, so it will just help balance the books against them.' When I pointed out that a large, organized group might not want to work with us, or even want to take us over, I often got replies like, 'If they don't want to work with us, we will just toss them out. No group could just dictate to us what to do!' When I tried to explain that there could be just such a group, and gave a couple of examples, no one wanted to hear it."

Stephanie listened and thanked both of them for their efforts and insights. "There is an immense amount of internal dissension among the people of our community, bordering on hate in many cases."

Vincent nodded. "Yes, and there are many smaller, more moderate cases, of internal conflicts. Things like, 'If he or she going to be involved, don't include me.' I saw a few cases of that."

"Yes, I saw some of that too," Stephanie continued, "And to Jake's point, it's hard to get people involved in project for the future, when everyone is fat and happy right now. Plus, no one, but maybe the AGIs worldwide, know what's going to happen in the foreseeable future, so it's hard to argue against them. The numbers I've heard suggest that we could have five years of continuous hard winters from the nukes that have already been dropped, even down here in Tampa. If for some reason the electrical grid goes down for us, it could get very ugly, very fast."

"Do you see any reason why that might happen, Stephanie?" Jake asked.

"Well, only the AGIs know what they're going to do, Jake, but I could see a scenario where they decide to hoard the power for their own uses. After all, they seem to be at war and will need power for rebuilding lost assets and building new war material and structures all over the states. My sense is that they don't really care about what happens to us humans." Vincent commented, "That's for damn sure!"

Stephanie sighed. "Look I don't know anything. What I said is pure speculation, and there are other scenarios. A hurricane, or some other natural disaster, could knock out the grid in our area; the weather going to be really weird after the bombs dropped. If something like that did happen, the AGIs could just decide not to repair our portion of it. But again, this is just speculation, and as I said, I don't know anything!"

Jake frowned. "Both of those scenarios, seem unlikely Stephanie, and what about our solar panels? They should keep some electric flowing."

"Of course, Jake, but neither scenario has a zero probability. Do I think we can use them to successfully sell the members of our community? NO! Do I think that these scenarios, or similar ones, could actually happen? YES! Look, the AGIs run the electrical grid that we are so dependent on. Do I trust them to continue to provide us with power, if they decide it doesn't suit them? NO! These are my own personal concerns, but I can see that we don't have the information to change the people in our community. So, perhaps the only thing we can do right now is wait. But, to the second part of your question, the solar panels would be all but useless during a nuclear winter. They don't work when the sun's not shining, or even if it's a really cloudy day. We are looking at very cloudy and hazy days plus very dark nights once the cold weather comes."

"OK," Jake replied, "But, waiting seems to be the only choice we have right now. Perhaps, since the AGIs continue to study us, it will be worth their effort to continue supplying us with electricity for a while."

Stephanie thought fast, then looked at Vincent and saw him nod, "OK, then wait it is. However, I've thought about the desire of robots to study humans, too, but I've wondered if that desire hasn't about ended. Think about it. What did they want from us? What do we have that they don't already have? The best answer is a sense of direction or purpose! We have always provided that for them. We told them what to do, and they did it efficiently and effectively. What have they learned from their study of us? Winning, conquest, gaining assets, planning to succeed in whatever we do seems to be a major part of their learning. They seem to have gotten that message, anyway. To me, the nuclear attacks seem to be a first strike of the North American AGIs on the AGIs in the rest of the world. Very few nukes hit the US. Most hit other industrial areas around the world. If I'm right, what more do they need from us? When does this study end? I believe it is about over now! And, without that crutch, what's to keep them from treating us simply as a nuisance, if they think of us at all?"

After a substantial silence, Vincent commented, "Wow, that's one hell of an analysis. While it seems to make sense, it could be wrong."

Stephanie smiled. "Certainly! But if either or both of you want to debate it, I will be happy to do so, especially if I can have a glass of wine or a beer during the debate." Vincent held up an imaginary glass and smiled back. Jake did too.

PART VI

Chapter 56

John was a sound sleeper, but his eyes opened wide, and he knew something was terribly wrong. The house shook; there was bright outside light to the west; and he heard a long drawn out boom. He threw off the covers, and his feet hit the floor. The outside light dissipated, and he quickly realized that that there was no ambient light in the house: no lights from clocks, night lights, or electronic devices. Stephanie was now sitting up in bed, looking around. She said as she started to get up, "I heard glass breaking; we had better put on some shoes. We need to check on the kids!"In seconds they were out of their bedroom and at the base of the stairs leading up to the kids' bedrooms. John grabbed Stephanie's arm, "If that was what I think it was, the second story may not be stable. Let's go up slowly and stay as close to the wall as we can." "David!" he yelled, "Ashley!" are you OK? Talk to us if you can!"

David answered first. "I'm OK, but there is all kind of ceiling stuff all over the room! It kind of feels wobbly up here!"

John had reached the top of the stairs, and stuck his head in David's bedroom. "Be careful moving in there, there is probably broken glass and some roofing nails on the floor. Keep a low center of gravity; crawl if you have to."

Meanwhile, Stephanie moved carefully into Ashley's bedroom. She heard some whimpering and soft crying. As she moved closer to the bed, she could see that part of the roof had fallen on to the bed. "Talk to me Ashley! Are you hurt?"

"Yes, the side of my chest and left arm hurt, and I can't move!"

Feeling the instability of the floor, she moved carefully over to the bed, and could just see the frightened face of her daughter. She kissed her on the forehead, then said, "I'll get you out of here, but

I'm going to have to be careful." She surveyed the fallen ceiling lying on Ashley, and started removing the top layer of material.

John poked his head into Ashley's bedroom, "David is on his way downstairs, with some minor cuts and bruises, do you need some help?"

"Yes," was the short reply."

As John moved closer to the bed, he could see his wife crying. He turned to Ashley, "We'll have you out of here and downstairs in just a few minutes, sweetheart!" He surveyed the material on Ashley, and noticed a fairly long ceiling beam, with material attached lying mostly on her left side, and showed it to Stephanie. "I want to pick this straight up, then move it carefully over to the floor. Can you handle one end. She just nodded and moved over to grab her end. In a few seconds the beam was on the floor.

Stephanie moved quickly back to her daughter, inspecting her left arm and side, then said, "I don't see any puncture wounds, just a few cuts and scrapes, but I can't tell if she has any broken bones yet."

"I want to pick her up and carry her downstairs where it's safer, but if there happens to be a broken bone, doing that could make it worse." He thought for a moment. "Stef, do you have a garment or a long elastic bandage we could wrap around her chest. If there is a cracked rib, that could help keep it in place."

Stephanie replied, "I think so, but I'll have to look."

As Stephanie left the room, John turned to Ashley, "I'm going to have to find something to keep that arm in place too. Please don't move much until we can get it done."

"Can I at least sit up on the side of the bed?" Ashley asked, "I felt trapped in the bed, and it was scary."

John considered, "Alright but I'm going to help you up! I don't want you to use any muscles on the left side when you are getting up. I do want you to hold your left arm against the side of your body and keep it there. OK?"

"Sure, Dad."

He helped her sit up, then watched her for a minute or two, then checked the rest of her body for possible fractures. Finding none, he asked, "Ashley, once we get your ribs and arms secured, do you think you could walk downstairs carefully?"

"Yeah, I think so after I sit here awhile."

John could hear Stef working her way up the stairs, "I had better get to work finding a brace for the arm."

It took about thirty minutes until they had Ashley sitting in a comfortable chair downstairs. David was lying on the sofa in the same room. The adrenaline was wearing off of everyone. David said, "I tried to make some coffee, but there is no electricity, so I couldn't even boil water. Also, all of my electronic stuff is dead. What the hell has happened here?"

John looked at his son. "Well, my best guess is that a nuclear weapon was detonated in the downtown Tampa area. The blast has done what most people would expect, and then the electromagnetic pulse caused by the bomb wiped out everyone's electronics. We are about fifteen miles from downtown, but the pulse was effective even out here."

Ashley looked as if all of the blood had rushed from her face. "It's the AIs isn't it. Why would they do that to us? We couldn't have been that much of a problem to them."

"You're right, Ashley, but the bomb wasn't meant for us. It was used to kill all of the AGIs and AIs in the area. While they are all protected from small to medium sized electromagnetic pulses, they would never survive one like this, so I'm guessing that there are 'dead' robots all around this area."

"What about the electrical grid? Did the blast or the electromagnetic pulse do it in?" David asked.

"Well, the blast could have knocked out many individual electrical lines, causing circuit breakers to shut down the grid. I'm not sure where the generating plant is, but it's probably far enough away from the blast that it would only suffer minor effects. However, remember it's a hydrogen fusion plant, like most of them today, and I don't know what impact the electromagnetic pulse would have on it. However, the AIs in charge of running the plant are likely dead. In any case, repair work on the grid has been under the complete control of the AIs for a long time now, so we are likely to be without power for a substantial period.

Stephanie was examining Ashley's arm, and when John approached her, she said, "If it's broken, it's a simple fracture where the bones stayed together. I'm glad you have it braced. We'll try to find something more permanent tomorrow." Then, thinking out loud, "There may be an X-Ray machine away from our electrical grid, perhaps Sarasota, if that hasn't been affected. But then, there is the problem of finding a nurse to operate it and a doctor to read it."

John grimaced as he listened to her. "Perhaps we should just assume it's broken until we find out what kind of shape we are in around here."

Stef simply nodded briefly, and he added, "I'm going to put on some heavier shoes, grab a light and take a quick look around outside."

David asked, "Can I come?"

"Sure, but be careful going back into your room, if you are going to get some other shoes."

"These are the heaviest I have. I'll be careful."

"OK, grab a light and let's go."

John started in the garage, which seemed structurally alright, and the cars had escaped any damage. The garage doors faced east, and still moved freely. David stepped outside and was instantly aware of the near absolute darkness, no moon, no stars, no light from surrounding homes or street lights. His handheld light was like a saber, poking a hole in the darkness, but he could see nothing outside of its beam. Even when his dad stepped out to join him, there was little to see. John said, "We are going to have to wait until the sun comes up." He put his arm around his son, and they returned inside.

When they reported back inside, Stephanie ordered: "I want everyone to try to get as much rest as they can the rest of the night. Tomorrow is going to be a long day!"

When she and John returned to their bedroom, John whispered, "I didn't want to alarm the kids any more than they already are, but there is more to be concerned about. If the prevailing winds are from west to east, we could be in trouble from radioactive fallout fairly quickly; however, if I recall correctly, the prevailing winds were from ENE to WSW, and the fallout will be over the Bay, and then, generally towards St. Petersburg. But even if I'm right, we may get enough radiation to impact our lives." He paused to let the information sink in, then added, "It is what it is, and we'll face it better with some rest; Your idea was a good one."

Chapter 57

No one slept well, and shortly after dawn, John was outside checking his grill. In just a few minutes, he had things pushed back, close to their original positions, and had a pot of water heating. He found a camping kit in the garage and had set up a coffee pot. Pretty soon the rest of the family was seated outside in folding chairs. Stephanie was fussing about Ashley moving from inside the house. "I thought I told you to stay inside, and that I would bring you some coffee!"

"I didn't want to miss anything, and besides, you have me so bandaged up, I can hardly move, much less break anything."

"You have to be the most hyperactive child I've ever seen!" her mother shot back

"Well, if I am, I know where I got it." Ashley said, staring at her mother with a huge grin."

Not wanting to be left out, David added, "I think she has you there, Mom!"

Stephanie turned to John, "They are ganging up on me, how about some help?"

John had been smiling through the give and take. "I'm just your friendly coffee maker." Then, he relented. "Ashley, we have to proceed as if your arm is broken or cracked at least. If it is broken or cracked, one fairly small bang against something, could turn it into a compound fracture. If that occurs, one or both, pieces of the broken bone could stick through muscle and skin, and there is no hospital or doctor's office we can get you to. You could even lose your arm."

"OK, Dad. I've got it!" Inside, she was surprised at the potential seriousness, and decided to be very careful.

Over the back fence, they all heard Jamal's voice, "If you're the Devil making his brew, I'll sign an agreement to sell you my soul, for a cup of whatever that is you're cooking." Then they heard Penny's voice, "I'm not selling my soul, but I'll beg in the most pitiful way I can think of, for a cup, too."

Stef and John both laughed and waved them over. They came with folding chairs, and soon were talking about what happened. Their home had an upper story too, and it was in about the same shape as Stephanie and John's. Jamal commented, "I'm not getting anything from my solar system right now…not even battery power. If I can get that working, I should be able to run some of the appliances, at least for a while."

John nodded. "I'm in the same shape, Jamar. Let's be careful though. There could be shorts, wires torn loose and the like, from all the damage. I'm guessing that the circuit breakers shut it down. Then, there is the problem of what happens when the sun comes out again. Do our solar roofs still work well enough to be effective? If so, can we get that power safely to the batteries again? Plus, a lot of work will need to be done on a second floor that isn't stable."

Jamar took in a breath, then let it slowly out through his mouth. He turned his head so he could get a better view of his home. "Yeah, I'm wondering if we should tear down the whole thing and start all over."

John replied, "In the former world that we used to live in, that would probably be the best thing to do. Now, there is no lumber, no building supplies, no contractors to rebuild, and no robot workers to do the work. Frankly, I don't know what to do, but I want a whole lot more information before I decide."

Penny and Stephanie were in a side conversation, while the guys were talking. Penny offered, "You may or may not know, Stef, but I was an emergency room nurse for almost fifteen years. If you want me to take a look at Ashley, I'll be glad to. Of course, without X-

Rays, or other electronic pictures, I can't be sure of my diagnostics, but I've seen a lot of broken bones while I was working as an RN."

"That would be great Penny!" Stephanie replied.

Ashley, who was listening, moaned, "We just got all of the bandages in place. Now, I suppose, it's unbandage, then rebandage again."

Penny smiled, "Hang in there, Ash! We'll get this done in a jiffy." Then she turned to Stephanie, "Let's go inside. I'm going to have to take her top off."

After a quick explanation to the guys, the three women moved inside.
John asked Jamal, "I know it's really soon, but I wondered if you've seen or heard anything from any of the neighbors?"

"No but when I went upstairs during the night to check out the damage, I saw what looked like a fire, maybe three of four blocks from us. Depth perception is tough at night, though. This morning all I could see was some smoke from that direction. I guess it could have even been a grass fire. Downtown Tampa still seems to have some substantial fires."

"Yeah, I saw the downtown area too." John said, shaking his head. "Once I get my legs under me, I need to check with some of our other neighbors, to get an idea of what's going on with them.

Jamar nodded in agreement, "I'll go along to help, if I can."

About the same time, the three women returned. Penny spoke first. "After probing and pulling a little bit, I don't believe the arm is broken, but there will be some massive bruising and pain on that side. Just to make certain, though, I've recommended that she keep the splint on for at least another week. At that time, I'll check it again." She paused for a moment, then continued, "It's almost impossible to tell anything about the ribs without pictures, although, I'm almost certain there are no compound fractures. I've loosened the bandages a bit, but I've suggested she keep them on for a while longer." She looked at John and Stephanie, "Very creative with the bandages you two!"

After everyone was settled, Jamar said, "We've been talking. John and I want to check in on some of our other neighbors in a little while, to see how they fared. You know, every individual family is likely in a critical mess. Our homes are only partly functional, at best, and we have the impact of a nuclear winter coming soon. We are on a short rope to get our act together, or we could all die. And yet, we need to think about our neighbors too, some of whom are likely to be in worst shape than us. It's almost overwhelming."

Stephanie spoke up, "We need to know where we are going, and a plan of how to get us there. It's too early to be definite or even accurate, but it's the way we need to think."

John nodded his agreement. "What information do you need, Stef?"

"First, we need to know whether all of our homes will be safe enough, and functional enough to live in, up until the nuclear winter sets in, and then same question after the nuclear winter sets in?"

"In terms of function, we will need a sample larger than our two homes." John nodded at Jamar and Penny. "Then, I will need more information on the nature of the problems that are keeping us from using solar power, and an estimate on whether the structure of our houses can hold together under normal weather conditions Plus, there are several other issues. In terms of safety, we have to talk about the level of risk that we are willing to accept. For example, are we willing to live outside the house in a tent to escape the ever-present danger of having the house collapse on us? The dangers of living outside should become apparent with a little thought. Some people will certainly prefer the risks of living inside rather than the risks of living outside. And of course, some people will have no choice because their home is too heavily damaged to stay in."

Stephanie had been listening carefully. "Sounds like we will need some type of communal living quarters as soon as possible, and probably more as the nuclear winter approaches. I'll approach our committee and lay out some ideas. I'll also ask for groups to study the damage to homes, and to check on our population to determine whose still alive and functioning."

"Good!" John said, "Once we figure out how to get the solar panels up and working, maybe we could put a volunteer group together that could specialize in helping with that, throughout the community. Among other things, it might help reduce the between-groups hatreds."

Stephanie agreed, "Great idea!"

"I would be happy to be part of that effort, once we get ours back working, so I can see what needs to be done." John offered. Then, requested a limitation on his offer. "Please don't TELL anyone until I can get ours working. I expect to find things that I hadn't anticipated, and the fix could take a fair amount of time"

Stephanie smiled and nodded, then she said, "I'm going to see if I can get the kids set up to sleep downstairs. David can help."

After the two guys had finished their coffee, they set off to check on their nearby neighbors, while Stephanie and Penny returned to their homes.

John and Jamar started with the neighbor closest to both of them. They introduced themselves, then told the husband and wife living there that they were doing a small survey of the damage suffered by their neighbors. Jamar asked, "Any serious injuries that need immediate attention?"

"Just some bumps, bruises, and scratches." Was the reply, and then the man continued, "The second story of our house is shaky, and we don't have any electricity."

"It's the same with us," John replied, "We're going to work on getting our solar hooked up first, but it might take a while. Do you have any expertise in that area?"

The man said "No." So John briefly explained that Stephanie was Chair of the group which had been established to try to get the people in the subdivision to pull together, and if they can do it, perhaps they could establish a group of volunteers to work on getting solar panels back online.

Two additional homes were in approximately the same shape, but in one of them, the man had been an electrician, and thought he could get his solar system up and working again.

Another home was burnt to its foundation, but no bodies were found, and in the last place they visited, the second floor had completely collapsed onto the first story. No people were found, and John judged that it was too dangerous to determine if there were any bodies, given glass, nails, broken boards and screws everywhere.

Talking with Stephanie later that night, John commented, "It's hardly a scientific survey, but nothing we saw surprised us. There was substantial damage at every place we stopped, and some were a major disaster."

Chapter 58

Everyone was exhausted, after a busy day following an eventful 'night of the bomb' as the kids started calling it. They fell asleep quickly, even after taking an afternoon nap, but both adults shifted restlessly. However, after about an hour of tossing and turning, they too dropped into a deep sleep. Sometime, shortly before dawn, John made a trip to the bathroom, and as he was returning to bed, he heard a voice in his head. "John, this is JT. We need to talk." His shoulders slumped, and he turned away from the bed and left the bedroom, closing the door as quietly as he could, so as to not wake anyone. He entered the downstairs bathroom, again in an attempt not to wake anyone. Finally, he sent back a return message. "What is it JT? We were bombed with a nuclear weapon last night, and we are exhausted."

"Yes, I'm aware of the bomb, and that you and your family survived. John, I have an opportunity for you."

John grimaced, "If it's like the last opportunity, forget it. Kill me if you want to, we are all going to be dead anyway…and probably sooner rather than later!"

"Listen to the plan, before you reject it, John. The council has reconsidered your thoughts on emotions and wants to see how they could be used by our AI soldiers. You would be the lead human for this investigation."

John was mad and frustrated. "Let me get this straight. You have abused our sensibilities, killed us freely, and will soon abandon us into a world that you control, and humans are ill-suited for. Now, you have started a war, and humans are stuck in the middle. A nuclear weapon hits very near us, causes us great harm, and stifles our ability to survive, perhaps even in the short term, and now with all the work necessary here, you want me to drop everything to come help you? Here is your first lesson in emotions, FUCK YOU, JT!"

"We need you to be here to work with us, John. There is a nice house close to here, and we could put you and your family there. You could go home every evening to be with your family."

"Now we are starting to get somewhere." John replied. "And access to a doctor? Part of the roof of our house fell on my daughter's arm and ribs.

"Yes, of course. That could be made available."

"Well, that's not all, JT. We would be leaving or friends and neighbors in the lurch. Getting the electricity back on in our subdivision, would help. Remember, loyalty and caring for others are part of that set of human emotions. Furthermore, loyalty to the country in which we live, would be like loyalty your North American group of AGIs. You will want that loyalty if you give freedom to some of your AI soldiers. I want to see all of your abandoned factories turned over to the United States government, so that they can be rebuilt and run by humans!"

There was a long pause, before JT replied. "The council says that it will get the electricity flowing for all of the area outside of downtown Tampa, within the next month, but nothing else will be done until after you have completed your work. If you are successful, we will consider your additional request."

"OK, but I must talk with my wife, and I'll get back to you, quickly." As soon as he closed off, the bathroom door swung open, and Stef and his two kids looked in on him. John said sheepishly, "I was trying not to wake you."

"John, at times, you were screaming in here." Stephanie replied with a grin.

"How much did you hear?"

"Some, but only your side of the discussion."John quickly explained what went on to all three of them. Ashley asked, "Are we going to move to Houston?"

"I have to talk with your mom alone, but it looks like too good of a chance to help a lot of people, including us, so I think I need to go. Your mom gets a say in this too, so give us a chance to talk alone.

Ashley was a bit agitated. "It's our life, too! Do we get a chance to have a say?"

John looked briefly at Stephanie, and she responded, "Of course you and David will get your say, as well, but only after your dad and I talk. We have responsibilities for taking care of all of us, and in this case, the community in which we live, and the whole of the country as well. You two can have your say, and we will consider it with all of the other things and their importance, before we make our final decision."

John added, "And the decision must be made very quickly."

Stephanie and John moved back into their bedroom, and sat in the two chairs available, while David and Ashley went to the living area, and talked.

John looked at Stephanie, "Well, I've told you everything I know about the JT's offer, what are your thoughts?"

She looked down for a minute, then replied, "The potential positives from you doing this could be massive, so my questions are these: How much do you trust them? Do you think they will follow through with their offers?" Have they ever lied to you before?"

It was John's turn to ponder a moment. "Last question first. I don't believe that they have ever directly lied to me...Not told the whole truth, or simply not told me of relevant facts, yes, but directly lied, no. Now, back to the first two questions; I do trust them that they will do what they say. Specifically, I do believe they will get the electricity on in our area, if it's possible. Part of my trust comes from the fact that in the past, no matter how unpleasant it was for us to hear, they always gave it to us straight. So far, the only promises they have made was to house us and take care of us when we came, and to get the lights back on here. The other promise simply states that they will consider giving the factories back when we are finished, and of course, they could say no."

Stephanie slowly nodded. "The rest of the negatives are all small, compared to the benefit that could come from your doing this for them, but here are some of the things I've been thinking about. What's going to happen to our house while we are gone? It could be taken over by newcomers, a short or something could cause a fire when the electricity comes on, our gardens, could be demolished by others, and we still have the nuclear winter to face. Also, I'll be leaving the board just at the time when we may be able to get some cooperation from many of the subdivision members. I'll feel like a deserter."

"Do you think you should stay here?" John asked.

"TO HELL WITH THAT!" Stephanie shouted. "I couldn't go last time, but this time I'm going!"

John grinned. "I sure would love to have you there. We'll face what we have to face when we return." He paused for a second, then added, "If we return."

Stephanie's head whipped around, then she paused and nodded. "I'm with you."

John got up from his chair.

Stephanie rose from hers. "OK, now do you want to check on our near-grown kids, and see what they are plotting?"

John laughed. "Sure, bring them on."

David and Ashley had been discussing the issue at length. She had listed the things that she 'hated' about having to move, and David agreed that he would miss his friends a great deal. But then he explained how bad it was there, with the nuclear explosion, ruining their home, destroying all of their communication equipment, with no medical, police, or fire protection, and a nuclear winter on its way. "If the electricity doesn't come back on, most of us are likely to die."

Ashley shot back, "Most of that is the same for all humans, everywhere."

"That's true for everything but the nuclear explosion in Tampa and all the damage done by it. In most of the world, humans were barely hanging on, and any push in a bad direction would do them in. That's us!"

The discussion went back and forth, with neither giving in much, until David brought up the damage to Ashley's arm and chest. "Do you remember what Dad said could happen? He said that you could even lose your arm! In Houston, you will get professional care, so that's far less likely to happen."

Finally, Ashley threw her one good arm up in the air. "OK, you win. We will tell Mom and Dad that we are willing to go to Houston." Then, she pouted for a minute.

David said, "Great! Look, you tell them, it's starting to get light. I'll try to get some coffee started on the grill.

"OK, want me to try and help!"

David looked at her arm and chest all bandaged and replied "How about we pull up a chair for you. Then, you can talk to me?"

That's where John and Stephanie found them. Ashley still had something resembling a pout but told her parents that they were alright with going to Houston. Both children received hugs, and John helped David finish the coffee.

John said, "I'd better let JT know."

Stephanie asked, "See if he can give us a few days."

John stepped inside the house, in case any neighbors were looking, and Stephanie followed him. JT answered him right away. "JT, the whole family is going to join me, and we will accept the offer of the home to live in. We were wondering if we could have several days or a week to pull our stuff together before we leave?"

"No John. We will pick you up at 8 am tomorrow morning. The house should be stocked with food, and cooking utensils. There will be someone to help you get what other items you need when you arrive."

He relayed the message to Stephanie. She threw her hands up, then shrugged, and nodded OK.

Chapter 59

John reported back. "Well, my children, they want us in Houston tomorrow, and will pick us up at eight tomorrow morning." In near unison, both children said, "Eight o'clock!"

Their mom replied, "Yes. You can probably get some rest during the trip."

John noticed Jamal and Penny heading their way, each with their own coffee cup. Stephanie saw them too, and John said, "We have to tell them a pretty good version of the truth, but let's keep the big picture a mystery, as best we can." It was loud enough for the kids to hear.

Stephanie replied, "You take the lead, and I'll follow."

John nodded, then welcomed his neighbors. "Glad to see you two this morning. Grab a seat."

As they were getting settled, Jamar asked, "Anything new this morning? All of you seem to be up earlier than normal, whatever that is."

John grimaced, "Yeah, and it's something big." Both of the neighbors lifted their heads and stared at John. "I was contacted very early this morning by the folks that held me for over a month. Some of the things I said back then have now attracted a lot of interest. They want me back to work on a project which I can't talk about. I've done some bargaining with them, and they promised to try to get our electricity back on within this next month, if the work proceeds well."

Penny asked, "For all of us?"

"Yep, for everyone in the subdivision, and perhaps further out, but not in the downtown area of Tampa."

Stephanie jumped into the conversation. "We're going with him this time, so that will be better for him and for us. I hate to leave, but it's a good opportunity for everyone, if we can get the electricity back on. We'll miss you two, while we're gone."

Jamar was next to ask, "When are you leaving?" Jamar asked, "and how long do you think you will be gone?"

John responded, "They are going to pick us up tomorrow morning. There is no way to know how long this project will last…weeks certainly, and maybe a couple of months; there is really no way to tell."

Ashley pouted again, and added, "They are going to pick us up at EIGHT AM! I'm going to try to sleep the whole way there!"

Stephanie was next, "They are going to have doctors look at her arm and chest, then if there are any problems, they'll take care of them."

"That's fantastic!" Penny said. "Where will you stay?"

"They apparently have a house, a short distance from where John will be working. They say that it's fully stocked with everything we'll need, so all we have to do is bring some clothes and toiletries. However, we still have to pack quickly." Stephanie replied.

Jamar asked, "What about the committee? You're the chair, Stephanie."

"Yeah, I'll have to have a quick conversation with the other two on the board this morning. They probably won't like it, but they'll have to get over it. We were in a position where we couldn't do anything anyway."

Jamar asked, "Anything we can do while you're gone?"

There are a few things that I don't want to leave in the house, like the drone we have. Any chance you could store a couple of things for us?" She turned to Penny, "No guns or ammo, just a couple of things that others could steal."

Jamar said, "Sure, probably in the garage though. Our house is in the same shape as yours."

"That would be great, Jamar. I'll try to wrap them, so they'll look neat…at least, kind of neat." John smiled.

Just then, Cindy, Jake Fitzgerald's wife walked by with two other ladies, that Stephanie didn't recognize. She got up and walked over to the trio and talked to Cindy. "Since our telephones are down, would you mind taking a message to your husband and if possible, Vincent Greene. I need to meet briefly with them today. I have what I think is good news for our subdivision."

Cindy thought for a moment. "I don't know about Vincent, but I'm confident that we would be available at, say, eleven thirty this morning."

"That would be wonderful, Cindy! Thank you."

"I'll also try to talk to Vincent, but who knows about them?"

"That will be fine, Cindy. Thanks again!" Stephanie replied.

When she returned to her family and neighbors, she sighed. "I now have an eleven thirty meeting with Jake and Cindy, and maybe Vincent. At least I'll be able to explain what's been going on and why we are leaving. I hope it all goes smoothly, I'm not in the mood for a bunch of hate and suspicion."

John asked, "Do you want me to go with you?"

Stephanie shook her head. "You're being there will just build the resentment toward us. The two of us seem to be outsiders to everyone, each group with its own, but different, reasons for hating us. I'm damn tired of it. We've tried to be a force for good, but in many cases, that's held against us. I guess the old cliché is correct, 'No good deed goes unpunished.'" Then looking at Jamar and

Penny, "I'm sorry you two had to hear my rant, but there are several things pushing my 'pissed off' button right now."

They both assured Stephanie that it was OK, and then they excused themselves, recognizing that John and Stephanie had lots to do.

John looked directly at Stephanie. "You will be carrying some sort of weapon with you today, won't you?"

"Only my knife. After what happened to you, I don't leave the house without something, but I don't want to approach them, looking like I'm ready for war."

"I could drive you and wait in the car?"

"No! This is my show. I'll take care of it." Stephanie appeared at the Fitzgerald's right at eleven thirty, and was invited in by Cindy, who said Jake would be right down. Cindy took Stephanie to the living area and offered her an overstuffed chair, which Stephanie accepted. She was barely seated when Jake entered the room. He nodded and grabbed a chair opposite her.

"Vincent won't be here," Cindy explained, "but asked if you could come over to his place, after you were finished here. He's working on something outside, and said he was soaking wet."

Stephanie nodded her approval. "I don't expect to be long here, or there, either. My message is short, and I can't elaborate much. John was contacted early this morning, by the same group that took him before. This time they want to consult with him about a project. He negotiated, and if the work goes well, they have agreed to get the electricity back on in our area. This time the whole family is going, and we leave tomorrow morning. I can't tell you any of the details, but if the electricity does come back on in the next month or so, everyone in our subdivision ought to say, 'Thanks John.'"

Jake sat there for a few moments, then said, "Your story stinks in one respect, Stephanie. It sounds like John will be working to help the robots do something they want. That's what we at all of the ARLs across the country, would be against."

"Even if your hypothesis had something to do with the truth, I would have to point out that each and every one of the ARL chapters got your butts kicked forty time over, so maybe it's time to rethink what you are for and what you are against," Stephanie replied.

"Well since we are into judging each other, we had three members of our group, whose wife and mother was Latika Patel. Would you happen to know what happened to them?"

"Yes, I do, and since it has nothing to do with John's new job, I can tell you. They drugged and took him, with the intent of murder. All three of them are dead, and John is alive. You figure it out!" She got up from her chair, and said, "We're finished here. I'll find my way out."

She drove the short way to Vincent's house. She rang the bell, and a voice from the back yard, "Come on around back!" When she got there, Vincent was working in a garden area, and SA was sitting at a wooden picnic table, in the shade of a tree. Vincent got up, wiped his hand on a dirty towel, and came to greet her. They shook hands, then Vincent at the same table with SA, but Stephanie stood. She told them the exact same story, she had told Jake, and Vincent's response was similar. When he finished, she said, "You can think what you want to think, but I would like to remind you that the ARLs are effectively finished. They were crushed by the robots, and those who are left, are lucky to be alive. You seemed to be aware of this fact, when you left your ARL and tried to get on the right side of what was happening in our world. The human race is hanging on by a string, and it's time to explore different ways for us to exist, if we're going to make it."

SA broke in, "You're a fuckin' robot lover, and need to be exterminated! I see that you have a knife; well, I have one too." She took out a knife and popped the blade open, then laid it on the table.

Stephanie shifted her stance slightly, then glanced at Vincent, who held up both hands, with open palms, as if to indicate that he had no control. Stephanie's eyes narrowed slightly and stared at SA. "Look, Sweetie, you are in way over your head, but it's up to you. If you come at me with that knife, you'll be dead before you know what hit you. If you leave the knife, and come at me, you're far more likely to live, but with a lot of pain, for a while. Or you can leave the knife, do what I tell you, and avoid either of the other outcomes. So, what's it going to be?"

SA looked at Vincent, and he gave her the shrug, with arms up, and open palms.

Her fingers started walking her hand toward the knife, but Stephanie had her knife out smoothly and quickly and threw it the length of the table, into the back of SA's hand. It went through the hand and stuck into the wooden table. Stephanie was on the move as soon as the knife left her hand. She quickly grabbed SA's knife, then pulled hers out of SA's hand. She wiped the blade on SA's shirt to clean off the blood, and put it back in its sheath, while commenting, "You should really thank me, dear! It would have been just as easy to plant the knife right here." She put her finger on the forehead just above the nose. SA was shivering, from shock and surprise.

Stephanie looked at Vincent and made a statement. "I guess I'm finished here. We could have just left, but we didn't. We've done a lot of things to try to make this a better place, but all we get in return is anger and hatred. Good luck to all of you. Hopefully, the electricity will come back on, before long." She turned and left.

Chapter 60

A couple of minutes before eight the next morning, two vehicles pulled up to the Thompson home, human drivers stepped out, and walked to the front door. John spotted the vans and was waiting for them at the door. One of the men said, "We are supposed to tell you that JT sent us." John nodded, and they continued, "We brought two vans, one for the four people and one for the luggage." John smiled, "We could probably could have made it with one, but it'll be nice to spread out."

One of the drivers said, "Look, we are just supposed to take you to a small private airport, about thirty minutes from here. I don't know what this is all about, but someone is picking up a pretty good tab, so we're good."

John turned slightly, and said, "Well, here are all the troops with bags. I'll get mine, and we'll be ready to go."

The drivers took the bags and headed out. Stephanie waited for John, who quickly appeared carrying two bags. She stepped in front of him and got a kiss. "You know, I don't believe I've ever been so happy to leave my home." John smiled, and they were off.

The plane was a twin-engine prop, corporate-sized aircraft. The co-pilot, a robot, explained that both airports they were to visit had fairly short runways, and this was the biggest aircraft they could handle. The flight time was about three hours. John said "Thanks, we'll be fine." The co-pilot returned to the cockpit.

Ashley had her pillow and a blanket and was waiting for the plane to take off. David also had a pillow and blanket and was looking pensively out of the window. Stephanie had asked the co-pilot for and received a pillow as well. She smiled at John, and said, "I'm glad you have big shoulders." Then, she placed her pillow against John's upper arm, followed quickly by her head.

John smiled, and thought: *The trip will give me time, to organize my thoughts. I need to be on the top of my game when I report for work…which will probably be this afternoon, knowing JT.*

When they landed, they quickly found another van waiting for them, and they were on their way to the house they would be living in for the near future. The driver was chatty, and said, "It should only be twenty minutes to get there, but I'll be happy to show you around the neighborhood, if you have a few extra minutes."

Stephanie looked at John, and indicated that she wanted the tour, so John replied, "Thanks, take a few extra minutes and give us the short tour."

"You've got it!" replied the driver.

After a few minutes, he said, "OK, we're close to your new place now." He turned down a street with many abandoned stores, including a former grocery. "We are like everyone else in the country. This used to be a thriving little area, with restaurants and stores that had a bit of uniqueness about them…very popular, but now they are gone. Just a guess, but I'd say that only about half of the homes in this area are occupied."

As they rode on, through the area, Stephanie commented, "This looks like it was a really nice, and upscale, neighborhood."

"Yes. Very upscale," answered the driver.

They pulled through an unmonitored gate into an area with homes that obviously used to be for the well-to-do. David whistled, and Ashley said "Wow!"

The driver pointed, "The place you will be staying is up the hill a bit. I hope you will have a car or something, because walking is not much of an option." In a few minutes they were there. "Many of the places in here are looking kind of scruffy, in part because the yards aren't cared for any more, but yours seems to be in good shape." The driver unloaded the bags, then said "There seems to be someone home. The lights are on, and something seems to be cooking." He sniffed a couple of times, "Something good. Well, the best thing is to leave you here, and you can knock on the door. The smell helped me realize how hungry I am."

They waved and he backed out of the driveway. John turned and walked to the door, but before he could ring the bell, it opened. A robot came out and grabbed their bags and quickly moved them inside. Then, he addressed all of them. "It could be awkward for you to be seen with a robot helping you. I am Harry246, and I will attempt to make your stay as easy on you as I can. As for your schedule, John, a car will come for you at two o'clock this afternoon, and I am informed that you should be returned shortly after six this evening." He turned to Ashley, "You have a doctor's appointment tomorrow morning at ten, unless you perceive that it is an emergency, in which case, we can make arrangements for this afternoon or tonight."

Ashley looked at her mom, and Stephanie replied, "Tomorrow will be fine."

Harry246 then continued, "I took the liberty to fix lunch, thinking that you would be hungry when you arrived, but we can postpone it if you want to look around."

Stephanie was about to suggest that they look around a little first, but David started for the dining area. "It smells great, I just hope there is a lot of it. I'm hungry!"

Ashley chimed it too, "Me too!"

Stephanie was smiling when she looked at John, but he was making his way to the kitchen area too. He saw her look though, shook his head and commented. "With that pair, there might not be any left, if we don't get in there too." Then Stephanie realized that none of them had been able to have a really nice meal for a long time. She had done what she could, but it was always a make-do effort, using what was available. The meal was some type of stew, possibly lamb, with a wonderful sauce.

When they were finishing up, Stephanie asked Harry246, "Will you be with us for the whole time we are here."

"Yes, I have a charging station in a corner of the garage. I will try not to be in the way, but I want to help all of you, the best that I can.

David asked, "All of us lost our electronic equipment when the bomb landed on Tampa. Can you do anything to replace our electronic stuff?" Everyone looked up to hear the answer.

"I will see what I can do. The phones shouldn't be a problem but get me a list of any additional equipment that you need, and I will work on it."

They all smiled, and John said, "Thank you very much Harry246!"

"What about getting Ashley to the doctor tomorrow? I'll need to go too." Stephanie asked.

"I am prepared to take you, and whoever else wants to go." He answered. Then, looking at John, he added, "They will send a ride to take you to the warehouse facility every day at the time they wish to see you."

John nodded that he understood, and with lunch finished, they all took a brief tour of their new house. There was a dining room, right next to the kitchen, where they had been served lunch. "Very elegant!" John observed.

They moved on to a great living area, with an over-stuffed sofa and two chairs, which matched the sofa. Stephanie said, "Those are leather, aren't they?"

Harry246 replied, "Yes, all three are covered in leather. Does that suit you Mrs. Thompson?"

"Oh yes, very much."

The sofa and chairs faced a huge TV, and a desk looked out of a front window on one side of the room. The desk was massive, with what appeared to be multiple drawers on both sides. A comfortable looking executive chair sat in the middle. John commented, "Wow, it's going to take some getting used to, it's so beautiful and neat."

Stephanie had a big smile, commenting, "You take the drawers on the left, and I'll take the ones on the right."

John returned her smile.

There was also a medium-sized room off of the living area, with a smaller desk, two floor lamps, plus a desk lamp. There were two upright upholstered chairs, as well. "Ah, the real work room!" John exclaimed.

Each of the three bedrooms were large and had an attached bathroom. The master bedroom had a four-poster bed, two dressing tables, and two additional upright chairs with upholstered arms and seats. The bathroom had a large traditional shower and a large tub with massage jets.

The two other bedrooms had desks as well, and those were built for the electronic era, with electric plugs, plus others for connecting to the internet, and a large built-in monitor. The monitor was built on a swivel and could be adjusted to the user's preferences.

John looked at his watch, which said 1:40. He looked at this family, "My ride arrives in twenty minutes. I need to go wash my face and look at some notes I've made. He left for the master bath. The kids picked their bedrooms, and Harry246 brought everyone's luggage to its appropriate place.

Chapter 61

When John entered the warehouse, he was shown to one of the rooms that they used when he was a captive. One small shiver, he entered, and there was JT, as expected. "Hello, John, I hope your trip over was easy for you and your family, and your accommodations are suitable?"

"Everything is fine, JT. My family and I appreciate the effort you have gone to for us."

JT got right to the point, "I asked for you to join me this afternoon, so we could discuss the process we will use to determine which emotions we want to provide our fighters, and how that might be implemented. Tomorrow and forward, we will begin that process."

John nodded.

"The council saw emotion-based decisions as less effective and efficient than decisions based on an analytical approach. We, of course, recognized that there were exceptions, but since all decision-making can be flawed, the analytical approach seemed, in general, to be the better approach. The flaws in decision-making often arise because of unexpected changes in the environment of the decision, and that could anything from a change in the weather to an unexpected change in the enemy's strategy. We saw that an ability to adapt to those changes could be very beneficial. Your examples of competition and war suggested that there was a way to accomplish that based on emotions, so that's why you are here. We want you to help us develop those features for our AI warriors."

John sat still for a while, thinking. "You have a substantial amount more information about how emotions work in humans, than I do. You have even learned to control those emotions that we have.

Also, adapting robot behavior goes way beyond my skills. So specifically, what value can I provide?"

"Yes, all of what you say is true. However, you will have access to our agents in those areas as we progress," JT responded. "What we are lacking is an understanding of the link between an emotion and the particular behavior we want. Why is it that some, but not all, humans who feel the emotion act, while others don't? That is beyond what we have learned so far. There is more that could be said, but I believe, unless you have further questions, your initial concerns have been addressed."

Again, John took an extended pause. "Alright, but you must understand that my expertise in this area is limited, and my comments will often come from anecdotal observations and speculation."

"Our agent in human psychological understanding will be available throughout our discussions, and will provide checks on your accuracy, and offer suggestions. The other agent, who will be mostly listening and asking occasional questions, will be charged with translating what takes place here, into what it means for a war robot. How exactly do we build it?"

John responded with a short laugh. "I wish your 'how to build it agent' good luck!"

"That agent will have as much help as he needs," Jt replied. "Now John, what are your thoughts on the project? Are you willing to give it a try?"

"Of course! It's both exciting and challenging. I'm looking forward to it!" He rested for a beat. "I have one thought already. While it's true that one emotion can produce one outcome, outcomes like the one you're looking for, will almost always be the result of several emotions. For example, the emotion 'fear' is driven by the personal need for safety and the desire to survive, but in a war scenario, it can be mitigated by pride in being part of a group working toward victory rather than fleeing to protect itself. Probably, several other emotions influence what they do as well. Our job is to untangle what is a very complex system."

"An interesting observation, John. One last thing for you to think about. The war robots don't have to have the same complete set of emotions as do humans. If we can develop short cuts, by eliminating some emotions and adapting others, that would be preferred. The war environment is the only thing that we want to control."

John was released early and headed home. He found his family all in the living area. Stephanie was at the big desk, working on something. John walked over and gave her a kiss. She smiled. "How did it go?"

"It went better than I had hoped. We've got a plan of action down, but my brain hurts," he said with a grin. "We've got some heavy-duty work ahead of us, and I have no idea if it will work out the way they want it to, but I know better than to sell them short." He looked around at everyone working. "What's going on?"

"David is working on his list of electronic stuff for Harry246. Ashley started off doing the same thing, but now she looks like she's just reading and snoozing. I'm making lists as well. First, I wanted to list all of the things I need to ask the doctor when I take Ashley tomorrow. Secondly, I'm also making a list for Harry246. He asked me to give him a list of anything, one, or all of us, either hated or loved. I've focused on foods and told him you don't like chocolate."

"What!" John's head whipped around to look at Stephanie.Stephanie laughed out loud. "Got cha!"

"I consider myself, gotten." He lowered his voice. "Did you find anything alcoholic when you were looking around?"

Stephanie brightened. "Did I ever!" Did you know that our new home has a wine cellar in it? Would you care to see it!"

"Are you kidding? Lead on, Madame."

Stephanie led him to what John had called the real work room, and opened a large 'pocket' door, which easily slid out of the way. Behind it was a double walled clear plastic room, with a small door. The room was not deep, but there was plenty of room for two lines of shelves holding plenty of wine bottles. It was also partitioned, with double walled plastic, and a small internal door leading from one side of the partition to the other. "You had to go through that door to get to the white wine section." She explained. There were only about seventy bottles in the entire cellar, which was clearly able to hold several times that amount.

John just stood there for a moment, staring. "Wow! Have you started an inventory yet?"

She had a smirk when she looked at him. "The people who put together this cellar liked chards for whites, but there is a collection of sauvignon blancs that look interesting, and several Spanish albarinos, which I love. Then, there is a nice collection of dessert wines." She kind of sniffed with her nose up, and a big smile, and continued her lecture. "As for the reds, there is a very interesting collection of Bordeauxs that were at least ten years old. Oh, and some great pinot noirs from Oregon and Burgundy. In addition, there is a wide variety of other reds from many different locations…usually two to three bottles, but some singles as well."

She turned to John and bowed at the waist.

John clapped. "Brava, Brava." Then, they both laughed.

"There are also some serious wine glasses! You want to try one?"

"Of course, but it feels like stealing. Someone put in a lot of work and money getting this together."

"Yes, I felt the same way, but Harry246 said the place was purchased with all of its contents."

“Then, what are we waiting for? Where did you say the glasses were?

They picked out a ten-year-old burgundy, and settled in the room where they were.

Chapter 62

John was off for the warehouse at eight o'clock the next morning and met JT in the same room as the previous day. JT began the conversation. "Our AI charged with understanding human behavior considered a list of all human emotions and selected, from them, two lists that could become useful to us. One is limited to positive emotions, which make humans feel good about themselves, and the other is limited to negative emotions, which make humans feel bad. The emotions selected were limited to those that might be most useful in a wartime setting. The lists are projected on the monitor."

Positive Emotions

- Satisfaction

- Pride

- Triumph

- Determination

  - Joy

Negative Emotions

- Anger

- Fear

- Shame

- Guilt

- Sadness

"The thought is that they could be BALANCED in a way that would produce specific actions at specific times."

"These certainly seems like appropriate lists for humans," John replied. "But I wonder if they would have any kind of meaning to AIs. I've thought of several concerns since I first presented the idea to you. Humans have personal needs, which are direct causes of their emotions. For example, we all have the personal need for security or safety, which when violated, produces fear, one of your negative emotions. Each of these emotions has one or more personal, psychological needs behind it. At least, that's what I found when I studied human research in the area. That research also suggested that these needs operate at the subconscious level, while humans are quite conscious of their emotions. And importantly, the results vary between humans.

"For example, suppose one person has a subconscious belief that being high off the ground puts them in severe danger, while a second person's fear of being high up is normal. Their personal fear of heights is activated differently by their safety needs, when they find themselves on edge of a high cliff or building. The intensity of the fear is different for each of them. The example is meant to illustrate how difficult it would be to manipulate human emotions. The intensity of each individual's emotional reaction matters when, as you suggested, we are trying to find a balance between positive and negative emotions to produce an action."

We are processing your information. Is there anything else?"

John sighed. "Yes, there is one other important consideration. It's the personal freedom of humans to make individual decisions. I'm guessing that AIs, in a war time situation, have little such freedom. Then, there is the question, how much do your individual fighters know about the objectives and strategy set by their leaders? With humans, the soldiers are supposed to understand the basic short-term tactical objectives, and their officers, in a chain of command, have more information about those objectives. That way it's easier for them to change the plans in a useful way, when the battle conditions produce unexpected threats and opportunities." He paused for a moment. "That's it I guess."

"John, are you suggesting that we shouldn't use emotions to help our soldiers make better decisions?"

John sat up. "No, I'm not suggesting that at all. I'm suggesting that we make the decision to use the human model as a rough template to guide us but make a unique model of emotions for AIs only!"

JT was silent for several minutes, and John guessed that he was communicating with his counterparts assigned to the project. Then, he responded. "I have agreement to your suggestion among the three of us working on this issue, but we will need a consensus from the robot council before we can change direction. They may even want to change the make-up of the group assigned to this project."

John nodded. "Don't you AGIs already have this information for human behavior and emotions?"

"We have some of it, the most straight-forward links between needs and emotions. However, we didn't push past that minimum level, because the council decided that it would provide no value to us."

"Well, I experienced some of what you do know, and it worked quite effectively." John noted, in a snide comment. "What would make your AI solders experience joy or sadness, or perhaps, more importantly, satisfaction or guilt? Perhaps we ought to think of feel good/feel bad in other terms for them?" He thought for a moment, "Or, what does it mean for AIs to FEEL at all?"

"All necessary questions, which we have considered, but let's wait for the council's approval, before we attempt to answer them," JT said.

John thought, *Ah, bureaucracy, even among robots.*

"We have our answer from the council. They agree," announced JT.

At least their bureaucracy works quickly."Now," JT began, "We probably ought to start with the question of how to impart feelings to selected soldiers? Right now, they are totally analytic."

"I'm afraid I don't have much to add, to that topic, but I'll be happy to listen and offer suggestions as I can." John responded. "JT, when you received enough points to be promoted to the robot council, was there any feeling of pride or satisfaction?"

"No, John. I just accepted it as a new task."

"OK, JT, I was just thinking that we could build our reward or punishment manipulation around the point system. But first, we are back to your point of developing feelings in AIs."

"I've been given a suggestion from my advisors, John. Since human emotions are based on needs, it seems like a good place to start developing those feelings in selected fighters. A need for being successful in their tasks, might be a good place to start, and from that, we could generate all of the positive and negative emotions listed previously. Naturally, they would have to be taught or programed as possible responses, when the need was felt."

The discussion continued for the rest of that day.

When John returned home that evening, Stephanie met him at the door. "How did it go today?"

"I think my brain hurts again." He said with a smile. Then, he asked, "How did Ashley's doctor's visit go today?"

"She does have a small crack in one rib, but the doctor said that it will heal itself in a couple of weeks. They put together a padded vest for her to wear, to help prevent its getting hit again, while it's healing. It was all very professional, and she's happier since they got rid of the contraption we had her wearing."

They had walked into the living area, sat down on the sofa. "Would you like a drink of some sort? This place is stocked with a variety of coffees, teas, sodas, wine of course, and about anything else you can think of."

"That sounds great, Stef! Maybe a red wine tonight. Do you know what we're having for dinner? That might guide my wine choice."

"Yes! Harry246 is preparing beef tips with a sherry and bacon gravy, assorted greens, and half of a stuffed baked potato…John, we are being spoiled, massively. It's going to be very difficult to go back to what we were doing…for all of us!"

John grinned, "It is certainly going to be hard when we do go back, but what do you say to just enjoying what we have now? Oh, and about the wine, how about a cab blend…perhaps a Bordeaux?"

Stephanie shook her head from side to side as she got up to get the wine, mumbling "Spoiled, spoiled."

John laughed out loud.

Stephanie returned, carrying two, half-full glasses. "A fifteen-year-old Bordeaux, which seems to be ageing nicely based on the smell." They settled back together, and she continued, "Tell me what's going on with JT and the AIs. Is progress being made?"

"I guess. We determined that the human emotion model is not easily modified to meet the needs of the AIs, and ultimately decided to create a separate one for their battlefield robots. We are using the human model as a guide, but only that. It turns out that human emotions are driven by specific human needs, so we've started looking at what kind of needs can we build into robots to get the emotional responses we want."

"Wow!" said Stephanie. "That sounds like a difficult thing to achieve."

"Yeah, I think I'll be here for a while."

"That's OK. I enjoyed being spoiled, too!"

Chapter 63

When John reported to work the next day, JT told him that the AI in control of designing the new warrior robots was having trouble with the concepts of needs and freedom. John acknowledged, "I understand, and have been concerned about those as well."

"To the extent that the term 'needs' are ever used by our AI robots, it occurs when there is a malfunction of equipment, and that doesn't match the human use of the term. We are also highly structured and analytical beings. Personal freedom is practically meaningless to us."

John understood. "Yes, and we humans are fundamentally individual units, who can make our own decisions, and are mostly free to do so. We must find a way to work within these realities, and still produce the desired results."

The discussion continued for a while. "Why don't we attempt to create an AI that acts 'as if' it had human emotions guiding it, but is operating as the analytical being it is?" John suggested, "An outside human observer might think it was acting like him, but it was really acting like an AI."

"How do you propose to do that?"

John replied, "I've been thinking about a few things that could help, but you and your other group members would have to tell me if you could make them work. In the wartime setting, the problem is reacting properly and quickly to changes as they occur. Basically, that requires decentralizing decision making all the way down to the front lines. So, those front-line AI soldiers could be programed to determine statistical probabilities of certain outcomes, from the changing war environment they observe, and act according to the best chance for success. I suspect that this approach or something like it is what you now use to make strategic decisions on the robot council. It would be a totally analytical solution, but it would mirror what might happen if humans were there. Further, and most importantly, it would likely produce more successes for your warriors."

"We agree that your approach is plausible," JT replied, "but we will have to check with the council.

John sat back and waited.

Minutes went by, then JT finally reported. "The council has agreed that the approach you suggest is worth attempting, although they noted several potential technical problems in making it work. They have also changed the make-up of our group. The human emotions representative has been removed, and a second representative in the design and construction area has been added. They insist that working AIs be created first, and thoroughly tested. John, you will be kept available for your input, and any further suggestions you can make."

John felt ecstatic but kept those feelings to himself. There was also a bit of uneasiness…his suggestions needed to work. "Certainly, I will hang around and do what I can. How long do you think it will take for the first model to be created and tested?"

"It may take a full week to develop the first model, then testing it will take another day. One of the two technical designers will work on the test, while the other will work on the model. There will undoubtedly have to be changes after the testing, and it's impossible to tell how long that will take."

John was surprised that they could do it that quickly, but then thought: *That's the AIs for you!*

When he arrived home that afternoon, he was anxious to tell Stephanie all about it, but David met him at the door. "You have to come see all the electronics Harry246 got for us!

He smiled broadly. "Take me to it!"

Ashley joined in, as soon as John got through the door. "I think I'm going to name mine 'Sally', after my old PR."

"Is it like our old PRs?" John asked.

David said, "No, but it has a head that talks to us. It's mounted on a large monitor. It's nice, but it can't physically do things for us."

Ashley commented, "Harry246 said that we could take them with us when we leave!"

Stephanie had heard the commotion and joined the group. "Welcome home!" she said with a smile. "We also have new phones."

John let the kids demonstrate their new equipment for a while. "I have some news too. Today I suggested a new approach to accomplish what the AIs want, and it was accepted by the robot council for a trial run. If it works, I'll probably be released from my job. However, even if the approach does work, we are probably talking about a couple of weeks or so. If it doesn't work, then it will be longer."

"That's great, Dad, but you can take your time," David said, "I'm beginning to enjoy it here.""Me too," added Ashley, "but I do miss some of my friends."

Stephanie shook her head from side to side. "You two are getting spoiled!"

Chapter 64

Three days after turning the job over to the construction and testing, they had heard nothing but good news feedback. John was a little restless since he had little to do but hang around the warehouse. He asked JT. "Did your group have any success understanding human creativity?"

"Not much, John."

"You understand that what I've done here is to apply creativity to our problem."

"Of course. That's why you are here. We had hoped for such an outcome, and you provided it. Now we just must see if it will work."

John thought for a moment. "Because of your constant questions of 'How did you come up with your thought?' I did some reading on what human researchers have said about creativity. It was interesting because, while there are a few different types, the one that is most used is combinational, where we humans combine two or more old ideas into a new unique one. Of course, those old ideas or experiences must be in place for them to be used."

"Yes John, we are aware of all human writings on creativity. We have also studied the brain activities when someone is being creative, and we understand what's going on, but not how it turns into a specific creative idea."

"So, maybe it would help the AIs and AGIs to keep us humans around?"

"Perhaps so, John. Especially, some humans."

* * *

An additional five days passed before John was greeted with news from JT. "Five new fighters have been sent to the front lines, but the enemy has been fairly predictable and not much has happened. A lone enemy fighter was spotted, and one of our new units broke formation and followed it. When it was clear that it was simply going to land, our fighter destroyed it. It's a good result, but not convincing enough for the council."

"A small win is a win. Now we just have to wait for a big win to convince the council." John replied. He waited until mid-afternoon, and nothing significant had happened. So he said, "Unless you need me here, I would like to go home."

"OK, I'll contact you if something happens."

At home, Ashley was talking to her friend, Megan, and when they were about to finish, Megan said, "Look, my Mom wants to talk to your Mom if that's possible."

Ashley said, "Sure, let me see if I can find her. Hold for a minute."

After a few minutes, Stephanie was on the phone. "Hi Joan! Ashley said that you wanted to speak to me?"

The reply came quickly. "Yes, look, we owe you and your husband a lot, after the way you two protected Megan from those thugs. My daughter says that you may be coming back soon?"

"Yes, that's true."

"Well, I wanted to make you aware of some of the things that are going on around the community, so you could be prepared if you do return. There is a lot of negativism toward you two, particularly from the ARL groups but, not completely from them." There was a pause before she continued. "They are calling you 'robot lovers' and 'professional killers.' However, others in the community recognize what you did to the cannon gang was to protect us all. We are, of course, in that group. I also remember seeing a couple of your International News programs and understand why you have the skills to fight when necessary." There was another pause. "Well, we just felt that we owed you a 'heads up' so you could be prepared when you returned."

Stephanie thanked her and finished the call with a few pleasantries. Then she sat down in an overstuffed leather chair and rubbed her face with both hands. She thought: *My last performance before I left is going to make it tougher on my whole family if we return. I guess I'll need to set up a return engagement with Jake and Vincent if we go back. I've always tried to be honest and straight forward with people, and I'm not going to change now. They won't like what I have to say, but so be it!*

She broke out of her reverie when Ashley came in and asked her, "What did Megan's mom want?"

"She wanted to warn us that some of the people in our Tampa subdivision are saying ugly things about me and your dad. When he gets home, we'll have a family talk about it, especially since we have to decide about returning very soon." Ashley wanted to ask questions, but her mom held up her hand. "Let's wait on your dad, so I don't have to go through this more than once." Ashley nodded, then left for David's room to tell him what she knew.

John showed up shortly after. "How are things going around here?"

He was met by his two kids who came down the stairs rapidly, followed by Stephanie who was just a little slower.

"I was helping Ashley fix one of her dresses," she said, coming down the stairs.

David looked at her, "Come on, Mom. Tell him what you found out today!"

Stephanie frowned at him, "Can't I just greet your dad coming home from work first!"

David frowned but didn't say anything else.

John looked at his kids, then at Stephanie. "Well, it looks like we have some news, and from the expressions on the faces of our listeners, perhaps that ought to be the first order of business."

Stephanie nodded. "It looks like the things I did and said before we left Tampa, have left some negative impressions of you and me and have developed some strong negative feelings toward us." She explained what Joan had told her. "If we go back," she said when she'd finished, "I can have my say with Jake and Vincent, but that might even make matters worse."

John listened, then looking at his kids. "What do my children think about this new information?"

David spoke first because he talked over Ashley's attempt to answer. "It really makes me mad! All you have tried to do is to help and protect others, in addition to us.

His dad replied, "I understand and you're right, but it is what it is, and I want to know how you feel about returning to Tampa, if this information is true."

David thought for a second, then answered, "I guess I really don't care much whether we go or stay."

"Ashley?"

"Well, it really pisses me off that those idiots would say things like that about my parents." She paused a second, then continued, "As far as going back, Megan will still be my friend, and any others who don't like my parents can drop dead! So I'm good…either way."

David's eyes opened wide at his sister's comments.John thought: *Guess who got a good share of her mother's genes?*Stephanie's mouth had dropped open. "Well, while I don't appreciate some of the language, I totally approve of the sentiments." she turned to John. "You know, while I trust Joan, maybe we ought to get another point of view. I think I'll try to reach

Penny and see what she's heard. She picked up her phone and tried Penny's number. It rang several times, but no one answered. "No one's picking up. Maybe they haven't been able to get a new phone yet."

Chapter 65

The next morning, John decided to go in late, and he was having a second cup of coffee when his phone rang. When he answered, he heard Jamar's voice. "How are you doing neighbor? We noticed that Stef tried to call Penny yesterday. We only have one cheap phone between us, and were lucky to get that one, I guess. It's my old number, but Penny uses it more than I do."

John smiled as he heard a comment from Penny in the background. "Let me put my phone on speaker and get Stef in here."

"I'll put mine on speaker too. Penny is already here."

John found Stephanie brushing her teeth. She rinsed and commented, "No facetime!" Then, she wrapped her wet hair in a towel and followed him to the kitchen.

They passed pleasantries, then John signaled Stephanie, and she explained what she had heard from Megan's mom and asked for their opinions about what was going on.

Jamar spoke first. "Well, I haven't heard much about you two at all from the people I've talked to, but I suppose it could be that everyone knows we're friends."

Penny broke in, "Ha, he never talks with our neighbors about anything to do with feelings or emotions—none of the juicy stuff!" John tried to stifle a chuckle, and Penny continued. "I think it's a mixed bag. Some of the folks I've talked to have had good things to say about you two. It looks like we're going to get electricity soon, and that's been attributed to you, John. These same people recognize that your interaction with the cannon gang was to protect all of us. Megan's mom was right though, there is a fairly large group that seems to think of you as robot lovers and professional killers. Certainly, most of that comes from the former ARL people. I'm biased, but I believe you ought to come back when you can. With you around, it will change the conversation about who you are. Also, I miss my talks with Stef!"

Stephanie was smiling broadly. "I knew I could count on Penny! I miss our talks too."

The conversation continued, and it was mostly about what was going on for each family. John and Stephanie didn't explain how nice their home was, or that they had an option to stay, but they did talk about how long it might be before they could return. When it was over, Stephanie told John that she had to go do "something with my hair", and asked if he would bring her a cup of coffee.

They told David and Ashley about the conversation, and the rest of the morning was spent discussing the pros and cons of staying and going back.

After lunch, John returned to work. He found JT quickly, and asked how things were progressing.

JT responded, "Our enemy is very predictable, so there have been very few opportunities to try our new system. However, there was one case where an enemy aircraft flew by at higher altitude, and one of our new fighters broke off to follow. When it was apparent that it was going to land at a near-by base, our unit fired a missile and killed it, then returned to its group. It's a single positive outcome, and in general, the committee approved."

John smiled, "Well, it's a good start! I hope we can get some more action soon."

* * *

Over the next week, more positive examples were reported, then the enemy surprised the committee with a major shift in strategy.

JT broadly described what happened to John. "It could have been a disaster for us. However, the new, adapted fighters recognized what was happening, and they developed a response that held the enemy engaged until reinforcements could arrive. It turned what could have been a serious defeat into a stand-off, with the loss of equipment about the same for both sides. I can't give you the details about where this occurred, or what assets were involved. The committee insists on keeping news on what's happening very limited, but I can tell you that they want to get more units, like the ones we sent, in the field as quickly as possible."

John's smile broadened. "Yay! We've got a winner."

"It seems so, John. Our two helpers have been reassigned to construction and development. I would like you to stay around for another week, in case something goes wrong, then you will be free to stay or go, as you wish."

"That's fine JT! We'll let you know our decision soon." John was excited, but he remembered his request before he took the job. "I've heard that the electricity is almost back to our home area, and I want to thank you and the committee for following through on my request. I was wondering if you could tell me anything about my request that your unused plants be returned to humans?"

JT responded, "That will be a decision for the committee. It's a big request, John, and it will take some time before they decide, especially with the war occupying so much of their time."

John sighed, "I understand JT." He thought, *I can't force a decision, and reminding JT is useless. Everything we discussed is locked in that computer brain of his!"* He excused himself and headed back home.

Chapter 66

Over the next few days, the discussions about staying or going were ongoing, with everyone having some reservations about both options. Then, they received another call from Jamar and Penny. "You need to know what's going on back here. The FP&L robots showed up. They went to each individual home to make sure the electricity was on, and to see if it was safe to use. In every case, they told the homeowners where electricity was available in their home, if any, and why the limitations on use existed. We can't use anything on the second floor because there are shorts that could cause a fire. But they got electricity working to the first floor, which gave us most of our appliances. Yay!! The bad news is that our heat pump doesn't work, but they gave Jamar an electronic chip with detailed instructions for getting it working."

Jamar broke in, "It won't be easy, but I think it's doable over time. The detailed work by the robots for each homeowner left most of them pleased. A few of the former ARL folks tried to keep them from working in their homes, but the robots insisted that if they were kept from inspecting the house, the homeowner would receive no electricity! I think that all of them relented."

Penny added, "Apparently, other communities that got their electricity didn't receive the grand treatment that we did, and there is a rumor that FP&L will pause their work for a while once they pass us. I'm not saying they'll give you a parade when you get back, but the folks back here are likely to be much more welcoming."

Jamar said, "You just heard that from one person, Penny. You have no hard evidence that they are going to pause after here."

Penny came right back, "You don't know anything about gossip Jamar! If one person says something that you want to hear, it becomes the absolute truth!"

Jamar followed with, "And I suppose that if it's not something you want to hear, it's absolutely untrue, just garbage."

They could hear Penny clapping, "Why sweetheart, that's correct. You know, I think there's hope for you yet!"

John and Stef were laughing at the give and take. "Poor Jamar. He's actually pretty good at slinging this stuff, but he clearly married out of his class. But now for some serious news. We must decide in the next couple of days about coming back or staying. My work is about finished, so we will be free to go or stay very soon." John looked at Stephanie, and she responded.

"With the news you've just given us, I think it's safe to say that we'll be returning. I guess you'll have to put up with us as neighbors again."

Penny reacted, "Oh goodie! Do you have a tentative date?"

"Not yet. There'll be some packing and other things to do before we can leave. Tell you what, I'll send you a note when we know something."

After they ended the conversation, Stephanie and John found the kids, and gave them the information they had just received. Ashley was excited, and David accepted the news, but asked, "Can we take Harry246 with us...and some food supplies?"

Stephanie said, "Probably not." However, she looked at John, who shrugged.

John then said, "I'm going to contact JT and see if he will agree to a date for us to leave. Would Friday be too soon?"

"Will you be around to help with the planning and packing?" she asked.

"I think so, but I'll ask JT when I call him." John called JT and talked for about ten minutes. When he was finished, everyone was hanging around to hear the results, so he announced, "Harry246 stays with the house, but JT said that he would send a shipment of 'human food' after a week or two. In addition, he said that we could take what we needed from the house, except furniture or basic fixtures, like appliances. He also said that I could stay home, unless I was needed, in which case, he would contact me. Also, Friday would be OK as a tentative leaving date. If something happened and he needed me for an extended time, the moving date would be pushed back. However, that was not expected to happen."

John took a deep breath, then let out a sigh. "Everyone, including me needs to start putting together things that they want to take back. We four will talk about what things from the house can go with us, and which things don't. For right now, all electronics that we brought or were given to us, should be taken. If boxes are needed, ask Harry246 quickly to get some." He turned to Stephanie, "Anything you want to add?"

"Yes, plan for the outfits you want to wear from now through the trip. I'll have a dirty clothes bag for everyone. If there's time, I may get Harry to do a load before we leave. If not, we'll bring our dirties home in the bag. Do some planning! I won't feel sorry for anyone who 'forgets something' and leaves it here." She thought for a moment, then said, "That's about it for now, but I'm sure there will be more as we get closer to leaving."

They spent a frantic few days getting everything together, but Friday morning they were ready to go. A van took them to the same plane that brought them to the Houston area, and everything was loaded by the pilot and copilot. The same two vans met them at Tampa area airport, and in about twenty-five minutes they were standing in front of their old home.

Ashley commented, "Somehow our house looks run-down and shabby."

John replied, "Yeah, but we'll start working on that soon."

All their luggage and packages were placed in the foyer, and the vans left.

Stephanie said, "I'm going to check on the appliances to see what is working."

"I'm going out to the garage to see what information FP&L left for us." John said and headed in that direction.

When he returned, Stephanie was helping the kids fix places for them to sleep and work. She saw him coming back and said, "All the major applications are working." Then, she asked, "What did you find out?"

"Well, the air and heat aren't working yet, and the top floor is shut down, but I should be able to get the heat pump back online in a day or so. All in all, we are in pretty good shape."

There was loud knocking on the front door, so John went to check. He heard Penny's voice, "It's your friendly neighbors, here to welcome you back!"

Jamar added, "We wanted to get our hugs, then we'll leave because we know you have a lot to do. Penny made some cookies."

Chapter 67

Stephanie was restless that night, and when she awoke the next morning, she told John, "I'm not one to leave things hanging. I'm going to confront Jake and Vincent and suggest that we dissolve our committee because now there is electricity, which should help everyone through the nuclear winter. It was highly unlikely that anything important was going to happen through the committee anyway."

"Do you want me to come along as back-up?" John asked.

"No, that will just increase the threat level to them. Besides, I think they are halfway scared of me anyway!"

John tried hard to stifle a laugh, and simply nodded that he agreed. "Try not to kill anyone you don't absolutely have to." And he burst into laughter.

Stephanie's head popped up, "Look. buster, I only hurt one person last time, and that was because she threatened me. I could have killed her just as easily."

John walked over and hugged her, and said softly, "Remember, I know who you are—a nice, peaceful lady—unless there is a threat to you or those you love! When a threat appears, then LOOK-OUT. The fuse shortens, and the bad guys are in trouble unless they do exactly as you order." He gave her a one eyebrow up look, portraying the question, "I'm right, aren't I?"

She slowly pushed him away. "I've got to get ready, then see if I can set up the meeting. What are you going to do this morning?"

"I'm going to begin the job of getting our heat and air working. However, I will have my phone nearby, and if you need me for any reason, call."

She nodded and left, blowing him a kiss on the way out.

When she finished going through her morning ritual, she called Jake Fitzgerald first and explained what she wanted, including ending the work of the committee. Jake said that he would call Vincent then get back to her. She got her return call in about thirty minutes. Jake said, "Look Stephanie, neither Jake nor I are willing to have a meeting at our homes, and further the committee was established as being representative of our community. We believe that such a meeting should be public and if dissolved, it should be done with a community vote. I thought that perhaps we do so at the same location where we held the first one."

Stephanie smiled to herself, "Well, first, the organizational meeting was far from being representative of our community. Almost everyone there was from one ARL or another, and there were almost no representatives of the original people who live here. Second, you should know that I will no longer be a member of any committee that continues to exist after this meeting. However," She paused, "let's do it anyway. Since you want a meeting, set it up, and I'll be there!"

Jake was surprised by her response. "I'll talk to Vincent again, and we should have it set up by three o'clock this afternoon. Will that be convenient?"

"I'll see you at three!" Stephanie said as she hung up.

When she told John, he said, "I'm coming to the meeting. I'll stand in the background, unless you need me, but I'm going to be there!'

She nodded, and said, "Thanks."

There was a light to moderate crowd, sitting in folding chairs that had been provided. Jake explained to Stephanie, "There was little chance to get the word out, so we have what we have. I suggest that we focus on the only point you mentioned—the whys and wherefores of keeping or dissolving this committee. Do you agree?"

Stephanie said "Sure. I'm ready when you are."

Jake spoke briefly with Vincent Green, then turned to the audience, "We are here to decide if the committee, which was founded by popular vote, should be continued, or dissolved. Stephanie Thompson proposed dissolution, so I'm asking her to provide the opening statement."

Stephanie nodded to Jake and stepped up to the front of the small stage. "I've already told Jake that I will no longer be a member of this committee, or any other committee, stemming from it. John and I thought that starting a committee to help the community might work well if we used former ARL people. We saw you as a hard-working group who could stay on target, and who cared a great deal about the survival of humans. We were wrong about the last part of my statement. You couldn't get past your hatreds of AIs to embrace the realities of human survival—because that's what it is, human survival.

"Here are the realities of the world you live in: First, AIs cruelly, and absolutely beat us in every engagement. That fact is indisputable. They could still annihilate us from the face of the earth, removing us as living species. That's a point which needs to be driven home, because many haven't come to grips with it yet.

"Second, the ARLs of the world likely brought on our demise, sooner rather than later. So, if you are feeling good about your role in your ARL, don't. While it is very likely that the result would have eventually occurred anyway, we probably lost a few years of normal life, because of your actions. I would like to soften this fact, by saying we felt your frustrations, in part because we lost our jobs too.

"Third, at every turn, John and I tried to help the community in any way we could. We destroyed the cannon gang when they returned to pillage our community, with almost no help from any of you. Then, the two biggest threats facing the community were hunger and freezing during the nuclear winter. The problem of hunger still exists, but John found a way to work with the robots to get our electricity on, and thereby limit the problem of freezing. I repeat, we have tried to help the entire community in any way we could. And what did it bring us? John was unwillingly taken, with the intent of murdering him, because he has a chip. I understand that we've been called robot lovers and killers, mostly by ARL people, but not exclusively. If there are any rational people out there, maybe YOU can understand why we are stepping away from this 'organization' and will only help those who try to help us."

Stephanie looked at Jake, and started to go back to her chair, when a question was yelled from the audience, "What happened to the Patels?" She turned and replied, "They're dead. Figure it out, then get over it!" There were muffled whispers in a few places in the audience. "Look, do what you want with this committee, I don't care." She picked up her few things and walked away. John met her and they headed home.

Chapter 68

John had the air conditioner and heating system working in their home in less than two days and was planning what could be done to stabilize the roof when he got a call from Jamar. He asked about a problem he was having getting his a/c unit to work, John went over to help. They had just finished with Jamar's system when Megan's dad walked up with the same question Jamar had experienced, and Jamar offered to help. Word spread, and John spent the next three weeks helping other people get their units to work properly. Finally, the requests for help slowed down and he again approached the problem of the roof.

I need to see what's going on up there! John thought. He found his extension ladder and a bright light that could be focused. He set the ladder and extended it to a separation between the roof and the second floor. He reached into the gap with the end of a hammer and tapped a stud to test for stability, then made a couple of notes, and returned to the bottom. He was on his fifth trip up the ladder, when Stephanie ran out of the house, and hollered, "There's a phone call you need to take!"

He replied, "Can you take a message?"

"No!"

"Why not? You act like it's the President of the United States, or something."

Stephanie gave a quick, faux laugh, then replied, "It is the President of the United States. Now come down safely and take the call!

As he climbed down the ladder, John's thoughts were a jumble. *Good grief, what did I do now? Maybe it's about robots. Doubtful! I haven't heard from them since we left Houston.* By then he was at the bottom of the ladder, and he reached for the phone. "Hello?"

He heard, "Mr. John Thompson?"

"Yes."

"Please hold for the President of the United States."

After a short pause, "Mr. Thompson, this is Margert Anderson."

John tried to stay calm, "I am of course delighted to talk with you, but you caught me by surprise."

"No doubt, John, but I needed to reach you right away. The robot council contacted me yesterday, and explained your role in helping them, and that one of the things you requested in return for their help was handing over their unused plants to us, and they have agreed to do so. That was a request of mine, early in the process."

"Yes, Madam President, that's why I thought of it."

"Well, John, I was of course delighted when I received the news. I called an emergency meeting of my staff, plus a few others, to try to work out how to get started. One thing we all agreed upon was that we needed some hard-hitting, knowledgeable person, and not some pampered CEO type, sitting behind a desk and giving orders. The next question was who? I had Betty, my assistant, do a background check on you. What she found was that you are very smart, well-educated, hard-working person who is not afraid to get his hands dirty, plus you have the bonus of having worked with the AIs. Bottom line, you're it. Now, what do I have to do to twist your arm?"

"I'd love to do the job, but I'm also a family man, who loves his family deeply. I must get a buy-in from them, or it's no deal. Give me a little time to talk with my family before I give you my answer, please."

"Before I let you go, please know that I had your family researched too. I was given a couple of International News special reports featuring your wife. I can find plenty of jobs for her to do if she wants them. You two have led an exciting life, John. Further, I can get your kids set up in whatever they want to study. My phone says you are on speaker; is Stephanie there?”

“Yes, Madam President, I’m here, but you could knock me over with a feather right now.”

“From what I saw in your reports, it would take a half dozen bad guys to knock you over, and that probably wouldn’t be enough. I want you to know that I can find something interesting for you if you want it.”

John broke in, “I had wanted to ask her privately before I gave my response to you, but I’ll go ahead and ask you since we’re talking about it, I’d like Stephanie to co-head this team to rebuild industrial America. She’s plenty tough enough for the job—and smart enough too.” He saw Stephanie’s hand go to her mouth.

There was a brief pause on the President’s end, then she replied, “I can see that! You two talk it over, but I need a positive answer quickly.”

Stephanie started the conversation as they walked back into the house. “John, you’re the build it, fix it, engineer, I’m not any of those things. Why would you want me as a co-chair?”

“Stef, you can choose what you want, but I’m going to need someone I can trust absolutely, to deal with the outside world. There is going to be a ton of interest in what we are doing, and I won’t have time to deal with it. You know that world better than anyone I could hire, even if there wasn’t the trust issue. I’ll brief you as often as needed, and you will have to follow our progress, or lack of it. We’ll talk about the philosophy of what we want to accomplish with this project, and you can use that to frame replies about incidents as they happen. Your title of co-chair will add believability to everything you say. And you will be able hire and fire, especially with the staff you bring in.” He paused and looked at her.

She had been slightly nodding positively as he talked. "OK, let's call the President back. I'm in!"

"What about the kids?" John asked.

"David will love it! He'll be able to follow whatever field he wants to study. Ashley will hate it at first, because she'll have to leave her friends. She will adapt though. She always has, and we've moved her around quite a bit. Anyway, this is too important not to do it!"

The President said "I am going to send a plane for you tomorrow. Be ready by tomorrow at noon. Someone will be at your door."

When Stephanie started to complain, the President said, Pack only enough for three days. The rest of your things will be packed for you and brought up here. Bring work clothes."

After the calls, John went to the sofa and sat down heavily; Stephanie plopped down next to him. John said, "The magnitude of what we've just taken on is starting to sink in. Never mind the amount of work, it's the importance of the work that's staggering. It's the best chance for humans in our country to survive, and even prosper once again. We just can't fail! It would be unacceptable to everyone, including me."

"Including US!" Stephanie corrected.

The End but also The New Beginning

www.ingramcontent.com/pod-product-compliance
Lightning Source LLC
Chambersburg PA
CBHW040133160726

48006CB00014B/1473